WHO IS MAGGIE

<u>**Also by Kim Malaj**</u>

Ember in Time Series
Castle of Teskom
Recover or Yield
Protectors of Time

Who Is Maggie

The Old Untold

Failed Book Cover Journals (A-Z)

Who Is Maggie

Kim Malaj

Who Is Maggie

In honor of my Great Aunt Myra Beth

She shared an infectious joy for three things:

Bob Barker on the Price is Right

Wizard of Oz

The Three Stooges

Cheers to sharing an infectious amount of joy for any interest.

1

"Monday freaking morning and the blue screen of death," Rozanne mumbles, stirring her coffee. Update seventeen of thirty-four displays in white across the blue screen.

The chime from the door startles Rozanne mid sip. She coughs and hastily straightens her slumped posture, jostling her full mug. It drips down the front of her pressed white jacket. She sets the dripping mug on the stained coaster below the counter and assesses the damage.

"Ah, crap!" She quickly removes the jacket and straightens her purple blouse.

A head with distinctive strawberry blonde locks appears above the shelves. The hair bobs up and down as the woman turns the corner and heads for the counter.

"Good morning, Mrs. Arber," Rozanne says, tapping the space bar.

Mrs. Arber smiles, reaching the counter. "Good morning, Rozanne."

"I believe your husband's prescription is ready," Rozanne says. "Which is great because the computer is still booting up."

Mrs. Arber nods and opens her purse, placing an insurance card for Mr. Arber on the counter.

"Any changes, or is this the same card?" Rozanne asks, impatiently clicking the mouse. The update text is still stuck on seventeen.

"No changes," Mrs. Arber answers, her voice so soft Rozanne barely registers her response.

"Great, let me look for what we have ready." Rozanne kneels to pick through the box labeled 'A' and finds two white bags for Benjamin Arber. "I found two. Do you know if there should be more?" she asks, turning back towards Mrs. Arber.

"Two is correct," Mrs. Arber answers.

Rozanne picks up the insurance card to confirm his date of birth before handing the card back.

Mrs. Arber places the card back inside her purse.

"How is he doing?" Rozanne asks, while pulling out a hand calculator to add up the copays.

"Recovering, thank you for asking."

"And Miss Maggie?" Rozanne looks past her down the aisle, expecting to find her curious daughter checking out the magazines.

Mrs. Arber tilts her head. "Pardon?"

"Sorry, I just assumed she was with you," Rozanne says, turning the calculator towards Mrs. Arber with the total. "The copay is eight dollars and sixty-five cents."

Mrs. Arber's eyebrows are knitted tightly together when Rozanne looks up.

"I'm sorry, is that total incorrect?" Rozanne asks, entering the numbers again. *It's the same total.* When she looks back up, Mrs. Arber shakes her head.

"Who is Maggie?" Mrs. Arber asks.

Rozanne tilts her head to the side. "Your daughter?"

Mrs. Arber shakes her head again.

Rozanne feels her cheeks flare up. "Oh. Okay. So sorry for the confusion. I think I need more coffee."

Mrs. Arber places a ten-dollar bill on the counter.

Rozanne gives her back the required change without meeting her eyes. She taps the space bar again, but the monitor still shows the update window.

"Is there anything else I can help you with?" Rozanne asks. She risks a look up, but Mrs. Arber is already walking away. "Have a good day!" she calls after her.

Rozanne slumps onto the stool and instantly regrets it. The dampness from the jacket seeps through her tan linen skirt.

"Great! Just great!"

She stands and twists to assess the damage. She walks back to the small kitchen with the jacket and collides with Monroe.

"Oh!" they say in unison.

She steps back and bumps into the door frame, hitting her elbow. Pins and needles shoot down her fingers. "Dang it! I will never understand why this is called a funny bone?" She shakes out her hand.

Monroe chuckles. "Sorry I startled you. Are you having a rough morning?" He checks his watch. "It's only five minutes past eight."

She frowns. "The computer started with the blue screen of death." He lifts an eyebrow. "It's updating. And I spilled coffee down this." She holds up her stained white jacket. She steps past him and walks towards the sink.

"Have we already had a customer?" He looks out at the small pharmacy. The four neatly organized aisles are customer free.

"Yea, the estate lawyer's wife, Mrs. Arber," Rozanne says, turning off the water and facing Monroe. "Have you met her?"

"Yes, her strawberry blonde hair is remarkable," Monroe says with a smile.

"And Maggie?"

He frowns.

"Okay," Rozanne says. "I may need a whole pot of coffee today."

"Who is Maggie?" he asks, filling his mug.

"I've seen a petite young lady with down syndrome here with Mrs. Arber every time she has come in," Rozanne says, dabbing her stain with a dry paper towel. "But today, when I inquired about her, she frowned like you just did. She even asked me who's

Maggie?" She looks up from dabbing. "And I said, your daughter. She just shook her head, paid, and left without another word."

"I would call that a blip in reality," Monroe says, raising his mug. "As far as I know, the Arbers don't have children."

Rozanne frowns. "She has the same strawberry blonde hair as Mrs. Arber. It's cut in a neat straight bob." She gestures toward her chin. Monroe just shrugs. "She has a few freckles across the ridge of her nose." Monroe shakes his head. "She is always wearing a pastel cardigan, over a flowery or plain dress, with knee high white socks and black shoes. You know, they look like ballet slippers." She raises a finger. "Mary janes!"

"I got nothing, kid," says Monroe. "I know almost every face in this town, and that description doesn't ring any bells."

"Really?"

Monroe nods. He fills a second mug and holds it up for her. "You're right. You may need the whole pot of coffee."

Rozanne frowns again but accepts the fresh mug.

Monroe whistles, walking out of the kitchen and past the counter to check and straighten the stock on the shelves.

Rozanne takes a long sip from the mug before placing it on the small kitchen table. She inspects the jacket. The coffee stain is clearly noticeable. She sighs and drapes it over a chair to dry.

She returns to the counter and wiggles the mouse.

The login window opens.

"Thank God!" Rozanne mumbles, logging in. She opens Mr. Arber's account to mark the two prescriptions as picked up and paid. She feels a ripple of unease from the nape of her neck down the length of her spine. There is a dependent listed on his account: Margaret L. Arber.

"Monroe, do you know Mrs. Arber's first name?" Rozanne asks, chewing on the corner of her lip.

Monroe looks up from one of the aisles, his white hair in bold contrast with the colorful diaper packaging on display behind him.

"Peggy," he answers.

She looks back at the screen and sighs. *Peggy is a common nickname for Margaret.* She closes the account and checks the incoming prescriptions.

The door chimes, and Monroe greets the postman.

She starts the printer for the new labels. She checks the details of each label with the details they have on file before moving them to the fill box on the counter behind her for Monroe.

Monroe returns. He steps behind the counter beside her. He sets a stack of magazines and a few envelopes on the counter.

"It's going to be a busy morning," Rozanne says.

"It's Monday." Monroe nods. "I asked Mr. Wier about Miss Maggie." He slips on his white jacket with 'Pharmacist' embroidered on his left lapel.

"And?" Rozanne drums her fingers on the counter.

"You definitely need more sleep or coffee." He raises his bushy salt and pepper eyebrows twice.

"Ugh!" She stomps her foot. "I swear she is real."

2

Rozanne's morning blurs with a steady stream of customers. She finishes her third cup of coffee by eleven.

Monroe fills the last awaiting refill. "How about some lunch?" he says to Rozanne.

"I just got here," Mary calls out from the back. "It's hot. Come and get it. I'll watch the counter."

Monroe slips off his white jacket and rubs his hands together.

Rozanne laughs at his response and her stomach groans in appreciation of the aroma of warm bread.

"I may need Tums to counter the amount of coffee from this morning." Rozanne holds her abdomen as they walk into the small kitchen.

Monroe laughs and waltzes over to Mary. "Lord, you're beautiful and all mine!" He pecks Mary on the cheek and rubs his nose to hers.

"And you the lucky devil!" Mary mocks. She turns to Rozanne. "How are you doing?"

"It's been a morning, but I'm so thankful you're here. It smells wonderful."

Mary smiles. "Homemade tomato soup with fresh bread and a fresh arugula salad with grilled chicken from the Mill Inn. Dressings are on the side."

"You're an angel!" Rozanne says, sitting across from Monroe.

Monroe is already halfway through his bowl of soup.

"There is dessert if you eat all your greens, Monroe," Mary teases, walking to the counter to help a new customer.

He snorts a laugh with a full mouth. "Rozanne, after forty-eight years of marriage, I hope you never have to bribe your spouse to eat more vegetables." He stabs a forkful of greens and frowns before taking the bite.

Rozanne laughs and smiles before taking in a large forkful of salad. Their banter is why she's never quit or moved on.

The small pharmacy has been a staple in this town for the last century. It has always been family owned and operated. Rozanne is only the second employee ever to have no kinship to the original owners.

Monroe finishes his lunch first and checks the fridge. He frowns and then opens the freezer. He pulls out one of the two single-serve ice creams.

"Hey you," Mary says, peeking her head in. "That's the sugar free one, right?"

Monroe squints at the container, moving it back and forth like he can't see.

"Seriously, you'll be useless by two if you eat a sugar-filled dessert now." Mary marches in and opens the freezer door, swapping his ice cream out.

His face falls, reading the label.

Rozanne presses her lips together, trying hard not to laugh.

"Sugar free and organic?" Monroe whines.

"Oh good," Mary says, patting his cheek. "You can read the labels."

Rozanne barks out a laugh in response.

Monroe glares at Rozanne, which makes her snort a little.

"Thank you for the ice cream, my dear," Monroe says with a grin not quite reaching his eyes.

"You're welcome," Mary says. "Rozanne, be sure you eat up! Otherwise, he'll finish yours too!"

"Yes, ma'am." Rozanne salutes.

Mary walks back to the counter.

Monroe sits down with a small pout and pops the top with his spoon. He takes in a spoonful and sighs.

"Is it good?" Rozanne asks Monroe.

"Of course, it's ice cream." He smiles and finishes the small serving without a single complaint.

"I'll finish up here," Monroe says, when the rush of the afternoon customers dies down just after four. "Head on home."

"I don't mind closing," Rozanne says, printing a few last-minute refill labels.

"No really," he says, placing a white paper bag on the counter. "I have to stay after and work on the books. But you could do me a favor and make a delivery on your way home."

"Sure, where to?" Rozanne asks, placing the verified labels in the refill box.

"Spa View Manor."

"The old creepy limestone building downtown?"

Monroe nods.

"They still have patients?" Rozanne takes off and hangs up her white jacket. Only a light outline of the coffee incident remains. "I thought it was condemned a few months ago."

"I think they're down to seven patients. The top two or three floors are condemned, but the second floor is still open." Monroe picks up the bag. "There are three compound cremes in here. Can you ask if they need any refills?"

"Sure, no problem." Rozanne pulls out her purse from the cubby below the counter and places the white paper bag carefully inside. "Have a good evening and don't stay too late."

"Yea, yea," Monroe says, waving her out. "Let me know if you have any problems. See you in the morning."

Rozanne leaves through the back entrance.

3

Rozanne shakes out her blouse. The warm afternoon sun is hot, and the humidity is at an instant damp level. A thrum of thunder is barely audible over the sound of the air conditioners working hard in the alley to cool the line of shops and cafes.

Fingers crossed that storm will bring in a cool breeze this evening. If I run my old air conditioner at full blast all night every night, it may not make it to July. Rozanne slides into her car and cranks up the air, simultaneously waving the door to give the hot, trapped air room to exit. Once the air coming out of the vents is not blasting hot, she closes the door and buckles up.

Rozanne backs out and drives slowly down the narrow alley and turns, entering the historic district. The town is not ancient but earmarked by many historic societies to keep the original esthetic, including the huge elm trees that line the street. It takes a committee to approve even the smallest change to the storefronts.

She rolls down the old brick street away from the Elms Resort that takes up acres at one end of the historic district. She navigates the late afternoon traffic to Main Street and turns right on Bluff Street. She slows and pulls into an empty parking lot.

She leans over the steering wheel to look up at the five-story limestone building. *No lights or movement.* Some windows look missing or broken near the top. *How could this still be open or safe?*

She cracks her door open to the sound of the cicadas' evening concert. She shoulders her purse, holding on to her keys and carefully climbs the broken, uneven stone steps to the front entrance.

The cicadas go quiet when she reaches the door. She whirls around, scanning the parking lot, shaking off an unreasonable shiver before pushing open the tattered front door. The door opens with surprising ease.

Her eyes land on a young lady who turns from the running water of a tiered marble fountain and smiles.

Rozanne blinks a few times. *It's Maggie. I'm not crazy.*

"Welcome to Spa View Manor." The young lady bows at the waist.

"Maggie?" Rozanne whispers.

The young lady straightens. She tilts her head to the side and smiles again. "You may take the main stairs to the second floor or use the elevator. Which do you desire?"

"You're Maggie, right?" Rozanne asks, too stunned to answer her question.

"My name is Margaret Penelope Vance," she answers with a soft lisp. "My family calls me Maggie. Are we family?"

Rozanne breathes out a sigh. "Maggie, my name is Rozanne. I work at the pharmacy in town. We've met a few times. Do you remember me?"

Maggie frowns and shakes her head.

"Oh," Rozanne says. "Well, no worries." She forces a smile and pulls out the white paper bag. "I have a delivery."

Maggie brightens with a smile and two quick claps. "Elevator or stairs?"

Rozanne steps further into the lobby. Her gaze floats up to the three large gold and crystal chandeliers and the beautiful light reflecting on the clean white marble floors. She admires several large carved marble columns framing the beautiful two-story vaulted ceilings. She spots a black iron gate in the corner and frowns.

"Is that the elevator?" Rozanne asks, pointing to it and chewing on the corner of her lip.

"Yes!" Maggie eagerly answers and walks in that direction.

"Stairs, definitely stairs," Rozanne says, a little louder than intended.

Maggie cowers and whirls to face Rozanne with a frown.

"Sorry," Rozanne apologizes. "I'm not so good with small, enclosed spaces."

Maggie nods and leads Rozanne to a wide marble staircase with dark wood paneling.

Maggie stops at the base and extends her arm up.

Rozanne takes a step up, and Maggie turns, walking away.

"Wait," Rozanne says. "Are you staying down here alone?"

Maggie stops and turns around. The glow from the chandelier highlights her strawberry blonde hair, so similar to Mrs. Arber's. She straightens her cardigan, sticks out her chin and bottom lip.

"I greet and direct," Maggie says with confidence.

"Oh! Well, thank you for your directions and friendly greeting." Rozanne smiles and nods towards her.

Maggie grins and nods once. Then she walks towards the fountain.

Rozanne slowly turns and walks up to the first landing. She inspects the details of the craftsmanship and not a cobweb or dust particle in sight. She continues up and finds a dark, narrow hallway with several doors on either side. *The elegance of the lobby stops here.* She hesitantly walks down the hall towards the only visible light. A small figure darts out of a door a few steps ahead.

"Oh!" Rozanne screams, jabbing her keys out in front of her.

A small boy looks up, points, and laughs before running back inside the door he came from.

12

She lowers her useless weapon of choice and exhales. A tall woman dressed in white is standing in the light, shaking her head.

"Sorry," she apologizes, "we don't get too many visitors. Are you dropping off for Monroe?"

Rozanne tries to laugh it off but feels it catch in her throat.

The woman in white is Mrs. Arber.

Rozanne swallows hard. "Mrs. Arber?"

"Heavens no!" the lady laughs. "I'm Minnie, my twin sister is Mrs. Peggy Arber."

"Minnie," Rozanne whispers.

"Yes," Minnie says, reaching for the white bag.

Rozanne hands over the delivery.

"We need two refills on these." She hands over two paper prescription slips.

"And Maggie?" Rozanne asks, tucking the two prescriptions in her purse.

"Maggie?" Minnie asks, her eyebrows knitted together.

Rozanne feels the color drain from her face.

"Darlin, are you okay?" Minnie asks.

Rozanne shakes her head. "No, not really! The young lady downstairs is Maggie. I've seen her with Mrs. Arber! Today Mrs. Arber claimed no knowledge of her, and now you? What gives?"

"There is no one downstairs." Minnie places a hand on Rozanne's shoulder. "I am the only staff member on duty this evening."

"She isn't staff!" Rozanne steps back. "Follow me."

"I'm sorry, but I can't leave this floor. I have patients."

"Fine! I'll bring her up here." Rozanne jogs down the hall. She reaches the landing and starts to descend the marble steps. "Maggie, can you—you've got to be kidding me!"

The lobby is vacant and dusty. The chandeliers are draped in decades of cobwebs, with two barely hanging. The fountain is in pieces and layers of graffiti cover nearly every wall.

"Everything okay down there?" Minnie calls from the second floor.

"Um, not unless 'okay' includes grand hallucinations!" Rozanne turns in a slow circle trying to gain her sanity.

"Maybe you should come back up," Minnie suggests.

Rozanne is already marching for the door. The sun is barely high enough to filter in through the dirt-stained windows of the lobby.

"No thanks, have a great night!" Rozanne shouts over her shoulder as she pulls open the door. She's relieved to see her car in the same spot. She half runs, half stumbles down the stone steps and wrenches open her driver's door. She throws her purse across the center console, spilling the contents all over the passenger seat and floorboard.

"What is happening!" she screams, slamming her door shut. She stuffs her wallet, the paper scripts, a long coupon receipt, a notebook, lip gloss, and loose change back in her purse, but she can't find her phone. She kneels on the front seat and searches between the passenger door and seat.

Tap, Tap

She jerks up, hitting her head on the roof of the car, and hastily pulls her skirt down before turning around. A face is pressed to the driver's window.

"What the—" Rozanne says.

A familiar face moves back, and he is laughing.

Rozanne sighs and swings open the door. "Gage! You nearly gave me a heart attack!" She unfolds from the seat, stands, and shimmies her skirt back down.

His gaze follows her actions.

"Why are you here?" Rozanne asks, looking him over. He has sweaty helmet hair, his riding jacket, leather boots and his signature grease-stained jeans. She looks past him, spotting his latest work in progress. The motorcycle looks half new, half rusted.

"I saw your car, or rather your rear bumper, on my test drive," Gage says, winking.

"Ha, ha." Rozanne rolls her eyes.

14

Gage's idea of a prank a few years ago was to place a new bumper sticker on the rear of Rozanne's plain white sedan every week until she noticed. He made it five weeks.

Gage turns and points at the building. "I thought this place was condemned."

Rozanne looks up at the dreary exterior. The sun is hidden by a few dark clouds, making the esthetic more ominous. She shivers. The windows are dark on every floor, including the lobby.

"I had a delivery for Monroe," Rozanne says.

"The pharmacy delivers to condemned buildings?" Gage asks, running a hand through his hair.

"Believe it or not, the second floor still has a few patients." She shakes her head, replaying the last ten minutes.

"They must have really heavy curtains," Gage says. "I drive by here a few times a week on my way home from the shop. It's always dark."

"Odd," Rozanne says. "But that somehow doesn't surprise me after what I just experienced." She sighs. "I've possibly had the weirdest day ever, and that was before stopping here."

"I'm done for the day," Gage says, looking over at his bike and back at her. "Do you want to grab dinner?"

"You're buying for that stunt!" Rozanne says, pointing to her car door.

He brings a fist to his chest, stabbing his heart. "Oh Rozanne, you wound me!"

"Good!" She grins. "Burnt ends?"

He immediately stops the theatrics. "Heart repaired! Race you there!"

Rozanne laughs and gets back into her car.

Gage straps on his helmet and straddles his ride. The motorcycle sputters twice before the thrum of the motor roars to life. He whirls two fingers in the air. She backs out of the spot and follows him to Kansas City Avenue, past the Mill Inn, and pulls into the old train depot that is now Wabash Barbeque.

The aroma of smoked meat fills Rozanne's nostrils the second she opens her car door. She inhales and smiles. *The sweet serenity of barbeque.* She walks around her car and opens the passenger door. Her phone falls out onto the gravel.

"Got it!" she says to herself and tosses it in her purse.

"Got what?" Gage asks, walking up beside her.

"I was looking for my phone earlier, before some rude boy scared the crap out of me!" Rozanne softly jabs her elbow into his side.

"Ah, but said rude boy is buying you dinner and drinks." He elbows her back.

"And drinks!" Rozanne sings. "Winning!"

Gage laughs.

The bell jingles overhead as they walk in. Rozanne jumps a little. Gage raises a single eyebrow. She shakes her head.

"You are extra jumpy today," Gage says.

"Weird day, remember?" Rozanne says. She recognizes most of the faces. Some regular pharmacy customers smile and nod. She returns the gesture as they weave through the tables to the only empty one in the corner.

They sit down, and a young blonde server makes her way over to their table. Her face brightens at the sight of Gage.

"Oh, hi Gage, the usual?" the server asks, ignoring Rozanne completely.

"Nah, not tonight, Roz," Gage says. The server's face crumples. "I mean Cora. Rozanne, what do you want?"

"A draft wheat beer, fried mushrooms, sweet potato fries and a pound of burnt ends."

Gage coughs. "Are we splitting the burnt ends?"

"Ha! What do you think?"

He laughs. "I'll have a Boulevard Tank Seven on draft if you have it, onion rings, and a half a pound of burnt ends." Cora nods, tucking her small notebook into her apron and walking back towards the kitchen.

"Heartbreaker!" Rozanne coughs.

"She's a baby," Gage says, "and Ron's little sister. No thanks!"

"As in Ronnie and Viola, Ron?" Rozanne asks.

"King and Queen of everything class of 2015, yes," he answers.

Rozanne looks over at the counter near the kitchen and sees it. Cora has the same blonde hair and light eyes as Ronnie.

"Hmm," Rozanne says. "I guess I don't remember much about the siblings of our classmates."

"You've never been great with faces," Gage says.

Rozanne turns in her chair to face him. "Really?"

He nods. "Last week, my mom came in for a refill and you asked for her name." He laughs. "She asked me if you have face blindness."

"In my defense, she changes her hair color every other month."

"You're missing the point. We were neighbors." He laughs at her frown. "You saw my mom more than you did yours growing up."

"That's not fair," Rozanne says, frowning. "My parents worked evenings." She turns away from Gage and focuses on the window. *Fucking drunk driver! Why does it still sting? I was fifteen. They're gone, Rozanne, that's reality.*

"I know, I know." Gage squeezes her knee under the table and mentally kicks himself for bringing up her parents. "Just saying my mom shouldn't be hard to recognize after seeing her daily years."

Cora arrives with their drinks before she can respond. She sets Rozanne's drink down in front of her.

"Bad news," Cora says to Gage, placing the bottled beer and a frosted mug. "The draft is tapped out and back ordered. And the kitchen only has one pound left of burnt ends."

Rozanne smiles at his frown. He scowls at her.

"Fine," he says, "give me a half pound of brisket and a quarter pound of burnt ends from her pound." Rozanne scowls at him. "Remember who is paying."

Cora's eyes widen, and she looks at Rozanne. "Oh, this is a date?"

"Never," they say in unison and laugh.

Cora's cheeks flush bright red. She quickly turns away and returns to the kitchen.

Gage pours his beer with expert precision and raises it up to Rozanne. He taps his glass with hers.

"To scaring the babies away," he whispers.

Rozanne snorts out a loud laugh, drawing attention from nearby tables. She cups her mouth and shakes her head.

"I can't take you anywhere," Gage teases.

Rozanne takes a long sip in response. He shakes his head.

"So, what really happened today?" Gage asks.

Rozanne explains the spilled coffee, the confusion with the customer this morning, the twin sister, and the "before and after" lobby this evening.

"Am I crazy?" Rozanne asks, before finishing her drink.

"Roz, that's a given," Gage says, his lips firm. "Who else would dare a boy twice her size to arm wrestle at eight years old and win?" His face breaks into a smile.

"Seriously!" She shoves his arm. "What happened today— do you have any rational explanation?"

"Rational," he says and shakes his head. "No, sorry."

Cora returns to the table and drops off their appetizers.

"Another?" Cora asks, taking Rozanne's empty glass.

"A water with a lemon, please," Rozanne says.

Cora nods, not making eye contact with either of them.

Rozanne pops a fried mushroom into her mouth and instantly regrets it. She opens her mouth to let the heat escape and breathes out in an effort to cool the food.

"Seriously," Gage says, unwrapping the napkin from the silverware and hands it to her.

She takes the napkin and swallows. "It was super hot!"

"Noted," Gage says, snagging one from her basket and blowing on it.

4

"Why did you let me eat so much?" Rozanne groans. She tugs on the waistband of her skirt.

"You kept stabbing my hand every time I reached for a fry or more burnt ends," Gage says, holding up his right hand with a four-prong indention.

"Sorry, not sorry," Rozanne says, opening her car door.

The sky lights up with lightning. They look up. A loud crack of thunder rattles overhead.

Gage straps on his helmet. "I'd better scoot. That is only a few miles away. You good to drive?"

"I had one drink before nearly a pound of meat," Rozanne says, patting her full belly. "Drive safe."

Gage nods, swinging a leg over and knocking back the kickstand in one smooth motion. He starts the engine on the first try, waves to Rozanne, and drops it in gear. He speeds off as the sky lights up again.

Rozanne slides into the car and pulls on her seatbelt. She checks her phone—two emails and one text alert. No missed calls.

Thunder rumbles and shakes the car.

She starts the car and pulls out of the deserted parking lot.

The bolts of lightning fall in quick, ominous, vertical streaks. She watches one bolt scorch the top of an old elm tree in the rearview mirror. The storm continues rolling east.

She slows and turns in to her long, narrow drive.

Her inheritance from her grandparents included her car and keys to a 1920s craftsman bungalow on five acres just outside of town.

The house lights come into view. She pulls around and under the carport. The outside lights flicker. *I still have power, for now.*

She installed the large flood lights after she found a strange man sleeping on her porch a month after she moved in. Her grandfather's shotgun and a lot of screaming made the man move on and never return. The following afternoon, she'd found the largest flood lights they had in stock at Morrow and Sons and installed them with the brightest bulbs available. She even removed the switch, so she didn't accidentally turn them off. No shadows possible in the front yard, wrap-around porch, or carport.

The rain pecks the metal roof of the carport as she climbs the four steps to the porch. She unlocks the front door and hears the chime of her phone. She sets her keys and purse on the foyer table and digs out her phone. The first text message is a payment reminder for the electric, and the second message is from Gage.

Soaked! But home.

She laughs and quickly types back. *Home and dry.*

A few mean face emojis arrive in response.

She types back one word. *Night.*

She loosens her skirt and sighs, rubbing her aching, full belly. She walks past the two bedrooms on the right and into a bedroom on the left. She hops over the squeaky floorboard near the threshold and peels off the day's clothes.

She starts the shower. The old pipes clang in harmony with the thunder just overhead. She streaks back through the house and grabs a flashlight from the kitchen junk drawer. She sets the flashlight in arm's reach of the shower and tests the water before getting in. She soaks, washes, and rinses her hair twice to get the smell of barbeque out. She shuts off the water just as the lights flicker and go dark.

"Dammit."

She finishes her evening routine using the flashlight. Then she walks back through the house to the porch. The solar lawn lights illuminating the path from the carport to the front steps are still bright except for two. *I need to add solar light replacements to my house crap I have to buy now that I am an adult list.*

She folds into the wide wicker hanging chair and adjusts to sit cross-legged. She turns off the flashlight and sets it in her lap. She wrings out her long brown hair and finger combs it out in sections, replaying the day.

"Is Maggie real or not?" she asks the sky

The wind howls swinging her chair.

"What was Spa View Manor?"

The rain pings with more gusto against the metal carport.

"Are Minnie and Peggy from here originally?"

The rain subsides to a faint trickle all at once.

"Am I actually crazy?"

BOOM, BOOM, BOOM

She jerks forward, tilting her balance. Before she can right herself, she falls out of the chair and smashes her face against the wooden porch. She untangles her hands from her hair and reaches up to touch her cheek. *Ouch.* It's moist. She pulls her fingers away and sees red as more lightning streaks across the sky.

"How in the hell did I manage that?" she mumbles, looking around for the flashlight. It's gone. *Likely rolled off the edge of the porch in my less than graceful tumble down.*

Her head throbs as she stands. She feels the trickle of blood fall down her face. She cups her hand under her chin and returns inside. She pats the foyer table down, finally palming her phone. She swipes her password sequence and opens the flashlight app. She immediately jumps back from the mirror hanging in the foyer, reflecting her bloody face.

"You've got to be kidding," she mumbles. The movement of her jaw creates a new stabbing pain. She steps closer to inspect the damage. Her right eye is already swollen and a large cut over her brow explains the blood, but her cheek is twice the size it should be compared to the left. She gently opens her mouth, reaches up, and touches a chipped tooth.

She highlights the video chat icon next to Gage's name and hits send. It rings four times before an image of a bare chest fills the screen.

"In the shower, call you—Roz?" Gage's wet, half shaved face fills the screen. The sound of running water stops. "Is it just the lack of light or is your face bleeding?"

"Help," Rozanne mumbles.

"Shit! Rozanne, what the hell happened?" Gage yells at the phone. The image on the screen goes to the ceiling and a blurred motion of a towel comes in and out of focus.

"Chair on porch," she mumbles and grimaces in pain. "Face plant."

"You fell out of the chair on the porch and did that much damage to your face?" Gage asks, his face filling the screen again as he pulls a shirt on.

"Yes," Rozanne answers.

"On my way," Gage says, half grinning. "Change. I can see through your top."

Rozanne glances down and covers her chest.

5

Rozanne manages a pair of sweats and a long cardigan over her damp top. She wraps a towel around her neck to catch the falling blood. She grabs her keys and purse. She is locking the front door when she hears Gage's new diesel truck pull into the drive. She manages the four steps down, but the pain is getting worse. She leans on the rail until he parks. The interior lights turn on as he opens his door. He is missing half of his beard. Rozanne points to his face, and he points back to hers.

"Pretty sure mine is looking far better than yours at the moment," Gage says, walking her to the passenger side. He helps her up on to the seat. "Lean your head back if you can." He slams the door and jogs around the truck. He drives slowly over the gravel, avoiding any extra jostling, but hits the gas once they are on the main road into town.

The emergency room is attached to a small hospital. The waiting room is empty when they arrive, giving them full access to Viola. She is sitting at the registration desk with her head down, glued to her phone.

"A little help here would be nice," Gage says, helping Rozanne to the counter.

Viola looks up and frowns. She takes one look at Rozanne's face and then scowls at Gage.

Rozanne groans after reading her name badge. *Ugh, Viola is the last person I want to see right now.*

"Hey, I didn't do this to her!" Gage says.

"Rozanne?" Viola asks, coming around her desk pushing a wheelchair.

"All me," Rozanne mumbles and lowers down into the chair.

Viola pushes the chair towards the trauma bay.

Gage follows.

"Oh, no you don't!" Viola snaps back at him. "She will not need you here for this."

"I didn't do this," Gage protests as the doors swing shut.

"He's right," Rozanne says, wincing. "I fell out of a chair and face planted on my porch."

"He hit you with a chair on the porch?" Viola asks loudly, gaining the attention of a passing aide. "Page the on-duty deputy and get Dr. Chamberlain."

The aide nods and grimaces, with only a glance at Rozanne's face.

"Not. His. Fault." Rozanne says louder.

"Hush now," Viola says, ignoring Rozanne's words. She stops the wheelchair, pulling the brakes and lifting the footrests. "Let's move you up here."

Rozanne stands, but the throbbing pain makes her knees wobble.

"Oh dear," Viola says, taking her arms, side stepping her to the bed.

A nurse walks in and helps Rozanne lie back. She snaps on a pair of gloves and pushes her still damp hair away from her face to evaluate the damage.

Viola watches.

The nurse looks up. "You can return to the desk."

"But…" Viola protests as a tall, thin woman enters wearing a badge that says Dr. Jean Chamberlain.

The doctor glares in Viola's direction. She cowers and backs out of the room.

"Well, what happened here?" Dr. Chamberlain asks.

24

The nurse steps back, giving her room to examine the right side of Rozanne's face.

"I fell face first from a hanging chair on my porch," Rozanne mumbles.

"The cut on your brow will require a few stitches, but the swelling along your cheek," Dr. Chamberlain says, gently pressing along her chin. "I will need a few images to assess the damage." She pauses to look back at the nurse. "Bring me a suture kit and put in the order for a head and neck X-Ray and head CT with contrast."

The nurse nods and steps out, closing the curtain.

"Did you try to stop your fall at all?" Dr. Chamberlain asks, examining her neck and shoulders.

"No," Rozanne says, pulling on her still damp hair. "I was finger combing my hair and was sitting on my feet."

The nurse steps in with a suture kit and bandages. "There is a woman by the name of Darcy asking to see you."

"Yes, please," Rozanne says.

Dr. Chamberlain shakes her head. "Not yet. This needs to be cleaned and sutured first."

The nurse nods and pats Rozanne's hand.

Dr. Chamberlain completes the final suture and steps back to assess her work. "You may have a slight scar just above your eyebrow." She tosses her gloves and looks at her chart. "You may visit with your friend for a few minutes, but try not to talk too much. A tech will be in to take you to radiology shortly."

"Thank you," Rozanne says, unclenching her fist and turning to the nurse. "Can you let Darcy in?"

The nurse smiles. "Sure thing, be right back with her."

The curtains part as the nurse leaves. Rozanne watches a whispered discussion between a deputy and her doctor. Darcy's worried frown appears in their place.

"What in heaven's name, woman!" Darcy says, coming to Rozanne's side. "Gage said you face planted on the porch?"

"Afraid so," Rozanne says, squeezing Darcy's hand. "Did you leave work for me?" She points to Darcy's dispatch operator badge hanging from the pocket of her Station 3 polo.

"Nah," Darcy says, pulling up a stool and sitting down. "Gage called me just as I was leaving work. He told me what happened. And he also said Viola was making a scene?"

"You know he didn't do this," Rozanne says, pointing to her face.

"Of course," Darcy says, shaking her head. "How's the pain?"

"Bike crashing off a ramp pain," Rozanne mumbles.

Darcy laughs. "And a week later, that fool out there was picking out his own cast colors. The two of you with arm casts for six weeks." She scrunches her nose. "Not sure whose smelled worse."

Rozanne flaps her elbow. "What can I say? We are smooth operators."

"And I believe whatever they gave you for pain has kicked in," Darcy says, bouncing her eyebrows. "In other news, Logan asked about you tonight."

"Oh?" Rozanne feels her left cheek burn.

"Did you two finally exchange numbers?" Darcy asks, raising her eyebrows.

"Yes," Rozanne says.

"Ah, yeah!" Darcy says, wiggling on the stool.

"But not sure this is a good look for an official first date." Rozanne gestures to her face.

"You've already discussed a first date?" Darcy asks.

"No," Rozanne says. "We haven't even had a conversation yet. I was going to text him tomorrow if he didn't call first."

"He is a medic and could help take care of you," Darcy says and winks. "And you never know he could like a few scars."

The curtain pulls back and a tech with 'Radiology' embroidered on their scrubs walks in. "Ms. Rayvern, we're ready for you."

Darcy stands and kisses Rozanne's left cheek. "I've got to go make sure my husband and kids haven't burned down the house. Call me tomorrow."

Five hours later, Gage comes to Rozanne's bedside.

The nurse hands him two prescriptions. "Fill these first thing in the morning." She hands him a full-sized piece of paper with an envelope attached. She taps the envelope. "These are the films with the diagnostic reports to give to the surgeon." She points to the top of the page. "Her appointment is for Wednesday at eight. Arrive fifteen minutes early to register."

Gage doesn't blink or respond.

Rozanne is half listening. The shot they gave her for pain is hindering the one eye she can open all the way.

"Do you have questions?" the nurse asks. "Because there is more."

Gage nods. "Why are you telling me all of this?"

The nurse frowns. "You are listed as Rozanne's emergency contact. She has you down as her only family member."

"We aren't family," Gage says, looking at Rozanne to agree. "We're just friends."

"Wisdom teeth," Rozanne says.

Gage frowns and then laughs. "Hell, paybacks are a bitch." The nurse frowns. "Roz had the pleasure of spoon feeding me after my wisdom teeth were removed," he explains. "She said one day she would need my help and I would step up and shut up." He motions his fingers across his lips and twists.

The nurse laughs and turns to Rozanne. "Well played." Then she turns back to Gage. "She has nine sutures that will dissolve, but please monitor them for any redness or swelling. She also needs a liquid diet until the surgical consult, minimal speaking, bed rest for six weeks, and keep ice packs ready to manage the swelling."

"Six weeks?" Gage asks.

The nurse nods. "And a very strict, do not leave her unsupervised for the first forty-eight hours, otherwise she will need to remain here for observation." She hands him a final paper with those instructions. "Any questions?"

"I'll do my best to manage her care," Gage says. "I promise."

6

Dawn filters through the woods as Gage pulls down Rozanne's drive. The morning light shimmers on the large pond at the edge of the property. The land slopes to a small, natural waterfall from a spring-fed river into the pond.

Rozanne stirs, as the truck bumps along the gravel and opens her left eye. Two figures stand from the corner porch swing. "Mary and Monroe?"

"I called them a few hours ago. I knew they would find out through the town gossip chain. Patient privacy doesn't really mean much here. I didn't want them to jump to conclusions."

"Ah, you wanted to cover your ass," Rozanne mumbles.

"Yes, to cover my ass from Viola's assumption, therefore the gossip."

"Wise move," Rozanne says, looking at the concern and pity on Mary's face as she approaches the passenger side of the truck. She opens the door and Mary muffles a cry.

"My child," she whispers.

Monroe's frown has reached a new wrinkle Rozanne didn't know existed. They help her out of the truck.

"We let ourselves in and prepped your room," Mary says, taking Rozanne's elbow. "And stocked you up with fruits, peanut butter, and yogurt. The freezer is full of frozen bags of peas and corn. The auxiliary women's group will bring over broths or soups every day."

"You don't—" Rozanne says.

"Yes, darlin' we do," Monroe cuts her off. "I promised your Grandma Anne we would fill her shoes if ever necessary and this, my dear, is necessary."

Gage holds the door open for them. They amble down the hall towards her room.

Rozanne's room is clean. Her bed has been made with fresh sheets and extra pillows. An extra side table from the living room is sitting beside the bed with a notepad and pen, a stack of books and magazines, a glass, a water bottle with several more bottles tucked in one corner, and an extra fan has been moved into the other corner.

Rozanne feels a tear fall down her cheek.

"We've made a room up for Gage across the hall," Mary says, and smiles. "You can ring him with this if you need him." She picks up a wood-handled brass bell, oddly similar to the bells from the church choir.

Rozanne's lopsided grin meets Gage's frown.

"Thank you," Rozanne says, resting on the side of the bed.

"Get comfy," Mary says, fluffing the pillows as Rozanne leans back.

"I'll head into town and fill these prescriptions," Monroe says, leaning to kiss her left temple. He whispers, "And smuggle some ice cream and pudding on my way back."

"I also have two scripts from Spa View," Rozanne says, reaching for her purse. Mary moves it closer to her and Rozanne pulls out the two small slips of paper.

Monroe smiles. "Great, I'll take those."

"I'll make some breakfast for Gage and let him rest for a few hours," Mary says, patting Gage on the shoulder. "Monroe can bring him back some toiletries from the pharmacy, including a bottle of shaving cream and a razor."

"You don't like the new look?" Gage says, fighting a yawn.

Mary pats his only smooth cheek and heads towards the kitchen.

Gage settles into the oversized chair in the corner near the bay window. "Do you think they can adopt me, too?"

"Ha, ha," Rozanne says.

"How's the pain?" he asks.

She holds up six fingers.

"Do you want to see the damage?" he asks.

Yes, no, ah hell, yes. She gives him a thumbs up.

He ducks into the bathroom and brings over a hand mirror.

"You sure?" he asks.

She glares at him with her left eye.

He lifts the mirror into focus.

The blood drenched face she saw in the mirror right after it happened is now a blue and purple swollen mass covering the right side of her face, from her chin to her hairline. She parts her mouth to examine her teeth. Only one tooth looks bad with a small chip.

Mary's footsteps start down the hall. Gage snatches the mirror and hides it behind his back.

"First round of peas," Mary says, holding a red wrapped bag of frozen peas. She unwraps the bag and shows Gage how to fold the cloth around and tuck it in. She hands the peas over to Rozanne and draws the curtains. "I'll come with another bag after I finish feeding and tucking in Gage." She winks at Rozanne before leaving the room.

Gage bites a knuckle until she is out of earshot. "I know you always said she was a saint. By heavens, you're right!"

Rozanne points to the bell and waves him out of the room. He minds her dismissal and disappears down the hall. She sighs and adjusts the ice pack before falling into darkness.

7

"Achoo!" Gage sneezes.

Rozanne startles awake and jerks her head to the side.

"Ugh," she moans. She slowly opens her left eye. The curtains are still closed, but she can make out Gage's figure. She slowly sits up, and a whoosh of pain fills her face.

Gage stands. "Sorry, I didn't mean to wake you," he says, coming to her side.

"It's okay. What time is it?"

"Noonish," he says, pulling out his phone. "Oh actually, just after one. You're due for a round of meds."

"I need the bathroom first," Rozanne says, plopping her feet to the floor. She waits for the throbbing to slow before standing.

Gage stands close but gives her the space she needs to make it to the bathroom.

"Do you want soup or a smoothie?" he asks, just before she closes the door.

"Smoothie."

"What kind?"

"Surprise me." She takes her time in the bathroom, washing her hands, and examining the damage. She's transformed from dark blue to eggplant purple since her glimpse this morning. She ambles back to bed.

Gage returns with a few pills and a purple smoothie. "Blueberry, banana, protein powder, and yogurt."

"Protein?" Rozanne asks, trying to get into a comfortably seated position.

"Mary's orders," Gage says and laughs. "She made a list of approved ingredients and amounts before leaving."

Rozanne tries to smile, but it hurts. She reaches for the smoothie. He hands it over and sets the pills on the side table.

She takes a sip through the straw and flinches.

"Is it bad?" he asks.

"Pain," she whispers.

"Noted," Gage says, "no straw."

She sips directly from the glass instead, pressing only against the left corner of her mouth. She swallows with ease.

Gage points to the different pills on the side table. "These are the ones Monroe filled this morning. The smallest is the pain medication. He said you can have two but to start with one."

He opens the curtains, and she points to his face while sipping.

"Yea, yea," Gage says, running his knuckles over his smooth jaw. "I'm almost positive Viola took a photo of my half shaven face while I was in the waiting room."

Rozanne chokes a little on the smoothie.

"No need for added laughter," he chides.

"Work," she whispers, pointing at him.

"Dusty is handling it," Gage says, plopping down in the chair. "He is finally getting to touch all of my tools. But he's a good mechanic and I trust that he won't burn the place down in my absence." He smiles and looks out the window. "The view from here to the pond is nice."

Rozanne's mind wanders to a previous conversation.

"The view from here is so nice," the lady says.

"You can thank my Grandma Edith," Rozanne's mom, Bonnie, says.

The lady turns and smiles. "Oh?"

"Edith made sure every window framed a piece of beauty around the property." Bonnie walks to the long narrow window next to the fireplace. "Stand here and tell me what you see."

The lady, curious, walks over to the spot and peers out the window. "My heavens," she whispers and walks closer to the window. "Is that weeping willow tree winking at me?"

Bonnie laughs. "Yes. My grandpa was clearing land for the house and Edith marked certain trees to keep. She used vines to tie back the branches." She points to the open curve of the willow branches. "She painted the lashes on the underside of a nodule on the tree and waited for my grandpa to notice." She smiles. "It was their first winter in the house and he was stacking wood for the fire when he caught sight of the tree."

"And was he amused?" the lady asks.

"He called Edith in to the room and pointed at the window. According to her, she just winked and left the room."

～✦～ ～✦～

"Earth to Rozanne," Gage says.

Rozanne watches a few ducks dive under the water of the pond before she sets down the empty glass and turns to face him.

"Present," she says quietly.

"Where did you go?" Gage leans forward, his eyebrows reaching his dark hairline.

She points to the window and reaches for the pills. She takes only one with a sip of water.

Gage stands and takes her empty glass from the side table. "I'm going to get you another round of frozen peas, unless you're still hungry?"

"Peas," Rozanne says, sitting up a little further in the bed. She reaches for the local newspaper sitting on top of the magazines.

She shakes it out and starts to read.

Cold Case Missing Persons: Margaret Penelope Vance is the only bold heading under the name of the newspaper at the top.

She gasps and immediately regrets it. She mumbles a curse.

Gage returns with the frozen peas.

Rozanne holds up the paper and points to the article.

Gage trades the bag of peas for the paper. He lowers to the edge of the bed.

"The Vance family were regular patrons of the Castle Rock Hotel after it was completed in 1905," Gage reads aloud. "On June 22, 1918, the couple left the hotel for dinner. When they returned to the family suite, their fourteen-year-old daughter, Margaret, was missing. She did not attend the formal dinners during their stays because of her condition." He looks up from the paper. "What condition?"

"Down syndrome?" Rozanne asks, lifting the peas from her face.

Gage's right eyebrow goes up. He continues reading. "After a thorough search of the hotel and grounds, the girl remained missing. They called in the local sheriff to assist. All guests and staff were questioned. The parents claimed they had left her locked in the hotel suite just before seven." He shakes his head. "Why would you lock a teenager in a room?"

Rozanne motions her finger in a circle at her temple.

He smirks. "Yea, sounds crazy to me too!" Then he continues. "But the lobby staff says she walked out to the garden gazebo just before eight. This was her evening ritual, according to some." He moves to sit more comfortably on the bed. "One housekeeper says she would often find the girl wandering the grounds during the family's previous visits, even though the parents claimed she was locked inside their suite." He moves the paper down to look at Rozanne. "Her parents sound awful!"

Rozanne frowns and nods.

Gage raises the paper again. "When the news of her disappearance was made public the next day, a former maid came forward and claimed the missing young lady knew all the servant entrances and secret doorways in the hotel. She would often play hide and seek with the staff while her parents were socializing." Gage smiles over the paper. "Ha! At least somebody acknowledges she's a human and not a pet to be locked away."

Rozanne gave him a thumbs up with extreme effort. Pain or no pain, she's never liked the woozy sensation when medication kicked in.

Gage reads on. "The parents were surprised and threatened to sue the hotel and charge the staff with child endangerment and kidnapping." He coughs. "More like charge *them* with abuse."

Rozanne makes a check in the air with her finger.

"After ten days and no further leads, the case went cold. It was shelved after a year."

"Date," Rozanne says.

"Date for what?" Gage asks.

Rozanne gestures for the paper. She points to the date the girl went missing, and then the date on the paper: June 23, 2018.

"One hundred years ago?" Gage asks.

"Ding, ding," Rozanne says.

"You saw a ghost?" Gage leans forward, his pupils double.

She raises one hand, palm up, and shrugs her shoulder.

"Rozanne, this is weird." Gage takes the paper back from her. "The article continues on the sixth page." He flips to the sixth page and drags his finger down until he finds the continuation. "On May 4, 1921, a young lady walked into the Castle Rock Hotel. A maid recognized her as the missing girl. She followed her towards the family's usual suite. The girl stopped near the door and tapped on the wood paneling. It clicked and opened. The girl ducked into the small opening." He looks over the paper. "Still conscious over there?"

Rozanne gives him a weak thumbs up.

He continues. "The maid attempted to follow her, but she could not get the panel to release. When she reported this to the hotel manager, she was dismissed. She made a report with the local sheriff, but it was misfiled and only found five years later when the office was moved to a new location." Gage laughs. "Figures they would drop the ball on this. Do you remember when they couldn't 'find' that rich lawyer's stolen car even though it was sitting in the police impound lot?"

She moves the bag of peas. "Ah, yea! The lawyer had found a loophole to dismiss all the evidence in a big trial and the arresting officer impounded his car out of revenge." Gage nods. "Didn't the police chief resign after that?"

"Oh, yeah." Gage snickers. "It was his nephew or cousin that hid the car."

She points to the paper. "Is there more?"

He nods. "The notes from the follow up to this report were dated September 1926. The Castle Rock Hotel was sold to Robert Ball by this date as an extension of the Ball Sanitarium. The sheriff found and interviewed the old hotel manager. He inspected the wood panels near the door to the suite in question, but it was a dead end. The small alcove was an old storage area."

Knock, knock

Gage looks up from the paper. "Was that Maggie? Is she here?"

"Go see who is at the front door?" Rozanne says, pointing in the direction of the hallway.

Gage wipes his forehead. "You could have played that up a little more."

"Next time," Rozanne says.

Gage puts the paper down out of her reach. "Don't read ahead! Be right back."

Rozanne sighs and hears the front door swing open. She hears a hushed conversation but can't make out the visitor. The front door closes, and the fridge door opens and closes.

Gage whistles a familiar tune as he returns down the hall and plops back on the bed, picking up the paper. He shakes it out dramatically. He stops whistling. "Now, where were we?"

Rozanne chucks the bag of peas at him.

Gage catches the bag and almost launches it back towards her, but he catches himself before throwing it. "What?"

"Door?" Rozanne asks, taking the bag of peas back.

"Oh! It was Viola and Cora," Gage says with a straight face and then burst out laughing. "Cora was waiting in the car, but Viola gasped when I swung open the door. She scowled at me before shoving a plastic bowl in my chest. I pointed to the blood droplets on the front porch leading from the wicker chair to the front door. She mumbled something and then said 'it's banana pudding' before marching back down to the car."

Rozanne laughs but abruptly stops holding the right side of her face.

"Now can I read again?" Gage says.

"Water," Rozanne chokes out.

Gage nods, stretching over her to reach the glass from the side table. She takes the glass and sips it dry.

"Thanks," Rozanne says, handing it back.

Gage stares at her before putting it back on the side table. "We can finish this later if you need to rest."

"I'm good," Rozanne says, resting the cool bag back on her face.

He adjusts the pillow between his back and the ornate footboard. He clears his throat and begins again. "But after pulling the cold case file and reviewing the case notes, the sheriff returned to the property. He asked the staff to show him the servant passages and found a false wall leading to the hallway near the suite entrance." He waggles his eyebrows at Rozanne. "It's getting good!"

"Interesting," Rozanne says.

"The hotel manager was taken to the station for further questioning but later released. No further information about why he was released was noted, and no formal arrests were ever made in the connection to Margaret Penelope Vance. The case remains one of our town's biggest mysteries. The current police station archives show at least eight more reported encounters with a young lady matching her description." Gage winks at Rozanne. "Make that nine."

"Ha, ha," she says, closing her good eye. The room remains quiet. She sighs and lets the drowsiness win.

8

Rozanne pain ripples from her hairline to her chin. "Ugh!" She grips the sheets and waits for the throbbing to subside. She inhales and slowly exhales, opening her left eye.

The afternoon light filters in over the light throw on the chair in the corner. The shimmering pond hints its late afternoon or early evening.

Thud

Rozanne sits up and immediately considers lying back down, but swings her legs over the edge and stands. The floorboards squeak under her weight.

"You up?" Gage shouts from the hall. He breathes heavily as he ambles to her doorway with two boxes covered in dust.

"What's that?" Rozanne asks, pointing at him.

"Research!" Gage says, winking.

"Dust!" She points to her face. "No sneezing!"

He nods, backs out, and ambles down the hall to the kitchen.

In the bathroom, her reflection makes her stomach turn. Her face from the left side is remarkably normal compared to the fifty shades of purple and mounds of swelling on the right.

"Dust free," Gage calls from her room.

She opens the door, assessing the stacks of old newspapers he is adding to one side of the bed.

"Are you hungry?" Gage asks, looking up.

Rozanne gives him a thumbs up before walking back to the bed.

"Soup or a smoothie?" Gage asks.

"Both," Rozanne murmurs after shifting on the bed.

"Great, be right back." He jogs out of the bedroom.

She hears him open and shut the fridge several times before the hum of the microwave begins.

She reaches for the yellowed paper on top of the stack nearest her. The date at the top of the old paper is July 1, 1918. She scans the headlines and finds no mention of the missing girl. She carefully opens each page and runs a finger over the headlines. On the fourth page, she finds the first mention of the Castle Rock Hotel. It's an advertisement for their upcoming fourth of July celebrations.

"That's it?" she mumbles.

Gage sets down the bowl of soup. "That's what?"

She points to the advertisement.

Gage hands her a smoothie and takes the paper. He thumbs through the rest of the paper and stops on the second to last page. "Bingo!"

He turns the paper towards Rozanne as she swallows a large sip of the cool banana and peanut butter smoothie.

He reads the bold text on the bottom corner. "Missing: Margaret P. Vance, 14, strawberry blonde hair, green eyes and goes by Maggie."

"That's it?" Rozanne asks, setting the smoothie next to the bowl of soup.

Gage nods. "Eat up. The soup is warm but not hot."

Rozanne takes the spoon, pointing it at him and down to the papers. "How did you know about these?"

"Anne," Gage says.

"Explain?" she says, taking a spoonful and savoring the warm soup.

"Your Grandma Anne always talked about the stacks of newspapers left in the attic. Have you been up there?"

Rozanne nods. Her great grandparents were one of the first to invest in the local paper with a handshake agreement to a lifetime weekly subscription.

"Great Grandma Edith kept them for these," Rozanne says, showing Gage the sewing pattern on the fifth page. "For the first eighteen years, every paper included a new pattern."

Gage grins. "That explains the other labels inside each box." He points over his shoulder to the hall. "It has the months and year on the outside but articles of clothing written on the inside." He hovers his hand over one stack. "These are from the months just after the girl is reported missing and these," he says, hovering his hand over the next stack, "are from the fall of 1926 when the case was opened again for more questions."

"That bored?" Rozanne asks, scraping the bowl.

"Curious," he says, picking up another paper. "Are you going to lick the bowl, too?" He winks and exchanges the paper he is holding with her empty bowl.

"Ha, ha." She glares at him.

He holds up the bowl. "Do you want seconds?"

She raises up her smoothie. "I'm good."

"Ready for another round of pain meds?" he asks, walking towards the door.

"Later." She holds up the paper.

He nods and heads to the kitchen.

Buzz

Rozanne reaches for her phone and thumbs her passcode to open. A few unread message notifications linger at the top, but one is from a number she doesn't have saved.

"Um?" she whispers.

Gage slides into the room.

"Did you give out my number?" she asks, shaking her phone.

"No," Gage says. "Why?"

"Odd." She stares at the message: *Maggie is real.*

She hands her phone to Gage.

"That's creepy," Gage says.

"Do you recognize the number?" Rozanne asks.

"No," Gage says, handing her phone back. He looks around the room. "Do you think somebody is listening?"

Rozanne's eyes dart around the room. "Gage? Are you messing with me?"

He shakes his head. "Did you tell anyone else about your encounter with Maggie?"

"Mary and Monroe know about my encounters at the pharmacy, and Monroe asked the postman if he knew anyone by that name or description." She shakes her head. "And of course, Peggy and her sister Minnie think I am nuts."

A shadow dances across the room. Rozanne slowly turns to look out the window. The evening dusk is a pink and orange fire, across the horizon.

Gage stands and moves across the room, blocking her view outside. "Roz, do you have new neighbors?"

"No." She sets the paper aside and stands. The room tilts as an aching pain slides down her face. Her knees soften and she leans on the side of the bed. "Why do you ask?"

"There is a girl standing on the far side of the pond."

"Not funny." Rozanne says, too forced.

Gage whirls to face Rozanne and takes two giant steps to help her sit back down on the bed. "You're dripping in sweat!" He feels her head with the back of his hand. "And burning up. I'm calling Monroe."

"No," she whispers, leaning back on the pillow. "It's just the pain. It is bad."

"Fine, an ice pack and a pain pill." He glares at her. "Don't move!"

Rozanne gives a weak thumbs up and turns her head to face the window as he bolts out of the room.

The natural light near the pond is nearly gone. A petite figure is walking away from the water's edge back to the woody hill that leads down to the creek.

Gage slides into the room with a pill and another frozen pea bag.

"Go!" Rozanne says, pointing to the window.

"Roz," Gage says, staring at her. "I can't leave you alone. Remember, doctor's orders."

"Two minutes, go!" She pops the pill in her mouth and sips a bit of water.

"Fine! Where's your flashlight?"

"Missing!"

He frowns.

She turns the flashlight app on and tosses her phone to him.

He catches the phone and shakes his head before jogging out of the room.

She watches him cross the yard. The beam of the flashlight moves up and down as he walks around the high side of the pond and disappears down the hill.

9

"Gage?" Rozanne calls out when the front door opens.

"No, it's Monroe." He shuffles down the hall to her open bedroom door. "Where's Gage?"

"Went to check on a girl," Rozanne says, pointing to the window. "Out near the pond."

"How long ago?" Monroe asks, walking to her side of the bed. "Are you sweating?"

Rozanne shrugs. "About ten minutes ago, maybe longer. He took my phone."

Monroe places his hand against her non-bruised cheek. "He left you alone without a phone?"

"It was my idea," she says, adjusting the frozen peas.

"Raise it up," Monroe says. "Let me take a look."

She removes the bag and watches the crease between his eyebrows deepen.

"All good?" She crosses her fingers.

"Not unless you like the color blueberry," he says. "Your swelling and the bruising are shockingly bad."

"Roz!" Gage shouts, as the back screen door snaps shut. "I think we need to call the sheriff." He jogs down the hall and slides to a stop. "Hey Monroe."

"Gage, your orders were to not leave Rozanne alone."

Gage throws his hands up. "I made that argument and lost." He points a finger at Rozanne.

"Why do we need to call the sheriff?" Rozanne asks.

"I didn't find the girl," Gage says, gesturing towards the window. "But there is an old pair of black shoes near the creek bed."

"Old shoes and you want to call the sheriff?" Monroe asks, folding his arms across his chest.

"They are small and there were two long white socks lying next to them." He bends, touching his leg just below the knee. "You know, the ones girls wear to here."

"Can you describe the… shoes?" Rozanne whispers.

Monroe turns towards Rozanne. "What's going on?"

"They're like um… small with a buckle across the top and a rounded toe." Gage says, handing her back the phone.

Rozanne types in 'Mary Jane shoes' and shows Gage the first image that pops up.

Gage nods. "Yea, but like older. Not dirty, just looked old."

"Monroe," Rozanne says, picking up today's paper. "Did you read the paper today?"

Monroe nods. "The cold case is old news, a local folk tale at this point. Why?"

Rozanne shows him the second article they found calling the missing girl Maggie and the text she had received from the unknown number.

He looks up from the phone. "The girl you saw with Mrs. Arber yesterday, you called her Maggie."

"Yes, I saw Maggie again last night at Spa View Manor."

Monroe shakes his head. "Mrs. Arber was quite concerned when she came into the pharmacy today." He takes the paper to the chair in the corner and sits down, removing a pair of reading glasses from his jacket. "When she asked about you, I just said you would be out for a few weeks."

"You think the text is from Mrs. Arber?" Rozanne asks.

"Maybe, but how did she get your number?" Monroe asks.

"You didn't give it to her?" Rozanne asks.

"No," Monroe says.

She makes eye contact with Gage.

46

Gage shakes his head. "Sorry Roz, I have no clue about the text message. But I think we need to call the sheriff to report what we saw and found this evening."

"Um, okay," Rozanne says, pointing to her face. "My pain pill is kicking in."

Gage steps across the hall and returns with his phone. "I'll step outside. My cell reception in here is spotty."

Monroe looks over the open paper and nods. "I've got eyes on her. Go ahead."

Gage walks down the hall and steps outside, closing the front door behind him.

"Monroe," Rozanne says, fighting the woozy sensation. "What did you mean by 'old news'?"

"Every five to ten years, a reporter finds the thread about the missing girl and writes a new article. It's never anything new, just a page filler for a slow news week."

"I've never heard of her before," she says.

"Are you sure?" Monroe says, putting the paper aside. "It made headlines about five years ago when the last heir to the Vance estate died with no will."

"All the Vances are gone?" Rozanne asks, sitting up a little straighter.

"All but the missing girl," Monroe says. "She was never declared dead."

"Why not?" Rozanne asks, fighting the wooziness.

"The wealthy grandparents of the missing girl had their inheritance set up in her name. If her parents declared her dead, the fortune would have been given away to charities." He frowns again. "Simply put, greed."

"Ugh." She lifts the pack from her face to take a sip of water. She looks past the glass to Monroe and swallows. "If the last Vance died, what is the connection with Mrs. Arber and her sister Minnie?"

"That's an excellent question," Monroe says, turning towards the door as Gage's footsteps pound down the hall.

"Okay," Gage says, gasping for a breath. "So don't freak out, but there was a report of a missing girl about the same size as the one we saw earlier. She was last seen wearing a school uniform with white knee socks and black shoes." He blows out a long breath. "They're sending every available deputy and a search party this way."

"I need to call Mary before she catches wind of this." Monroe waves his phone and steps out of the bedroom.

"Is this real or am I in some kind of nightmare?" Rozanne asks, placing the bag of peas back on her face.

"Too real." Gage takes the stack of papers from the bed and turns to leave the room.

"Wait," Rozanne says. Gage turns back to face her. "Why are you taking those?"

"I think a real case and a cold case is too much to digest at the moment." He gestures to the window. "Right?"

Rozanne fills him in on the details about the Vance family fortune Monroe shared.

"Do you think the cases are related?" Gage asks.

"No," Rozanne says, "well at least I don't think so."

10

Red and blue lights whirl around the yard as additional squad cars file down the drive.

A loud, quick knock on the front door makes Rozanne jostle the bag of peas.

Monroe raises his hand and motions for Gage to stay with Rozanne. He answers the door to a buzz of conversation and a few radio chirps.

"The kids are here in the back bedroom," Monroe says. He widens the door and gestures to the two deputies. They remain standing on the porch. "Rozanne is on bedrest."

The first deputy removes his hat and steps across the threshold. "And you are?"

"Monroe." He turns towards the hall. "My wife, Mary, is on her way here with dinner for me and the kids. Will you let your other deputy near the road know?"

A radio chirps. Rozanne hears footsteps in the hall.

Gage straightens and stands between the door and Rozanne. The deputies enter.

"I'm Deputy Morris." He takes out a small notebook and pen from his belt. "Can you walk me through what you saw, exactly?"

"Just before dusk," Gage says, walking to the window. "We saw a young girl standing on the far side of the pond."

Deputy Morris turns towards Rozanne. "You saw this too?"

"Yes," Rozanne answers. "Gage saw her first and left the room to fetch me a pain pill. I watched the young girl turn and walk towards the woods." Rozanne lifts the bag to expose her face. "I would have checked on her, but this…"

The second deputy whistles long and low. "That's some bruise." He sneers towards Gage and rests his hand on the baton at this hip.

Gage raises his hands. "I was only her ride to the hospital last night."

Deputy Morris frowns. "How did the injury happen?"

"I fell face first out of a chair swing onto the front porch."

Gage nods towards the door. "Her story is consistent with the blood droplets on the front porch."

The deputies make quick eye contact. The second deputy steps out and walks out to the porch.

Deputy Morris looks down at his notes and focuses on Gage. "When you returned to the room, what happened next?"

"Rozanne tossed me her phone with the flashlight on and ordered me to check on the girl."

"Ordered?" Deputy Morris looks over at Rozanne.

"I'm not supposed to be left alone until after I see the doctor again."

The deputy nods. "Are you renting the property?"

"No, I own it," Rozanne says, waiting for his next question. He only stares at her. "I inherited the house and land from my grandparents."

"From your grandparents," Deputy Morris says, raising his pen. "And your parents?"

"They were killed six years ago by a drunk driver," Rozanne whispers. "They're buried out in Elmira next to my grandparents."

"My condolences." The deputy jots down a few lines. He turns to Gage. "And your relationship to Rozanne?"

"Friend."

The deputy nods. "And what did you do next?"

"I went out the back door and jogged to the high side of the pond and down through the woods to the creek." He shakes his

50

head. "I didn't see the girl, but found a pair of black shoes and white socks near the water."

"Can you show me the path you took from the house to the creek?"

"Yes," Gage says, nodding his chin to Rozanne. "It's the same worn path Roz and I always take."

The deputy raises the corner of his mouth. "Just friends?" He stares directly at Rozanne.

"We've been friends since we were six," Rozanne says, looking past the deputy to the window. "He knows the woods here better than I do."

"And how do you know Monroe?" the deputy asks.

"He's my boss at the pharmacy," Rozanne answers.

"He makes house calls?" the deputy asks.

"Only because my Grandma Anne made Monroe and his wife Mary swear to look after me."

Mary barges into the room as if summoned. "And because we love her like our own."

"And you are?" The deputy frowns at the second deputy standing at the door behind Mary.

"Mary." She comes to Rozanne's side of the bed and kisses her temple. "Weren't you listening?"

"Ma'am," he says. "You just interrupted the first witness statement we've had for a local missing girl."

"It's only getting darker," Mary says. "Go on, get outside and look. Gage can show you where they saw what. Rozanne needs to rest."

Gage bites his knuckle to keep from laughing as the deputy tries to respond. He ends up closing his mouth and exiting the room.

"Mary," Rozanne chides.

Mary snickers. "Well, I'm not wrong."

Monroe walks into the room with a wide grin. "Why did the deputy look like somebody stole his lunch money?"

Mary waves her hand in the air. "Rozanne should rest and talking is painful, right?" She looks down at Rozanne.

"A bit," Rozanne says.

Monroe laughs and holds up an ear thermometer. "She felt a little warm. Can you check?"

Mary pushes back Rozanne's hair and gently slides it into her ear with practiced precision. "How close is the nearest house from here?"

"The Clevengers own the land on the other side of the creek," Monroe says, leaning on the bedpost. "But the house there has been empty for the last decade. And the Kings' ranch is about another two miles to the east. To walk would be maybe twenty minutes through the woods and another ten minutes through the pastures."

Beep

Mary sucks in a breath as she removes it from Rozanne's ear. "You're right, 99.6°F." She shows the output to Rozanne and then to Monroe.

Mary heads for the bedroom door. "She is off limits to anyone else this evening." She returns from the hall closet with a quilt and unfolds it across Rozanne's bed.

"It's June in Missouri." Monroe shakes his head. "Not really quilt season." He winks at Rozanne as he moves out of Mary's way.

Rozanne half smiles and feels the drowsiness kick in.

11

Gage follows the deputies to a group gathering near the pond. A few volunteers are handing out reflective vests and flags along with flashlights. Gage takes an offered vest and slides it on. He scans the crowd, a mixture of law enforcement, and a few locals from town and the school.

Deputy Morris hands Gage a large flashlight and nods to a uniformed officer behind Gage. "Patrol Sergeant Littrell will take the lead. Shine the light ahead of him to show him where you walked earlier."

Gage nods.

"Alright," Deputy Morris shouts to the sea of faces beside Gage. "The first group will start here." He points to the pond and the woods down the hill. "Groups two and three fan out to the east into the tree line." He holds up a reflective flag on a thin metal stick. "Flag anything that seems out of place. Her name is Penelope. Her family calls her Penny. If you find her, immediately, radio the group lead."

Gage stiffens and turns to Littrell. "Is her first name Penelope, or is that her middle name?"

"First, I think," Littrell answers. "Why?"

"Um…" Gage stalls, unsure how to answer.

"Let's go people," Deputy Morris commands.

Littrell marches forward.

Gage sighs and follows. He shines his light on the worn path.

Littrell pauses and marks a boot print in the dirt near the high side of the pond.

Gage looks at the tread of his own boot. They match the print in the dirt.

"Nervous?" Deputy Morris asks, leaning close to Gage's ear.

Gage jumps forward and whirls to face him. "Dude! Personal space ever heard of it?"

"Hmm," Deputy Morris says and nods. "Keep moving."

Gage hesitantly turns back towards the path and shines the light near the edge of the pond. "There are a few springs on the property. The grass can be slick."

Every three steps, Littrell pauses and marks another print. Gage shines his light on the path and directs them down a steeper part of the hill.

Littrell slides a bit, breaking off a few branches to catch his weight.

The deputy mumbles, "Way to disturb the scene."

"We are close to the creek," Gage says. He nods to Littrell. "And the shoes and socks are just there." He points his light over to the edge of the trickling water.

The patrol sergeant and the deputy freeze.

Gage walks forward, but the deputy clamps his hand down on Gage's shoulder.

"Stay," Deputy Morris says. He nudges Gage behind him, unsnaps his holster, and keeps his hand on his sidearm.

Gage attempts to see past him, but the light only goes as far as the creek.

Littrell doesn't move as the deputy passes.

The deputy shines his light over the rocks next to the shoes and socks. He pauses the light over jagged blue rocks with flecks of silver. They're lined up in the shape of a small arrow pointing across the creek to another arrow made from similar rocks. The second arrow points back across the creek to the shoes.

"The arrows weren't here earlier," Gage says.

Deputy Morris turns to him. "Are you one hundred percent sure?"

"Yes," Gage says, pointing to the boot print next to the black shoes. "I squatted right there to inspect the shoes, but I've watched enough TV to know better than to actually touch something. I would have had to step on the rocks."

Littrell walks forward and inspects the print. "He's right. The print impression is deeper than the others." He shines a light directly over the arrows. "And the rocks look dry and clean."

"And not from this creek," Gage blurts out.

They turn away from the rocks to face Gage.

"I've played in this creek nearly my entire life." He points up and down the creek. "I've never seen rocks like this here." He bends and picks up a few from the creek's edge. "It's mostly just dull gray or brown pebbles, never bigger than a quarter."

Deputy Morris nods and clicks his radio. "Search lead."

"Copy."

"Is the rock shop owner, Lorraine Michaels, still here?" Deputy Morris pans his flashlight over the ground around the socks and shoes.

"Yes sir," the lead responds. "In the third search group."

"Copy," Deputy Morris answers, fixing his beam of light on the white socks. "Send Ms. Michaels and the evidence team with lights down to the creek."

The area around the path to the creek, the arrows, shoes, and socks, are marked off with stakes and yellow tape.

Gage watches a tech photograph the socks and shoes. They bag, label, and seal each of them individually before placing them in a larger bag.

Another tech gestures towards Gage's boots. "I will need to make a cast of your boots to compare to the other prints we find."

Gage nods.

Deputy Morris walks to Gage's side. "Do you know if there are any wells on the property?"

"Two," Gage says, pointing back towards the house. "There is an old pump house about fifty feet from the house to the west of the drive and a second old well in the woods further east towards the Kings' property."

"Do you know if they are still actively used?"

"The one close to the house, yes," Gage answers. "The second was used until about six or seven years ago. Roz never mentioned why they stopped using it."

"Who are they?"

"The Kings," Gage says. "I think they used it for their livestock."

"But the well is on this property?"

"Near the border with the Kings' ranch, but yes, technically on her side of the property line." Gage tilts his head to the side. "Why is all of this important?"

"Just checking all the boxes." He directs the evidence team to set up the lights around the marked area. "Ah, Ms. Michaels."

"Please, Lorraine is fine. How can I help?"

Gage watches Deputy Morris motion her over the yellow tape. She steps over and follows him towards the creek.

The deputy shines his light over the arrow. "Do you recognize these rocks?"

She squats to get a closer look. "May I pick one piece up?"

The closest tech gives the deputy a thumbs up.

The deputy nods.

She picks up a piece and stands. She hovers her flashlight, turning the rock over, and then squats again near the water and rinses it off. "It looks like a shard of kyanite."

"Is that something you would expect to find in this area?" Deputy Morris asks.

The young woman shakes her head. "No, in fact, it's typically found only near the Appalachian Mountains."

"Odd," Gage mutters.

She bends over the rest of the shards and glances up. "They aren't that rare. We stock them in our shop. But if I remember right, they are very…" She stands and scrunches her nose. "Symbolic."

"How so?" Deputy Morris asks.

"Historically, they were left near a trail to point out nearby graveyards," she says. "Most notable during the wagon trail days during the Gold Rush era."

Gage shudders.

"Thanks." Deputy Morris writes the information down and escorts her back over the yellow tape. "Please leave your contact information with the search lead if you haven't already."

She nods but squints across the creek.

"Is there something else?" Deputy Morris asks.

She points past his shoulder to a tree on the far side of the creek. "A large crow just landed on a branch of that tree."

Gage turns his flashlight in that direction, panning the beam of light from the roots hanging over the creek slowly up the trunk of the tree.

He pauses. A piece of bark is missing and an arrow pointing up is carved into the tree.

"What the hell?" Deputy Morris mumbles.

Gage's beam follows the trunk of the tree up to the branches.

A screeching call from the crows scream in unison and four large crows dive towards them all at once.

Gage drops the flashlight. The techs scramble behind trees and duck, covering their heads.

Gage steps in front of Lorraine as one crow dives straight for her. She ducks and screams as the crow buzzes over Gage's head, missing him by inches. Then, the birds fly off into the night.

"It's clear," Gage whispers down to Lorraine. She looks up and past him to the other techs now standing and dusting off their pants and jackets.

"Thanks," she says, standing. "Are you a cop?"

"God no!" Gage says.

Deputy Morris coughs behind him.

"No offense," Gage says to him.

Deputy Morris walks between Lorraine and Gage, raising his flashlight to Gage's face. "Have you seen the arrow on that tree before?"

Gage closes his eyes and turns away from his light. "No, never." He laughs. "But there is one tree on the property that you may find a little strange."

"Why is that?" Deputy Morris asks.

"The willow tree has eyelashes painted on the trunk of the tree."

Lorraine laughs.

The deputy frowns. "Why?"

Gage smiles. "Art. Well, Edith's interpretation of art."

Deputy Morris scans his notebook. "Who is Edith?"

"Roz's Great Grandma."

"We've got something," a tech hollers near the creek.

Gage lifts a foot to cross over the yellow tape.

Deputy Morris shakes his head. He points at Gage and Lorraine. "Stay put."

They nod. Lorraine stands on her toes and strains to see.

The tech is squatting near the edge of the creek, holding the beam of a flashlight between the two arrows. A shiny copper penny is wedged between two rocks just above the stream.

"A penny," Deputy Morris whispers. "Collect it as evidence." He taps his radio. "Search lead."

"Did he say penny?" Gage murmurs. Lorraine nods.

The deputy walks away scanning each tree with his flashlight surrounding the taped off scene.

"Copy," a man's voice answers over the radio.

"Status?"

"Group two cleared the woods to a fence line to the east, and the third group is circling back, covering the land from the road to the house."

58

"Copy," Deputy Morris responds and turns back towards the techs.

A crow swoops over his head. He ducks and watches it land on a branch of the tree across the creek.

"Creepy," he mutters, panning the beam of his flashlight back to the arrow in the tree. Something glints in the light. He slowly pans the beam back over the trunk. "I think there is something embedded in the arrow."

A tech jumps the creek and climbs up the embankment. He changes the flash settings on his camera and focuses the lens on the arrow. He snaps a few times and looks at the viewfinder. "Sir, I believe we have another coin."

The deputy jumps the creek and scrambles up to the tree. He rolls to his toes to level his eyes with the arrow. He places his light just below. "It's another penny." He follows the light past the arrow to the branches and finds the beady eyes of the four crows looking down.

"Can you make out the year on the penny?" a tech asks, who is standing close to Gage.

The deputy places the light directly over the coin. "1918."

Gage coughs to cover a curse.

"Same," the tech says, holding up the evidence bag.

"Did you just say shit?" Lorraine whispers.

Gage shakes his head. "It's been a long, weird day."

"Two one hundred-year-old pennies, a pair of socks, shoes and foreign rocks," Deputy says, reviewing each item. "Plus, three arrows."

The tech beside him says, "Plus four crows."

They all look up as the birds take flight. They fly north.

"Gage, do you know what's on the land north of here?" the deputy shouts, flashing his light towards him.

"An old farmhouse," Gage says.

"Occupied?" the deputy asks.

"No," Gage says.

"Who owns the land?"

"It was Billy Clevenger," Gage says. "But he died a while ago. Not sure if the family took it over."

Deputy Morris jots down the name and points to Gage and Lorraine. "You two head back up and check in with the search lead. I'm sealing off this area."

"And Gage," the tech says, "just leave your shoes on the front porch. I'll take the mold and return them by dawn."

Gage nods and tilts his head toward Lorraine. "Ready?"

Her eyes are focused across the creek. "She's only fourteen." She shakes her head and turns to Gage. "Do you think we'll find her?"

"I hope so," Gage says, picking up the flashlight and scanning the path. He walks back up towards the house. Lorraine follows.

They hear bits of radio chatter and something about dogs as they clear the woods near the pond.

The yard around the house is flooded with people and large lights. A few tents and tables are set up near the drive.

"I hope Roz can sleep through all of this," Gage mumbles.

"Who is Roz?" Lorraine asks.

Gage nods his head towards the house. "The owner of the property."

"Why isn't he out here looking like the rest of us?" Lorraine asks.

"Roz is short for Rozanne, and she is on bedrest."

Lorraine stops walking. "Rozanne, the girl who works at the pharmacy, Rozanne?"

Gage turns, and Lorraine is scowling at him.

"What is that look for?" he asks.

"You're the Gage who beat up his girl?" She folds her arms across her chest.

"Jesus, the gossip in this town only gets worse." He shakes his head and walks away from her towards the house.

60

"But it's true, isn't it!" Lorraine says, following him. "You two were together right before she showed up in the emergency room with her face smashed in."

Gage whirls around and points a finger at her face. She jumps back. "You have no idea what you're talking about." He takes off the reflective vest and throws it on the ground. "Unbelievable."

12

Monroe stands from the porch swing as Gage stomps up the steps.

"What's wrong?" Monroe asks, assessing Gage's frown.

"This damn town's gossip train of lies and drama," Gage says, swinging open the front door.

Mary pokes her head out from the kitchen. "Muddy boots, stay outside."

Gage stops with one foot hovering over the threshold, then brings it back down on the porch. He turns back towards the steps and bends to unlace his boots. He slides them off.

Monroe chuckles. "Nothing gets past my Mary."

"It's all good," Gage says. "I actually need to leave these out here, anyway. A tech will swing by and pick these up."

Monroe nods but keeps his eyes focused on the crowd. "Did they find anything?"

"Yes and no," Gage says, fighting a yawn. "I'll fill you in after a hot shower."

Monroe nods.

Mary stands in the kitchen doorway, assessing Gage as he walks in. "I'll warm up some of the casserole after you shower."

Gage nods with a smile. "Thanks, give me ten minutes."

Mary steps out on the porch. "What happened?" she asks Monroe, closing the front door.

Monroe loops an arm around her. "Pretty sure the rumor that Gage is responsible for Rozanne's injuries has reached the height of town gossip."

Mary groans. She looks up at Monroe. "I answered at least ten phone calls today to squash this rumor out." She straightens. "I'm calling Viola's mother."

Monroe chuckles. "You realize Viola is the same age as Rozanne and Gage?"

"Yes," Mary says. She balls her hands and places her fists on her hips. "And Vi's mother is the biggest gossip in town. Where do you think she got it from?"

Monroe laughs and leans against the porch rail. He checks his watch. "It's almost midnight."

"Even better!" Mary turns and marches back inside.

A tech walks up to the porch. "I'm here for the boots."

Monroe points down to Gage's boots. "All yours." He nods to the crowd. "Are you wrapping up or just getting started?"

"The deputy is splitting up the group to search the farm north of here." They take the boots. "Thanks."

Monroe waves. He steps inside and closes the door as Gage emerges from the hallway. "A tech just picked up the boots," Monroe tells him. "Are you hungry?"

"I can always eat," Gage says.

"Now you listen here!" Mary shouts into the phone.

Gage turns to Monroe, eyes wide.

Monroe just smiles.

"Gage would never do such a thing," says Mary into the phone. "And I've seen the evidence with my own two eyes here on the porch. I'm still on the board at the hospital. I'll call the other members in the morning and file an official complaint." Mary paces in the kitchen. "What will that do? It will open an investigation against Viola for violating patient privacy!" Mary smiles and points to the phone when she turns to face Gage and Monroe. "And she can be sued for slander for her lies. I'll make sure my second call is to the prosecuting attorney." Mary pops a piece of the casserole into the microwave and sets the timer before pressing start. "You're calling her now?" She cuts a slice of bread and plates a salad. "I also want her to publicly apologize to Gage and to Rozanne." The microwave dings. "She has till noon tomorrow."

Mary disconnects the call and turns to Gage with two plates. "Hungry?"

Gage stares blankly back at Mary.

Monroe puts a finger under Gage's chin and pushes his hanging jaw back up.

Gage blinks. "Mary, um, you didn't have to do that?"

"Do what?" She smiles and puts the plates on the table.

Monroe chuckles. "Our saint, Mary, will do what she wants." He pulls out a chair for Gage. "Have a seat."

Gage moves to the offered chair and sits. "It smells great, thanks."

"You bet," Mary says, setting down an open beer next to his plate.

He lifts his beer. "To saint Mary."

Monroe raises his fresh mug of coffee. "To saint Mary."

Mary snaps a dish towel at Monroe. It hits his hip. Monroe frowns. Mary smiles and twirls the towel. "Saint what?"

Gage chokes on his beer. He coughs into his elbow.

Monroe shakes his head and sits across from Gage.

Mary fills a mug and sits beside Monroe.

Gage scrapes his salad plate and forks the last bite before moving on to the casserole.

Monroe sets his mug down. "Care to share what you saw down there?"

Gage nods and swallows. He explains the rock arrows and pennies.

"Pennies," Mary says, holding up a hand. "Isn't the missing girl named Penny?"

Gage nods. "That's not all. There is an old tree that hangs over the creek." Monroe nods. "And a third arrow is carved into the trunk of the tree with another penny stuck inside." Gage shakes his head. "Both pennies are dated 1918."

"That's odd," Mary says, taking a sip of her coffee.

"True," Gage says, finishing the last of the casserole. "But that year is significant." He nods to Monroe.

Monroe shakes his head. "Sorry, not following."

"Margaret P. Vance went missing in 1918. And the P stands for Penelope."

Monroe whistles.

Mary shakes her head. "The missing girl's full first name is Penelope."

Gage points to Mary. "Precisely. And the shoes I found by the creek are not new, they looked old." He shakes his head. "Monroe, what else do you recall about the Vance family?"

"They were wealthy," Monroe says and shrugs. "Not sure how that helps."

"Like old money or rags to riches?" Gage asks.

Monroe shrugs.

"That's a great question," Mary says. She stands and fetches her phone from the counter. She swipes open the screen and taps it a few times. She turns the phone to Gage. "I can't read without my glasses."

Gage takes her phone.

"Bingo!" he says as he starts to read. "The Vance family were the first successful investors of a mining operation in the Appalachian Mountains. They mined coal, iron ore, minerals, and precious jewels for nearly eighty years. Everett Vance was the first one to discover kyanite on American soil." He looks up from the screen. "The shop lady called the rocks kyanite."

"That's definitely a connection," Monroe says, twisting his mouth from side to side. "But do we share this with the deputy?"

Knock, knock

Gage jumps, knocking his head on the hanging light.

Mary rushes past Gage. She swings open the door. "Deputy," she says with a nod.

"Mary." He nods back. "We're done with Gage's boots." He sets them down just inside the door.

"Thanks," Gage says, walking towards the door.

"We will start our search of the woods again at first light and extend it north past the creek. We will have a team with dogs here in the morning." He looks past Gage to the hall. "I have a few additional questions for Rozanne."

"If it isn't urgent," Mary says. "I would prefer that you wait until morning. She was running a slight fever this evening after all the activity."

Deputy Morris nods. "Maybe Gage can assist." Gage nods. "The search team found a treehouse on the property."

Gage frowns and looks at Monroe.

Monroe shrugs.

"I've never seen a treehouse here," Gage says.

The deputy shakes his head. "It's in the willow tree that you mentioned down by the creek."

"Not possible," Gage says, walking to the long window next to the fireplace.

Several lights are pointed up at the tree. He leans closer to the window. A small platform is lit under the willow branches.

"That's new," Gage says, walking back to the door. "Roz, will have to explain it."

"In the morning," Mary says firmly.

"Yes, ma'am, it can wait. There will be a deputy on call through the night and into the morning." He nods to the tent set up outside. "Please let them know when she is awake."

Mary nods. "Good night, deputy."

Deputy Morris tilts his hat and closes the door.

13

"Why are dogs barking in my yard?" Rozanne mumbles, switching on the bedside lamp. She squints at the brightness of the light. She inches up and off the bed slowly. Upright and steady, she walks to the drawn curtains and peeks out.

The yard is full of people, squad cars and a few dogs on leashes. The early crest of dawn seeps through the tree line on the east side of the property.

"Oh dear," she whispers, staring out at the pond past the crowd. "It wasn't a nightmare." She recalls the young girl.

Rozanne flinches when a girl appears closer to the woods, on the far side of the pond. She blinks and shakes her head, but the girl is still there.

Rozanne raises her hand up to wave, but a person walks into her line of sight and stops. She takes a step to the right, but the girl is gone.

"Gage," Rozanne says, moving toward the bedroom door. "Gage!" she shouts, in spite of the pain.

The door swings open, missing her by an inch. She stumbles back.

"Shit!" Gage shouts, diving forward. He clasps her forearms and steadies her before she falls back. "Are you okay?"

One tear falls from her left eye. "I saw her!"

"What?" Gage asks, searching her face. "Who?"

"The girl from last night," she says, sucking in a breath. "Just past the pond, closer to the woods."

Gage looks past her towards the window. "Rozanne, the curtains are closed."

"I know," she says, stomping her foot. The jolt of movement makes her nauseous. "I peeked out when I heard the dogs barking and I saw her."

Gage frowns.

"I swear!" She pokes his chest and shakes her head. "A person walked into my line of sight and then she disappeared again. But she's so close."

"Okay." He looks down at his boxers and back at Rozanne. "I'll throw on some clothes and let the deputies know what you think you saw."

She back hands his shoulder. "I know I saw her!"

"Fine," he says, placing a protective hand over his shoulder and backing out of her reach. "Get dressed. Deputy Morris had a few more questions for you, and I have one as well."

"Go!" Rozanne gestures to the bedroom door. She hears Gage curse and stumble before his footfalls race down the hall as she closes her bathroom door.

She faces the mirror and immediately shuts off the lights. Her reflection is too frightening to endure before coffee. She navigates the room without stubbing a toe and finishes at the sink. She gently brushes her teeth and lets down her hair. She hesitantly turns on the light and focuses only on untangling the knots with her brush.

She pulls her hair to the right side and loosely braids it down the front. She risks one look up. She immediately turns away from the mirror and opens the bathroom door.

She heads to her closet and slides open the bi-fold doors. She considers a camisole and blouse but pulls out a hooded wrap dress. It has long sleeves, but it is thin. She grabs it and shimmies out of her shorts and tank. She's tying the dress when Gage knocks on the door.

"Roz, you decent?" Gage asks through the door.

"Yes," she says, taking one last look in the full-length mirror. She pulls up the hood.

Gage looks her over as he opens the door. "The deputy is waiting in the living room."

Rozanne follows Gage down the hall.

A tall man turns and extends his hand.

"Rozanne, my name is Deputy Clawson."

She shakes his hand and smooths out her dress.

The tall deputy is young, maybe a few years older than her and Gage.

"Deputy Morris had a few additional questions that I'm here to ask, and I have one from the sighting this morning." He hands Rozanne a pen and paper. "I was instructed by a woman named Mary to keep this brief."

The left corner of Rozanne's mouth curves up. "Ask away."

"Can you describe the girl you saw by the woods a few minutes ago?"

"She was wearing a white top, navy or black skirt," Rozanne says, chewing on the corner of her lip. "I can't recall anything else."

He nods and jots down her response. He flips back a page. "How long have you lived here?"

"Three years."

"And when did you build a treehouse in the willow tree?"

She looks up and shakes her head. "What willow tree?" she asks Gage.

"Edith's winking tree," Gage says. "You didn't know about it either?"

"No!" Rozanne holds up a finger and walks to the long window. She stares at the uniformed people surrounding the tree. She turns back to the deputy. "I don't understand."

"The search party found food wrappers under the willow tree and wood tacked to the far side of the trunk. They climbed up and discovered a large wooden platform."

She stares at Gage.

Gage raises his hands. "I was equally surprised."

The deputy looks over his notes. "The other deputy reported you inherited the property."

"Yes," she says.

"And you don't recall ever noticing a treehouse on the property."

"Never." She points to Gage. "But there was that guy on the porch."

"What guy?" the deputy asks.

Gage nods. "A few weeks after Rozanne moved in, she found a guy sleeping on the front porch. She chased him off the property and installed the lights around the house to keep any other drifters away."

"Can you describe the man?" the deputy asks.

She holds up a finger as she writes a list of what she can recall:

Late thirties, early forties
Black and white beard
Long, thin dark brown hair
Blue eyes
Narrow face
Six feet or a little shorter.
He wore a long khaki jacket over a dark shirt, jeans
Red shoes
And carried a ratty green canvas bag

She hands him the list. He reviews the description.

She turns back towards the window. "Was anything up there?"

The deputy places the slip of paper in his notebook. "Empty water bottles, a stash of canned tuna, a flashlight, and an old sleeping bag."

She rubs the prickly skin on her arms.

"Have you ever seen or heard anything in the woods before last night?" the deputy asks.

She turns away from the window. "Mostly just birds, occasionally deer or rabbits."

"Do you have more questions for her?" Gage asks, pointing at the clock hanging over the mantle. "She needs to eat something to take her meds before we head out."

"Just one," the deputy says. He shifts to stand between Gage and Rozanne. "The night you, um, fell, are you sure no one else was on the porch?"

"Why?" she asks.

"The techs checked the swing," the deputy says, keeping his eyes glued to Rozanne. "It would have been difficult to fall the way you did without force."

She doesn't blink. "Gage was not here and did not harm me."

"We know and confirmed his account of events with a few witnesses," the deputy says.

"Excuse me?" Gage asks. "You did what?"

The deputy ignores his question. "His neighbors recall him on a loud motorcycle that evening and then him leaving again in a truck after your phone records show a call to him."

"When did you look at her phone?" Gage walks around the deputy to face him and to block Rozanne.

"I didn't," the deputy says, taking a step back. "The deputy at the hospital did when there was a question about her injuries. All possible assaults are submitted to the county sheriff for follow up."

"Viola!" Rozanne mutters.

Gage turns to face Rozanne.

"It's her fault," Rozanne says.

"Who is Viola?" the deputy asks.

Gage turns back to the deputy. "Town gossip and hospital admission clerk working the emergency room on Monday night." He shakes his head. "She immediately made false accusations and even had the nerve to come by here yesterday afternoon with banana pudding."

The deputy laughs. "I'm sorry. Small towns are still very trippy for me. I didn't grow up where everyone knows everyone. It's pretty odd how small towns operate."

"Welcome to our hell," Rozanne mumbles.

"Do you think the treehouse and her face plant on the porch could be connected?" Gage asks.

Rozanne grabs Gage's elbow for support as her knees soften.

"I wouldn't say connected, yet." He looks over Rozanne's shoulder at the window. "It's a pretty easy tree to hide in and not be seen from here."

Rozanne squeezes Gage's arm.

Gage looks down. "I think I should follow Mary's orders and get you some pain meds before the car ride."

The deputy nods and walks towards the front door. "Thanks for your time, and I hope you have a speedy recovery." He pauses as he steps onto the porch. "One last thing. The well on the east side of the property. It's no longer in use?"

"Correct," she says.

"Do you know why?" he asks.

"Kings drilled a new one."

"Great, thanks again."

The front door closes.

Rozanne whimpers and points at her face. "Pain."

Gage helps her into the soft chair near the window and rushes into the kitchen. He returns with a frozen bag of corn.

Rozanne lifts the bag to her face, but it trembles under her shaking hand.

"Shit," Gage says.

She closes her left eye and tries to steady her breathing. She takes in a long, deep, shaky breath and mentally counts to eight before she exhales.

Gage clears his throat.

She opens her good eye.

He has a single pill on the palm of his hand and a glass of water. "Swallow. I'll get your smoothie started."

She swallows the pill with a few sips of water and sets the glass on the table beside her. She closes her eye and starts the breathing exercise again. Her pain eases.

Gage rattles a drawer closed and returns with a smoothie. "Better?" he asks, handing her the cool glass.

"Is my flashlight in the junk drawer?" Rozanne asks, taking the glass.

"It's daylight Roz."

"Duh!" She takes a sip and swallows.

Gage returns to the kitchen and opens a few drawers. "No flashlight." He returns to Rozanne and frowns. "Was I supposed to look for it?"

"It rolled off the porch when…" she says, pointing to her face.

Gage shrugs. "I can check. Why is this important?"

"They found a flashlight in the treehouse."

Gage exits the house and jumps off the porch. He then walks slowly around the perimeter of the house.

Deputy Clawson is walking with a small group of volunteers when Gage comes around the corner.

"Hey," Gage says, jogging up to the group. "Quick question."

"Sure," the deputy says.

"Rozanne said her flashlight rolled off the porch the night she fell."

"Okay?" the deputy says.

"And you found one in the treehouse?"

The deputy taps his radio. "Charles, can you bring the flashlight from evidence over to the house?"

"Copy," a man responds.

Gage and Deputy Clawson watch a man jog from the willow tree to the front porch carrying a clear bag with a flashlight.

"Thanks," Deputy Clawson says.

Gage opens the front door for the deputy.

The deputy sits in the chair across from Rozanne. "Gage mentioned you had a flashlight roll off the porch the other night?"

"Yes," Rozanne says, still pressing the bag of corn to her cheek. "The power went out during the storm."

"Can you describe your flashlight?" he asks.

She shows him a description she had written of the flashlight. *Black handle, yellow rim around the top, and a white paint stain near the switch.*

"Sounds similar enough," the deputy says. "Is this it?" He uncovers the clear bag from under his arm.

She drops the bag of corn. "Yes."

"That bastard," Gage mutters, pacing between the front door and the kitchen. He turns to the deputy. "Find this creep and put him away!"

The deputy stands. "We're on it. If you can think of anything else, let us know."

Rozanne nods and stands. She turns to Gage the second the door closes. "What the actual fuck is happening?"

Gage shakes his head. "I wish I knew." He looks over her head. "You have about two minutes. We need to get moving to make your appointment on time."

🚪

Rozanne walks down the hall back to her room. She sets her purse on the bed after checking for her phone, insurance card and driver's license. She runs her tongue over her teeth and steps into the bathroom. She overhears Gage answer his phone as she rinses off her toothbrush.

"She's in pain," he says as Rozanne walks down the hall. "We are leaving now." He pauses and turns for the front door. "Yes, I will tell her."

Rozanne follows him out and locks the front door.

"Thanks Monroe," Gage says. He pockets his phone and takes Rozanne's arm as she steps down the first step.

"My legs aren't broken," she mumbles.

"True," he says. "But your balance is crap even when you aren't on pain meds."

"Ouch," Rozanne says. "Tell me how you really feel."

"Truth hurts," he says, as she slides into the passenger seat of her car.

"Why are you driving my car?" Rozanne asks.

"Monroe's orders." Gage smiles and shuts her door. He's still smiling as he slides into the driver's seat. "Oh, and before I forget, you need to check your social media accounts."

"Why?" Rozanne asks, buckling up.

"Also Monroe's orders. Via Mary."

14

Deputy Clawson returns the flashlight to the evidence team. "Put a rush on the prints pulled from this." A tech nods.

He walks towards a group of volunteers just as Rozanne and Gage exit the house. He watches Gage help her down the steps and open her door. He reviews the report from Deputy Morris. 'Just friends' is written next to Rozanne and Gage, with a large question mark. He laughs. *I would bet a hundred bucks that boy is madly in love with her.* He draws his attention away from the car as it pulls towards the road and addresses the next search party.

"Deputy Clawson!"

Deputy Clawson holds up his hand with a finger raised as he continues instructing the next search party. "Mark anything out of place with a flag, but do not touch—"

"Sir, a minute!" the tech interrupts.

Deputy Clawson glares in the tech's direction.

The tech holds up a bag.

Deputy Clawson nods to another deputy and steps away from the group.

"What do you have that couldn't wait?" he says, towering over the tech.

The tech turns over the bag, exposing a Colorado driver's license. "This was tucked in the lining of the sleeping bag we recovered from the treehouse."

Deputy Clawson takes the bag. He examines the photo of a man with auburn hair and blue eyes. "Belver Potts. Hmm, does he have a record?"

"Yes," the tech whispers. "And it matches a name of a man that assisted with the search last night. The search lead ran the list of names that assisted for any priors and this guy was flagged."

Deputy Clawson turns and scans the current search group.

The deputy turns back to the tech. "Scan the ID and send it to all deputies and local officers with a P.O.I. tag."

"Sir?" the tech asks.

"Person of interest."

The tech nods and jogs back to the crime scene unit van.

The search party starts their march forward and a few phones chime at once.

The deputy pulls his phone out from his belt to check the message. As requested, the image of the ID had been sent, along with the words "P.O.I. missing person search." A second alert pings while he zooms in on the expiration date: March 23, 2003. *Fifteen years?*

He opens the next new message. It's from an unfamiliar number. The message is five words: *A penny for your thoughts?*

The deputy looks up from his phone. He scans the woods and the people still lingering by the tent. No one is looking in his direction. He jogs to the crime scene van as the tech jumps out.

"Problem with the text?" the tech asks with their hand on the door.

"Not unless you sent this cryptic crap to my phone," the deputy says, holding his screen up to the tech.

"No, sir," the tech says.

"Sorry," the deputy says, shaking his head.

"No problem," the tech says, stepping aside. "The guys can run the number through the database."

The deputy ducks inside the van, taking a seat next to a tech on a laptop. "I need a phone number checked immediately." The deputy hands him the phone. "I received this message right after you guys sent the text out."

"Yes, sir," the tech says, typing the numbers in. A blue circle in the middle of the screen spins, and then an owner registration number pops up. The tech whistles.

"What is it?" the deputy leans forward to look at the screen.

"The first four numbers indicate the service provider." The tech looks up from the screen. "It's a pay as you go phone."

"A burner phone?" the deputy asks.

The tech nods and clicks to copy the number. The tech opens a second window and pastes the number in. "We can find out when it was last activated and how the payment was made."

"At least that's something," the deputy says, pulling out a notebook and pen.

"Got it," the tech says, pointing to the line. "It was activated three days ago and paid for in cash." He right clicks on the address and clicks search. "At the local Casey's gas station across from the hospital."

"Thanks!" the deputy says, stepping out of the van. He adjusts his radio. "8615 to dispatch."

"Go ahead, 8615," the operator answers.

"Do you have an officer near the hospital?" Deputy Clawson asks.

"Yes, sir," the operator says.

"Please send me their number," the deputy says.

"Stand by," the operator says. "10-4."

Ping
The deputy opens the text and dials. He paces a step each time the phone rings. He makes it four steps and pauses.

"Officer Clay," a woman answers.

"This is Deputy Clawson. I'm with the search party east of downtown. We just had a suspicious text from a burner phone. It was bought with cash three days ago at the Casey's across the street from the hospital." He pauses when he hears the engine of the officer's car start. "We don't know if the P.O.I. and phone are related."

"Copy," Officer Clay says. "I'm turning into the parking lot now."

"Call me back directly," Deputy Clawson says, walking towards the search lead. "I don't want the chatter over the radio. The P.O.I. could be with the search party."

"Understood," Officer Clay says.

Deputy Clawson pockets his phone.

"Deputy Clawson," a sheriff admin says with a shout and waves at him.

He jogs to the admin.

"We had a call from a deputy that is covering the farm north of here," the admin explains. "We have a possible match for the P.O.I."

"Bring him in for questioning as quietly as possible," the deputy says.

The admin nods.

Deputy Clawson walks over to the search lead and holds a torn piece of paper with the number for the burner phone. "Can you compare this number to the volunteer contact information for today and yesterday?"

"No problem," the search lead says. He taps his laptop and types in the number. "Nothing from yesterday. I haven't finished entering today's information. Give me ten minutes, tops."

Deputy Clawson's phone rings. He nods to the search lead and steps out of the tent.

"Clawson," he answers.

"We have a match," says Officer Clay. "The clerk on duty was working the day the phone was purchased. She rang up two phones during her shift. One was bought by a teenage girl and the other was bought by a man matching the description of the P.O.I." The officer pauses as the store door jangles. "I showed her the copy of the ID and she confirmed it was him, but that he had a reddish-brown beard."

"Did she see a vehicle?"

"She says he left on a black bicycle."

"Anything else?"

"She says his clothes were nondescript, but dirty. And he's missing half a pinky."

Two uniformed deputies and a man with a volunteer vest emerge from the woods near the pond and walk straight for Deputy Clawson.

"Good to know," Deputy Clawson says. "Any cameras on site?"

"Yes."

"I'll put in the formal request and have an officer swing by with the paperwork," Deputy Clawson says. "Thanks officer. Good work."

"Just find the girl, deputy."

He ends the call and greets the two approaching deputies with a nod. They nod in return. The man between them doesn't look up from the ground.

Deputy Clawson points to a white tent. They lead the man over to the tent. A table and two chairs are set up inside. One deputy leads the man to a chair and the other steps out and hands Deputy Clawson a wallet.

"What's this?" Deputy Clawson asks, opening the wallet.

"The man had this in his jacket pocket," the deputy says.

He looks at the driver's license. The name next to the photo is Billy J. Clevenger.

Deputy Clawson shakes his head. "I thought the owner of the land north of here was dead."

"Check the expiration date."

"Expired over twenty years ago," Deputy Clawson says. The deputy nods. "Did he identify himself as Billy?"

"He hasn't spoken a word to anyone," the deputy says.

The radio on the deputies' shoulders crackle. "Deputy Clawson," a man says.

Deputy Clawson steps away from the white tent. He clicks his radio and answers, "Copy."

"We have a woman here requesting access to the home," the man says. "She says she lives here with Rozanne."

"Stand by," Deputy Clawson says into the radio. He hands the wallet back to the deputy and points to the tent. "Start with the basics."

15

Gage pulls into the surgical center parking lot. He told Rozanne the details and odd connections from the search last night during the commute.

"Mary's phone call to Viola's mother was epic," Gage says, putting the car in park.

Rozanne sighs. "Thank God that's over."

"Hey, my driving isn't bad," Gage says, opening his door. He jogs around the car and opens her door. "And look at the service I'm providing!"

"No," she says, getting out of the car. "I meant Viola and her gossip." She winces and sucks in a breath.

"Is your pain that bad?" he asks.

"Yea, with any movement," she says as they walk. "I still can't believe Viola did a video apology."

Gage laughs. "You can thank Mary later."

"She's the best ally to have in your corner," she says, entering the large lobby. "What floor?"

"Fourth," he says, holding up a card.

"I hate elevators," she whines.

"I know," he says, "but would you rather have four flights of jarring pain or less than a minute of panic?"

"Fine," she sighs.

The elevator doors open. A young woman makes eye contact with Rozanne. She lurches back a step with a look of horror.

"I know," Gage says with a smile, winking at the woman. "Isn't she pretty?"

The young woman ducks her head and bolts past him.

"Seriously," Rozanne says, nudging Gage as they walk into the elevator. "I even turned the lights off in the bathroom this morning."

"Your hood is covering most of the damage," he says, tugging her hood down after punching the four. "I was confused by your outfit choice this morning, but I get it now."

The elevator door closes.

"Says the guy who wears the same outfit," she whispers, "every single day."

Gage looks down, inspecting his black shirt and jeans. "I wore a red shirt last week."

The elevator starts up.

"Free motorcycle racing shirts don't count," she says, shaking out her hands and focusing on the display as the numbers change.

Gage places a hand on her shoulder. "Roz, take a breath."

She exhales when the elevator doors open and shakes out the back of her dress, damp with sweat. She follows Gage through double doors to a large desk. The receptionist smiles up at Gage. Her smile falls when she catches sight of Rozanne.

The receptionist focuses on her screen. "Welcome. May I have your insurance card and a photo ID?"

Rozanne opens her purse and hands her the insurance card and her driver's license.

The receptionist forces a smile when she looks up. "I'll make a copy of these." She places a clipboard with a few forms on the desk. She nods to the waiting area. "Take a seat and fill these out. Please sign on the lines highlighted in blue."

Rozanne settles in a chair away from the three other people. Gage takes a seat across from her. She finishes reading and signing the forms. She scoots forward to stand, but Gage pops up from his chair and takes the clipboard.

"Thanks," Rozanne says.

"You look really rough," he whispers.

Rozanne raises her middle finger to scratch her neck. He chuckles and walks to the desk.

He returns pocketing a card and hands her back the insurance card and driver's license. She points to his pocket. He winks.

"Her number?" Rozanne asks.

He smiles and nods.

"Rozanne," a nurse calls from an open door.

Rozanne raises her hand.

"Come on back, we're ready for you."

She stands and walks towards a nurse in dark purple scrubs.

Gage walks beside her and points to the scrubs, and then to Rozanne's face.

Rozanne sighs.

The nurse frowns at Gage. "He finds your injury amusing?"

Gage stops smiling and shakes his head.

The nurse smiles at Rozanne. "Do you want him in the room?"

Gage runs two fingers over his mouth and twists at the corner of his lips. Rozanne rolls her eyes.

The nurse laughs and stops at an open door. "You, sir, have a seat. Rozanne, follow me to the scale."

Gage salutes and plops into a chair next to a cabinet with a sink.

Rozanne follows the nurse down to a scale near the nursing station. The nurse motions for her to step up.

She slips off her shoes and steps onto the scale.

"Great," the nurse says. "How tall are you?"

"Five foot six," she says, slipping her shoes back on and following her back to the open door.

Gage straightens in his chair. He smiles at the nurse as they walk in.

"A little too late to charm this old lady," the nurse says to Gage. "Rozanne, have a seat here." She pats the end of the exam table. "I need to take a few vitals and go over your medical history."

Buzz, buzz

Gage pulls his phone out of his pocket. "It's Deputy Clawson."

Rozanne nods, and he steps out, closing the door behind him.

"Hi," Gage answers, walking towards the waiting room.

"Gage, is Rozanne with you?" Deputy Clawson asks.

"Yes," Gage says.

"Does she have any roommates?"

"No," Gage says, nodding to the receptionist as he steps outside the office suite.

"Great, small town busy bodies," the deputy grumbles.

Gage hears the deputy click his radio and say, "Negative, escort her off the property."

"Any luck this morning?" Gage asks, but his phone lights up with the call ended screen. He shrugs and pockets his phone. As he walks back into the office suite, the door to the patient rooms swings open.

The nurse pushes Rozanne out in a wheelchair.

"Oh good," the nurse says, handing Gage a piece of paper. "Take her down to the second floor. A patient tech will be waiting."

"Sure thing," Gage says, taking the handles of the chair from the nurse. He pushes the wheelchair out of the office suite. He stabs the down arrow. "Only two floors this time," he says. "What's on two?" He turns the paper over before Rozanne can respond. "Why does this say Pre-Surgery Checklist?"

The elevator door slides open.

"Gage," Rozanne says, gripping the armrests of the wheelchair as he pushes her in.

Gage pushes two. He turns and kneels to her level. "What's happening?"

"Surgery," she says, pointing to the paper. "It will be at least five hours, maybe longer."

"What do I tell Mary or Monroe?" Gage asks, looking at the paper.

Rozanne opens her purse and pulls out her phone. She takes the paper from Gage as the door slides open. She snaps a photo of the surgery written at the top of the page and texts it to Gage as he wheels her out of the elevator.

Gage's phone pings.

"That's a text from me. Show Monroe the text and tell him my will is where Grandma Anne kept hers."

Gage frowns. "Roz, you're not going to die."

"Ducks in a row," Rozanne says. "Be back before five."

Gage shakes his head. "Are you serious?"

"Do you want to leave your purse with your husband?" the patient tech asks, looking over Rozanne's shoulder.

"Not married!" Gage and Rozanne say in unison.

"My bad," the patient tech mutters. "Even so… your purse?"

Rozanne looks at Gage. He shrugs. She lifts her purse but hesitates and says, "The keys are in the outside pocket, otherwise stay out of the inside."

"Yes, ma'am," Gage says, taking her purse with a slight bow. "See you before five."

"Thanks," Rozanne says.

The patient tech holds up his badge to Rozanne. "I'm Winter."

Rozanne squints at the badge. "First name or last?"

He laughs as he pushes her wheelchair through a set of automatic doors into a room divided with curtains. "First."

She rubs her arms and looks over her shoulder. "Is it always this cold in here? Or does that come with your name?"

Winter smiles and walks around the chair to lift the footrest. "It's the nature of the surgical wing, not the person." He winks. "But we have an endless supply of warm blankets for the patients."

Rozanne stands.

Winter lowers the stretcher to chair height.

"On the bed is an envelope for any jewelry or a watch. It will be sealed and returned to you after surgery. The bag is for your clothes and shoes. There are two gowns. Please tie the first one in the back. The second you can wear as a robe, loose in the front." Winter lifts the gowns and holds up a pair of socks. "And these are to keep your feet cozy. Do you have any questions before I step out?"

"Is my doctor good?" Rozanne asks, her tone shakier than she expected.

Winter laughs. "One of the best. If I were in your skin right now, his are the only hands I would want to operate on me."

"In my skin," Rozanne says with a laugh.

Winter shrugs. "In your shoes, doesn't really apply to a maxillofacial surgeon."

"True," Rozanne says.

Winter steps out and closes the curtain.

Rozanne changes into the gowns and socks. She settles on the narrow bed under a blanket.

A nurse walks in, scooting an IV bag and a tube hanging on a pole, along with a tray of other tubes and syringes.

"Name and date of birth," the nurse asks after setting the tray on the bedside table.

"Rozanne Rayvern, June 10, 1997."

The nurse nods and wraps the patient information band around her wrist. "Any known allergies?"

"None," Rozanne says.

"Great," the nurse says, sliding on a pair of gloves. "I'm going to start a line for the fluids and medications. We'll be administering all medication for the surgery through it. One poke and done." The nurse hesitates. "Are you squeamish around needles?"

"Not at all," Rozanne says and half smiles.

"Got it," the nurse says and keeps the promise of one poke and done. The nurse pulls back the curtain and motions Winter over.

Winter adds a second warm blanket and releases the brakes on the bed. He hums and pushes the wheeled stretcher down the hall.

Rozanne watches the fluorescent lights overhead. "Is a song stuck in your head?" she asks as he slows to turn into another room.

"An old hymn," Winter says. He sings, "It is well."

"Do you sing to all of your patients?" Rozanne asks.

Winter lines up her stretcher next to another bed in the center of the room.

"A tradition or habit," Winter says. "We're going to transfer you now." Winter nods to another person dressed in scrubs at the foot of the stretcher. "On three." They each grasp a corner of the sheet under Rozanne. "One, two…"

They lift and transfer her over. A woman leans over Rozanne into her line of sight.

"My name is Dr. Morris," she says. "I'll be administering and monitoring your anesthesia."

Her name rattles Rozanne's brain. "Deputy Morris?"

The doctor tilts her head to the side. "My brother."

16

Gage parks in front of the pharmacy. An elderly couple walks by his car hand in hand. He watches the man hold a nearby café door open for the woman. She pats the man's leg as she passes through the door. The man catches Gage staring and winks at him.

Gage chuckles and gives him a small wave. He grabs his phone and hops out of Rozanne's car.

The pharmacy door jingles, and Gage steps around a customer browsing the magazines near the entrance.

Mary looks up from the counter with a smile, but her smile falls when she catches Gage's face above the shelf as he rounds the corner.

"Who is with Rozanne?" Mary whispers, leaning over the counter.

Gage holds up his phone. "I come bearing a message."

"Monroe, can you come to the counter?" Mary says over her shoulder.

Monroe comes around the corner with a white bag. "Gage, what are you doing here?" He looks past Gage. "Where's Rozanne?"

"In surgery," Gage says, holding up his phone to show Monroe the text from Rozanne.

"You left her there alone?" Mary scolds Gage.

Gage shakes his head. "I'm following Rozanne's instructions. First, come here and explain her surgery. Next stop is to check on my shop and then return to the surgery center before five." He holds up a finger. "She also asked me to tell Monroe, her will is in the same spot where Anne left hers."

Mary frowns and takes Gage's phone to look over the text. "How serious is this surgery?" She looks up at Monroe.

"Fairly standard repair for her fractured cheek," Monroe says. He bends and pulls out a brown book. He hands it to Gage.

Gage takes the worn leather book and thumbs through it. The thin pages are gray and covered in loopy handwriting. "Is this Rozanne's journal?"

"No," Monroe chuckles. "It was resting against the back door of the pharmacy this morning with a note." He hands Gage the blue post-it.

"Find Maggie." Gage frowns. "Any idea who left this?"

"My first guess is Mrs. Arber," Monroe says.

Gage carefully opens the cover. A date is faded in the top right-hand corner of the page. "1917?"

"Really?" Mary asks. "Well, you mind those pages with care."

Gage nods at Mary and takes a step back bumping into a man behind him.

"Sorry," Gage says, stepping aside to allow room for the man to place his items on the counter.

The man smiles and points at him. "Hey, don't you run the body shop out on 10 Highway?"

Gage nods.

"I just rolled by on the way here," the man says, nodding towards the door. "There was a guy out front with a fire extinguisher standing over a charred bike."

"Oh, no, no, no," Gage says, waving to Monroe and tipping his head to the man. "Got to run, thanks!"

Gage charges out the pharmacy door and dances around a woman walking her small black dog. "Sorry," he says and skids to a stop. A white delivery van is parked directly behind the car. "You've got to be kidding me!"

90

He yanks open the car door, tosses the journal into the passenger seat, and taps the horn.

A man steps out of a store a few doors down and waves two fingers in the air.

Gage sighs and slides into the car. He slams the door and starts the engine. He digs out his phone and dials the shop.

"Auburn Automotive, this is Dusty."

"Please tell me you didn't burn the old Scout bike?" Gage says, watching the delivery driver stroll back to the van.

"Hey Gage," Dusty chokes out. "How's Rozanne?"

"Dusty," Gage says, placing the car in reverse, "answer the question!"

The white van finally moves out of the rearview mirror. He punches the gas and flies out of the spot.

"I can explain!" Dusty says. "Kind of… dude, really, it wasn't my fault."

"Dusty!" Gage yells, turning right. He winds up directly behind a large blue public bus on the two-lane highway. He checks the oncoming lane but mumbles a curse at the steady stream of traffic. He punches the passenger seat. "That was a vintage bike, man. The parts are nearly impossible to find!"

"Dude, I know," Dusty says.

"I leave you alone for two days," Gage says, braking for the bus. He watches the handicap lift unfold and mumbles a curse. "Gather your tools."

"Are you going to fire me?" Dusty asks.

"Dude," Gage says, pounding the steering wheel. "I'll answer that when I get to the shop."

Beep

Gage looks at his screen. "I got to go."

"Gage," Dusty says.

Gage presses the screen to accept the new incoming call. "Hello."

"Gage?" the male caller says.

"Yes," Gage answers.

"Deputy Morris." He clears his throat. "Is Rozanne home?"

"No, sir," Gage says, watching the bus pull forward. "She's, um… still with the doctor."

"Deputy Clawson just filled me in on Rozanne's flashlight with the found belongings." Deputy Morris pauses for a muffled conversation. "Will she be home this evening?"

Gage inches forward, keeping his distance from the bus and assessing the oncoming traffic. "I can't say for sure," he says, throwing on his blinker and punching the gas to pass the bus. "I will know more once I return to the surgery center this afternoon."

"We can come to her," Deputy Morris says.

"Sir, Rozanne is in surgery at the moment," Gage says, turning into the shop. He mumbles a curse. The old Scout is charred past recognition. The tires are sagging from the wheels and nearly melted into the pavement.

"Ah, I see," the deputy says.

His response snaps Gage back to the conversation. "Is there anything else you need at the moment?" He shuts off the ignition and slides out of Rozanne's car. Dusty is standing in the shop door with a bag slung over one shoulder.

"I am keeping a deputy on regular patrol around this area for the next few days."

"Great." Gage sighs, walking around and assessing the bike. "I hope you at least have a lead for finding the missing girl."

"Me too," the deputy says.

Gage taps the screen to end the call and kneels next to the bike. He sniffs the seat. "Dusty, why does the seat smell like diesel?"

17

As Deputy Morris exits his patrol car, a tech calls him over.

"What do you got?" the deputy says, walking up to the white van.

"The guy carrying the wallet isn't Billy Clevenger," the tech says. "The thumb print we lifted from the wallet is a match for this guy and the Colorado license we found."

The tech holds up a wanted flyer.

"You're sure?" the deputy asks, examining the grainy photo and the outstanding warrants listed below.

"I will need a full set of prints to confirm," the tech says. "But the thumb was a ninety-six percent match according to the lab. We also ran the prints from the treehouse to compare. One confirmed match, two partial prints match."

Deputy Morris smirks. "Great job." He nods to the house. "The owner will not be home for a while, but I'll get a set of her prints to compare to the other evidence."

"It sounds like the K9 unit is headed back," Deputy Morris says. He turns to face the woods past the pond. "Do you know if the search party has found any additional arrows carved into the trees around the property?"

"No sir," the tech says. "Beyond the evidence near the creek and the treehouse, only a few pieces of trash were marked for collection."

The deputy holds up the wanted flyer. "I'm keeping this. Please let me know if you're able to pull any additional prints to match this guy."

The tech nods.

Deputy Morris sets off towards the white tent.

Deputy Clawson ducks his head to exit the tent and shakes his head as Deputy Morris approaches. "He's not talking."

"He might now," Deputy Morris holds up the paper. "A print from the wallet and treehouse match this guy."

"Belver Potts," Deputy Clawson says, squinting to read the text. "Armed robbery and vehicular manslaughter?"

"And wanted by the feds," Deputy Morris says. "So, if they see we have a confirmed fingerprint match." He looks at his watch. "We've got two, maybe three, hours tops before they come knocking."

"I'll follow your lead," Deputy Clawson says, stepping aside.

Morris nods and walks into the tent.

A man is hunched over a cup of water behind a folding table between two deputies who straighten at the sight of Deputy Morris.

Deputy Morris nods to them and they step out. He takes a seat across from the man, and Deputy Clawson remains standing to his right.

"My name is Deputy Morris. I am the lead investigator for a missing girl, and you, sir, are not a local. Can you share who you are and how you ended up as a volunteer with our search?"

The man raises his gaze up to meet Deputy Morris's eyes.

Deputy Morris stares at the man's grey eyes. The deep wrinkles around his eyes and crossing his forehead would suggest the man at least resembles the one in the grainy photo. Deputy Morris waits for the man to respond while assessing his sharp-angled cheekbones, the auburn beard and the dirt lining the creases of his neck just above the shirt collar.

"I am a drifter," the man says. "Right place, right time to lend a hand."

"And where did you drift from?" Deputy Morris says, leaning forward.

"I followed the river down to the creek and followed the creek up to the woods over yonder," the man says, nodding in the direction of the willow tree. "I try to stay near running water, if I can, during the summer months."

"You admit to squatting on private property?" Morris asks, crossing his arms over his chest.

"The area was marked as safe," the man says.

Deputy Morris frowns.

"Down by the creek there is an arrow on the tree," the man says. "A drifter code. An up arrow indicates the area is safe to make camp as long as it's up."

"Did you see the missing girl Tuesday evening?" Deputy Morris asks.

"No," he says, shaking his head. "I was wiped out from the storm the night before and was asleep up in the tree until the flashing lights and people showed up."

"And where were you Monday?" Deputy Morris asks.

"I made a trip to town to buy some additional food and was back up in the treehouse before dusk."

"And where did you go to buy food?" Deputy Morris asks.

"I stopped at Casey's, Dollar General and John's Super."

"Do you have receipts for the items you purchased?" Deputy Morris asks.

"No." He frowns. "I don't keep much but the clothes on my back and an extra pair of clean, dry socks."

Deputy Clawson places two hands on the table and leans down to meet his eyes. "Why are you chatting away now?"

The man furrows his brow. "I didn't want to repeat myself. I knew from the chatter that a Deputy Morris was the lead and returning mid-morning."

"And this isn't your first run in with the law?" Deputy Morris says, flipping over the paper on his lap and placing it between them and the man.

The man smiles, showing his surprisingly straight, white teeth.

Deputy Clawson points at the man. "Belver Potts."

"Present," he says, and winks at Deputy Clawson.

"And this?" Deputy Clawson says, holding up a clear plastic evidence bag with the recovered black wallet.

"In the pocket of this jacket," Belver says, patting the sleeve of his denim jacket. "I found it hanging on the back of an old tractor on the far side of the creek. I hadn't opened the wallet and was going to return the jacket back where I found it when I moved on."

"The only place you're moving on to is a courtroom," Deputy Morris says, tapping the paper.

Belver chuckles. "Squatting on private property is a misdemeanor, at best." He nods to the house. "And that's only if the owner chooses to charge me."

"The owner you assaulted on her own porch?" Deputy Clawson says, pounding his fist on the table.

Belver raises his hands. "I've never been within a hundred yards of her."

"Lie number one," Deputy Clawson says, holding a finger up in the air.

"I came to the house once during a thunderstorm," Belver says. "But only after she left with a guy in a truck. I was soaked through." He shrugs. "I took cover under the porch awning until the rain let up."

"You pushed her," Deputy Clawson says.

Belver shakes his head.

"We have evidence that says otherwise," Deputy Morris adds.

Belver shifts in his chair but keeps eye contact with Deputy Morris.

96

"You are wanted in three states, including this one," Deputy Morris says. "We are charging you for the assault, trespassing, squatting, harassment, and theft. And possibly kidnapping, but we can check your whereabouts after you are locked up."

"I've never hurt or taken anyone." Belver glares at Deputy Clawson. "Harassment? Theft? What are you talking about?"

Deputy Clawson smiles and nods at Deputy Morris.

"We know about your burner phone," Deputy Clawson says. "And the text you sent is considered harassment."

Deputy Morris chuckles. "You have the right to remain silent…"

"I don't have a phone," Belver says. He stands and the chair falls back. "Theft of what?"

Deputy Morris stands matching his posture. "The wallet, jacket, and flashlight."

"I found the jacket and wallet," Belver interrupts. "I said I didn't take anything out of the wallet. And the flashlight was lying on the ground."

Deputy Morris continues, "Anything you say can and will be used against you in a court of law. You have the right to an attorney. If you cannot afford an attorney, one will be provided for you."

"Take off the jacket and place your hands behind your back," Deputy Clawson says.

Belver squares his jaw.

Deputy Clawson rounds the table and Belver leaps back, but Deputy Morris is there. He grabs his wrist and cuffs it in one smooth maneuver. Belver bucks in response, but Deputy Clawson grabs his other hand and Deputy Morris places the other cuff around his wrist.

"You're making a mistake!" Belver hisses.

18

Rozanne raises her hand to her nose and pats her face. *Numb. Is that a tube?* She opens her left eye.

Gage's face hovers into focus. "Hey sleepy head."

Rozanne blinks and tries to sit up.

"Easy," he says.

"What's on my face?" Rozanne mumbles.

"You have a drainage tube from surgery," Gage says. "You also have bandages along the right side of your face." He chuckles. "Think—half mummy."

She glances around the room noting the furniture and the bathroom door. "I'm home?"

"Yes," Gage says.

"But how?" Rozanne asks.

"You were awake and talking when I wheeled you out of the surgery center," Gage says. "But you fell asleep in the car and again when we got you inside."

"I don't remember anything after being wheeled into the operating room," Rozanne says, glancing at the window. "It's dark?"

"Yea, it's almost ten," Gage says. "You're due for a pain pill." He holds up a pill and a glass of water.

Rozanne pops the pill in her mouth and takes a few sips of the water.

"Are you hungry?" he asks, taking the glass.

"Not really," Rozanne says, reaching up to her face. Gage swats her hand away. "Hey!"

"Doctor's orders." Gage sets the glass down on the side table.

She frowns, attempting to sit up further. Gage fluffs a few pillows, and she settles back with a grin. "Tell me what happened today."

"That's a long list," Gage says, walking to the opposite side of the bed. He stacks a few pillows against the footboard and sits. He leans back on the pillows and sighs. "The search party cleared out earlier this evening. A man was arrested for multiple outstanding warrants and was also charged with squatting on your property."

"What man?" Rozanne asks.

"He's a drifter named Belver," Gage says, shaking his head. "The deputy says the guy claimed the arrow on the tree by the creek is a drifter code for a safe place to camp as long as you find high ground. And the deputy wanted to assure you the guy you found sleeping on the porch and this guy don't physically match."

"Did he admit to this?" she asks, pointing to her face.

"Not exactly," Gage says. "He mentioned taking refuge on the porch during the storm, but only after I picked you up that night. He claims that's when he found and took the flashlight."

Rozanne rubs her arms.

"Are you cold?" Gage asks, leaning forward.

"No, just chilled by the idea of a man being so close for who knows how long without me noticing." She glances out the window. "Did they find the missing girl?"

"They didn't find any additional leads on the missing girl, and they couldn't link the drifter to her disappearance."

"I swear! I saw her this morning!"

Gage picks up and rattles the pain pill bottle. "Sorry, but you're not exactly in the best frame of mind."

"Ugh," she groans.

"The other news is not too great," Gage says.

She sits up a little higher and nods.

"My shop was broken into and vandalized… either that or Dusty is lying."

"Wait, what?" she says, leaning forward.

"My old Scout bike caught fire today," Gage says. "It's burnt beyond repair. Dusty claims he was welding on another bike and a spark hit the fender. It was instantly engulfed in flames."

"And you don't believe him?"

"It's not exactly possible," Gage says, frowning. "But I could smell diesel on the seat and over the tank."

"Do you keep any diesel in the shop?"

Gage nods. "We have a small can of it, but it was full when I checked."

"So, either Dusty is good at covering his ass," she says, "or someone deliberately dumped fuel all over your bike?"

Gage nods. "Dusty swears he locked up good last night, but he said the garage door wasn't all the way down this morning."

"Did you call the cops?" Rozanne asks.

"And tell them what?" Gage asks.

"That somebody destroyed your bike and nearly committed arson!"

Gage shakes his head. "The person I should call—is freaking Vi!"

"You think she did it?"

"No, but I imagine her gossip may have motivated someone to think I deserved it."

Rozanne shakes her head. "You need to tell the local police, at least." She holds up her hand and wiggles her fingers. "Maybe there are prints on the door?" She stares at her hands palm up. They are covered in black smudges. "Wait, why are my fingers like this?"

"Deputy Clawson took your prints when you returned home," Gage says. "You told him he had a nice smile and then drooled down your top."

Rozanne pushes his leg. "Seriously?"

Gage laughs. "Yes," he says, blocking her famous back hand. "You were awake and talking when he came in."

"I… I don't remember any of that!"

"Monroe mentioned you may have some memory lapse because of the anesthesia," Gage says. "Speaking of Monroe," he rolls off the bed and picks up a book from the chair in the corner, "he found this leaning against the back entrance to the pharmacy. I think it's a journal."

"It looks old," Rozanne says, touching the leather cover.

"It is," Gage says. "The year, 1917, is written on the first page."

"What?" she says, carefully opening the cover. "Holy smokes!"

"I know, right?" He circles back to the end of the bed and sits down. "I haven't read past the first page."

"Who left this?" she asks, squinting at the cursive handwriting.

"The only thing left with it was a post-it that said, 'Find Maggie.'"

She looks up from the page. "You're joking."

"No," Gage says, making a cross over his chest. "Monroe thinks it was Mrs. Arber."

She thumbs the pages. "Can you read it? My pain pill is just kicking in."

"We can wait till tomorrow," Gage says, taking it from her.

"Just the first entry," she says, folding her hands and placing them under her chin. "Please."

"Fine." Gage sighs. "No interruptions."

She makes the gesture of zipping her mouth shut.

"Original!" Gage snorts a laugh. He lifts the journal and reads to her.

December 20, 1917

Today was my first day at CR. Training started before dawn. I was issued a new dress, apron, and a frilly head piece. I felt like a little doll. The manager ran down the list of rules for two very long hours. A few of my favorites were we're to be invisible but always available and never use the main corridors, including the main entrance. It's like we are ghosts that hover just out of sight and clean when no one is looking. All the rooms are booked for the next two weeks. We are expected to work every day until the day after New Year's Day. I told mama when I got home, and she looked straight through me without a word. Maybe I'm already a ghost. Fingers crossed. I don't get lost tomorrow. Every servant staircase and hall passage looks identical.

"CR is Castle Rock?" Rozanne says, fighting the drowsiness.

"Maybe," Gage says, closing the book. "I won't read ahead." He stands and sets the book on the dresser near the closet. "Do you need anything else?"

"Just going to brush my teeth and then go straight back to bed."

"I'm still across the hall," he says. Then he points to Mary's brass bell on the side table. "Ring if you need me."

"Bless Mary's heart," she says, sliding out of the bed.

Gage chuckles and shuts her bedroom door.

Rozanne leans against the bed and waits out the throbbing in her right temple. It subsides. She sighs and walks to the bathroom. She stares in the mirror. "Half mummy. Ha! More like a freak show."

She makes it back to bed and taps her phone. She has twenty-three text message notifications, eight missed calls, and ten new email notifications on the screen. She pauses at a text sent from an unknown number. A small grainy image fills the screen. She taps to zoom in and out and then all at once she sees it.

She rings the bell and yells, "Gage!"

"What?" Gage says, swinging open her bedroom door and pushing a hand back through the sleeve of his shirt.

"Tell me what you see." She holds up her phone.

102

He walks to the bed and bends to look at the screen. He shakes his head. "It's dark, maybe a window?"

She zooms back in and out again.

He points at the phone.

"Please tell me you see a girl in the window?" Rozanne whispers.

"Roz," Gage whispers. "Who?"

"Maggie."

"Who sent this?" Gage asks, focusing on the image.

"Unknown number."

19

Gage steps out of the front door and breathes in the cool night air. He raises the phone to his ear.

The call connects after the first ring.

"Morris."

Gage leans against the porch rail. "Deputy Morris, my name is Gage."

"I know. I saved your number," the deputy says, fighting a yawn. "What do you need at this hour?"

"Rozanne just checked her phone for the first time today," Gage says. "There was a text message from an unknown number with an image of a girl in a window."

"What girl?" the deputy asks.

"The image… it's not that clear," Gage says, "but with the missing girl and the search… Rozanne didn't want to hold something like this back."

"I'll send an officer over with a tech," the deputy says. "I was going to call you in the morning, but since you woke me up. How did you know the shoes by the creek were old?"

"They looked too solid, or maybe the right word is chunky. All the new shoes are flimsy and shiny."

"Hmm," the deputy says.

"Was I wrong?"

"No, not at all. The shoes by the creek were from a Kansas City shoe company that shut down production during the first world war."

"Oh, wow." Gage paces the front porch. "And the socks?"

"Still tracking down that information," the deputy says.

"What about the rocks and the pennies?" Gage asks.

"Also still processing," the deputy says. "Expect a white van and a patrol car in the next twenty minutes."

"Yes, sir," Gage says, ending the call. He pockets his phone and pushes the front door open. He trudges into the kitchen and opens the fridge. He stares at the various dishes and picks out the banana pudding. He opens the lid. "Gross." A filmy green layer covers the top. He turns on the faucet and promptly dumps the contents down the drain. "Gossip and Viola's pudding be damned."

He finishes washing the dish and places it in the rack with the other dishes that need to be returned. In the distance, he hears the train whistle blow. He checks his phone for the time: five past eleven. He leans against the counter and mindlessly scrolls through his newsfeed until headlights stream through the front windows.

He walks out onto the porch and watches a patrol car park. An officer exits the car.

"Are you Rozanne Rayvern?" the officer asks.

Gage laughs. "Do I look like a Rozanne?"

The officer checks his phone. "Then you must be Gage."

"That I am."

"What kind of name is Rozanne anyway?" the officer asks, walking to the front porch.

"It's a type of geranium," Gage says, pointing to a basket of small purple flowers hanging from the porch.

"Interesting," the officer says, admiring the flowers. "They're pretty. Deputy Morris mentioned a text message with an image. May I see it?"

"Just a second," Gage says, stepping back inside to grab Roz's phone from the entry table. He steps back outside and hands the officer the phone with the message open. "It's a dark photo. If you zoom in and out, it comes into focus."

The officer looks up as a new set of headlights block his view of the image. A white van rolls to a stop next to the patrol car. A small thin woman hops out and walks towards the porch.

"And here I thought we had wrapped up this location," she says, showing her badge to Gage. "Is that the phone with the mystery image?"

Gage nods, and the officer hands her the phone.

"And it's your device?"

"No, it is Rozanne's phone."

"Give me two minutes to get her consent," she says. "And a few minutes with the phone and I'll bring it right back."

Gage opens the door and directs her to Rozanne's room.

The officer leans against the porch rail and stares out at the woods.

"I really hope we find this girl soon," the officer says.

"How many days has it been?" Gage asks, stepping out of the doorway.

The tech nods to them as she exits the house. She hops off the porch and jogs to the van.

"She was reported missing on Monday around five in the evening," the officer says, "but we didn't actively start working the case until Tuesday morning."

"And it's Wednesday," Gage says, checking his phone, "well, almost Thursday. Why the delay from Monday to Tuesday?"

"The parents made the call on Monday," the officer says, facing Gage. "But the responding officer assumed the girl went to a friend's house after school. It's pretty common. Teenagers forget to tell the parents."

"And she was last seen where?" Gage asks, leaning with his back to the house.

"According to the report," the officer says, turning to point out towards the pond. "Here on Tuesday evening near sunset."

"Roz and I don't know if it was her for sure," Gage says. "And by the time I made it outside, the girl we saw was gone."

"The clothing description of the girl you two saw matches the description from the mother and the teachers at the school," the officer explains. "Dark blue dress with a white shirt, white knee socks and black shoes."

Gage frowns. "I don't recall giving a clothing description to anyone."

The officer shakes his head and pulls out a phone. "This is the typed transcript from the call you made on Tuesday night."

Gage reads the transcription.

> ***Caller:*** *There was a girl we don't recognize on my friend's property near her pond. I went out to check on her, but I only found a pair of old black shoes and two socks near the creek at the edge of the property. The girl was gone.*
> ***Operator:*** *Can you describe the girl?*
> ***Caller:*** *A small teen maybe in a dress or skirt with long white socks and dark shoes.*
> ***Operator:*** *Hair color?*
> ***Caller:*** *Brown or light brown*

Gage shakes his head. "Shit!" He looks up at the frown on the officer's face. "Sorry. It's been a few eventful days and I don't recall describing her at all, but…"

"Wicked!" the tech yells from the van.

The officer turns towards the van as the tech pokes her head out.

"I need additional eyes to confirm what I'm seeing," she says, waving them over.

Gage and the officer step down off the porch. They head to the side door of the van. When they poke their heads in, she taps the space bar on the laptop.

"Tell me what you see," she says, pointing at the screen.

Gage stands aside and lets the officer climb into the van first. The officer leans in close to the screen, but then jolts back immediately. "Is that…"

Gage climbs into the van and examines the pale faces of the tech and the officer. "That bad?"

She nods to the screen.

Gage squats and focuses on the enlarged, grainy image from Roz's phone. A girl in the window is pointing at the sidewalk visible in the reflection in the windowpane. A tall figure is holding hands with a girl, matching the description of Penny.

"Can you zoom in here?" Gage asks, pointing to the reflection of the buildings in the windowpane.

The tech zooms in on the area Gage indicates.

"It looks like an old sign off Broadway," Gage says, pointing to the left-hand corner of the image. "That's the top of the sign above Ray's, the old diner." He points out R and A on the screen.

The officer leans over Gage's shoulder. "You're right."

The tech enhances the image of the figure walking with the girl. The features of their faces remain too blurry to make out, but the image on the tall figure's shirt sleeve sharpens.

"That's a medic symbol," the officer says. "I need to make a call." The officer ducks out of the van.

Gage whistles. "Were you able to track the number of the person who sent the text?"

"Just the carrier of the line, but no identification," the tech says. She pans back to the girl in the window and taps her into focus.

Gage gasps.

The tech turns to him. "What?"

Gage pulls out his phone and taps in an image search for Margaret P. Vance Missouri. A black-and-white photo appears in the search results. He taps the photo and zooms in on the girl next to two adults and holds it against the screen.

She takes Gage's phone.

"How do you know this girl?" she asks.

"What girl?" the officer says, coming back into the van.

"He just identified the girl in the window," she says, without looking up from her laptop.

"Who is she?" the officer says.

"A ghost," Gage says without thinking.

The tech stops typing and turns to look at Gage.

The officer points a finger within an inch of Gage's nose.

"Stop messing around," the officer says, sliding a hand to the cuffs on his belt.

"I'm not," Gage says, pointing to his phone. "I pulled up an image of a girl named Margaret P. Vance. She went missing from the Castle Rock Hotel in 1918. There was a recent article about her in The Standard. I read it to Rozanne on Tuesday before we saw the girl by the pond."

The tech pulls up the newspaper and clicks on the article. She scrolls down and looks back at Gage. "There is no picture attached to the article."

"Okay, this is going to sound nuts," Gage says. "But Rozanne saw a girl just like this—with short hair, a cardigan and a similar dress—on Monday at Spa View Manor. Her name, according to Rozanne, was Maggie."

"Spa View Manor is condemned," the tech says.

"I thought so too," Gage says. "And the top floors are condemned, but they still have a few residents on the second floor."

"Why was Rozanne there?" the officer asks.

"She was delivering a few things from the pharmacy."

"And this girl Maggie was just hanging out at Spa View?" the officer says.

"It was Rozanne's observation, not mine!" Gage says, shaking his head. "I told her she was nuts."

"Hold up," the tech says. She pulls up a map of downtown. She points to the screen. "Here is the old manor and here is

Ray's." She overlays the map with the image. "This could be from one of Spa View's windows."

Gage and the officer stare at the screen over the tech's shoulder.

"If this is our missing girl and this is the person who took her," the officer says, pointing to the figure with the girl in the reflection. "Where could someone take a teen and go unseen for days?"

"There are several homes near the manor that were abandoned after the last flood," the tech says, opening a new map. She types in the cross streets Broadway and Main. A live camera feed shows an intersection. She points the camera north over Main and zooms in. She points out the three houses. The street is too dark to make out much. "They will be torn down in a few weeks." The officer furrows his brow. "My cousin is in charge of the demo."

Gage fights a yawn. "Hope this was at least helpful."

The tech hands Gage back his phone, along with Rozanne's.

"It's something," the officer says. "I would expect a visit from a deputy tomorrow to get a statement from Rozanne about what she thinks she saw at the manor."

Gage nods. "I'll let her know." He ducks his head, exiting the van. "Thanks for coming out here so late."

The tech smiles and nods. "It's worth it if we find her."

Gage nods, and the officer follows him to the front porch.

"If you or Rozanne get any more messages from unknown numbers," the officer says, nodding to the phones, "call Deputy Morris immediately."

"Of course," Gage says. "On a separate note, I own the body shop, Auburn Automotive, out on 10."

"Go on," the officer says.

Gage continues, telling him about the fire, the partially open garage door, and the distinct smell of diesel.

"Did you call in the fire department or the police?" the officer asks.

"No," Gage says, sticking his hands in his pockets. "We keep a fire extinguisher onsite. My mechanic put out the flames and wheeled the bike outside before anything else caught fire. I didn't call it in because I wasn't sure if my mechanic was covering his ass or if it was an arson attempt. But there were some nasty rumors that I hurt Roz."

"Does she have any admirers who may wish you were out of the picture?" the officer asks.

"Roz and I are just friends," Gage says. "The whole town knows we grew up together. We were neighbors most of our childhood."

The officer nods. "I'll have an officer swing by the shop in the morning. Any cameras onsite?"

"Unfortunately, no," Gage says.

An engine starts, and Gage and the officer turn towards the driveway. The tech waves at them before she backs up the van and turns for the drive.

"I should head out too," the officer says.

"Sure," Gage says, taking a step up onto the porch. "Have a good night."

"You too," the officer says, returning to their patrol car.

Gage watches the taillights disappear before going inside. He cracks open Rozanne's door. Her snoring is semi muffled by the bandages. He tiptoes over and plugs her phone in, placing it on the side table. Rozanne moans and reaches a hand for her face. Gage gently redirects it, tucking it under the covers.

He tiptoes out and plops face down on the bed in his temporary room. "Please, no more drama or trauma tomorrow," he mumbles into the covers.

20

Gage turns off the blender and listens. *Was that the doorbell or Roz's bell?*

Knock, knock

He walks to the front door and looks out. Deputy Morris is standing on the front porch.

Gage opens the door. "Come on in," he says, gesturing towards the kitchen. "I'm just about finished with Roz's breakfast."

Deputy Morris removes his hat and steps across the threshold. "We found Penny."

Gage takes a step back into the door. "Is she…"

"Alive? Yes." The deputy frowns.

"Oh, but that's good, right?" Gage says.

"I wish it was that simple." The deputy shakes his head. "She is in critical condition. The questions we have, unfortunately, are more urgent than ever. We found her, but not who took her."

"Where?" Gage asks.

"In one of the abandoned homes near Spa View Manor."

"Oh, the photo…" Gage shakes his head and closes the door. He faces the deputy. "How can we help?"

"The officer and tech have filled me in on the text message and the link to that old cold case," the deputy says, nodding towards the hall. "Is Rozanne awake and able to give me a play-by-play of her encounter with the girl at Spa View?"

"She's awake, but in the tub. She should be out in a few." Gage walks to the kitchen. "Can I get you anything to drink?" He pours the smoothie into a glass.

"Coffee, if it's ready, would be great."

Gage nods to the full pot of coffee. "How do you like it?" He pulls two mugs down from the cabinet.

"Black, one sugar."

Gage places a tablespoon of sugar in one mug before filling and handing it to the deputy. "The coffee is maple something. You can blame Roz if it's too sweet."

The deputy grins, taking a small sip. "Not too bad."

Gage preps his coffee, picking up his mug and Roz's smoothie. "Let me make sure she is out of the tub."

The deputy watches Gage walk down the hall. He wanders over to the long narrow window, admiring the view of the winking willow tree. The rising sun just passing the woods to the east creates a halo of light around the highest branches.

"Deputy, come on back," Gage says, from the open door to Roz's room.

The deputy turns away from the window and walks down the hall. He nods to Rozanne from the door.

"Come on in," Rozanne says. "Sorry for the delay."

"No problem." He steps in and walks to the window.

Gage moves the chair from the corner closer to the bed.

The deputy sits and pulls out his notebook.

"Gage mentioned you found Penny," Rozanne says. "Is she home with her parents?"

"No, I'm afraid her recovery…" the deputy says, and swallows hard. "It's a wait-and-see situation at the moment."

Rozanne frowns. "Oh, no."

"We really need to clear a few things up," the deputy says. "And hopefully catch this guy."

Rozanne nods. "I am pain med-free at the moment. Ask anything you want."

"What can you tell me about Maggie?" the deputy says, locking eyes with Rozanne.

She blows out a breath. "She's either a hallucination or a super creepy haunting." She bites the corner of her lip and scrunches her nose. "I can start from Monday morning up until last night, but I am warning you, it will sound a bit nutty."

The deputy looks from Rozanne to Gage.

Gage nods.

"If you promise that you won't take me away in a white jacket to a looney bin," Rozanne says. "I will promise to be as transparent as possible."

The deputy shakes his head. "I know the girl in the old photo Gage showed the tech was from an old cold case, so I can't be too shocked, right?"

"Buckle up, deputy," Gage says, grabbing the old newspapers from the dresser.

"Monday morning," Rozanne says. "I had a customer come into the pharmacy. Long story short, I assumed the customer had a daughter, Maggie, with her on previous visits, and I mentioned her to the customer. I was met with a confused frown. According to Monroe, the customer doesn't have any children." She shrugs. "I remembered the girl with such clarity I had a hard time believing him."

"Can you describe the girl?" the deputy asks.

"Strawberry blonde hair, cut in a short bob under her chin. She had a few freckles across the bridge of her nose and was always dressed very proper."

The deputy looks up from his notebook and scrunches his nose.

Rozanne continues. "Right, details. The few times I saw her, she was dressed in a blouse and skirt or a dress with a cardigan. Usually, pastel colors of pink or yellow. She would always be wearing knee-high white stockings and black shoes."

Gage coughs.

Rozanne looks up at him.

He locks eyes with her. "And her condition."

Rozanne sighs. "Maggie has down syndrome and speaks with a soft lisp."

The deputy sits back. "That's a lot of details for a ghost."

Rozanne shrugs and takes a sip of her smoothie.

"And how many times do you think you have seen her?" the deputy asks.

"Four or five times inside the pharmacy," Rozanne says, setting the cool glass down on the side table. "And once at Spa View Manor on Monday evening." She pauses. "It gets a little weirder."

The deputy smirks.

"I stopped by Spa View to deliver a few things for Monroe."

"What time was that?" the deputy asks.

"Near five," Rozanne says. "The place from the outside was dark and looked condemned, but when I pushed the front door open it was an elegant, spotless, grand lobby. It had a tiered marble water fountain, beautiful, glowing chandeliers, and Maggie."

Rozanne pauses to adjust a pillow. She continues. "Maggie turned towards me and said, 'Welcome to Spa View Manor. You may take the main stairs to the second floor or use the elevator. Which do you desire?'"

"She greeted you like she worked there?" the deputy asks.

"I didn't have that thought at first, but I did address her as Maggie. She said her name was Margaret Penelope Vance and only her family called her Maggie. She asked if I was family." She shakes her head. "I introduced myself and told her we had met at the local pharmacy, but she didn't seem to have any memory of our encounters."

Rozanne picks the water back up from the side table and takes a sip. She winces a bit.

Gage moves for the door. "I'll grab some peas."

The deputy looks at the door and back to Rozanne.

Rozanne chuckles. "Frozen peas."

The deputy smiles before draining his coffee. He sets the mug on the side table. "Okay, so what happened after the introductions?"

"She showed me to the stairs after I refused the tiny elevator," Rozanne says. "But she didn't follow me upstairs. And when I questioned whether she should remain down there all alone, she said, 'I greet and direct.' That was the first time I thought she may have been a resident, staff, or even a patient of the manor."

"And the staff?" the deputy asks.

"There was only one staff member on duty. And they played dumb. They claimed no knowledge of a girl in the lobby or anyone by the name of Maggie."

The deputy shifts in his chair and tugs at his shirt collar.

Rozanne blows out a breath. "Here's the kicker. The customer from that morning and the staff member on duty are identical twins. I thought I was being punked. I literally ran down to the lobby to get Maggie, but the lobby was dark. Dust and cobwebs were everywhere. I bolted out of there beyond freaking out."

Gage slides into the room. "Mary just pulled up." He tosses the wrapped pack on the bed next to Rozanne and jogs back down the hall.

Rozanne settles the cool pack gently over her bandages.

Deputy Morris points to the papers on the bed next to Rozanne. "And those?"

"Gage pulled the papers down from the attic after I explained my encounter with Maggie and the recent newspaper article talking about the cold case."

"You have an archive of old papers up there?" the deputy says, looking over his head.

116

"My Great Grandma Edith kept the old ones for the sewing patterns on the fifth page." Rozanne opens the old paper to the fifth page to show him. "She stopped the collection after the sewing patterns were discontinued."

He nods. "I imagine she was part of the Great Depression generation. They were known for holding on to things."

"Understatement of the century," Mary says, from the bedroom doorway. "Edith would have been considered a hippie and hoarder if she grew up in our day and age."

Rozanne smiles. "Grandma Anne would have probably agreed with you on that."

"I'm making breakfast," Mary says. "Deputy Morris, I'll set a place for you." The deputy opens his mouth, but Mary waggles her pointer finger at him. "I insist you eat before leaving."

"Yes, ma'am," the deputy says, grinning.

"Great," Mary says. "Rozanne, ring the bell if he stays too long."

"Yes, ma'am," Rozanne says with a salute.

Mary smiles and returns the salute before heading to the kitchen.

"Is she always so bossy?" the deputy asks, shifting in the chair.

"She's wonderful," Rozanne says, narrowing her left eye to a slit.

The deputy chuckles and thumbs through his notes. "Okay, back to business. Did you see anyone outside of Spa View when you left?"

"The parking lot was empty when I went in and came out until Gage knocked on my window."

"Why was Gage there?" the deputy asks, leaning forward.

"He was out test driving a motorcycle from the shop. He stopped to see what I was up to."

"And you didn't find that odd?" the deputy asks. He glances towards the open door.

"No. Gage always test drives between the shop and his house, just in case it acts up. Then he can easily walk it back to either location." Rozanne laughs. "And my car has a very distinctive bumper sticker collection. It's pretty easy to spot."

Deputy Morris scribbles down a few lines. "And after your run in with Gage outside of Spa View."

"Gage and I had dinner at Wabash." Her stomach rumbles loud and she looks down. "Sorry, that was my last real meal, and my stomach knows it."

The deputy nods. "And after dinner?"

"I went home, alone." Rozanne shifts the bag and winces. "And then called Gage for a ride to the hospital about an hour later."

"Right," the deputy says. "I assume Gage told you about the arrest and charges against the man that set up camp in your tree?"

"He did."

"He is scheduled for a bail hearing later today." The radio on the deputy's shoulder crackles.

"Deputy 8413," the dispatcher calls.

Deputy Morris taps his radio. He responds, "Copy."

"We have a 10-66 reported near Bluff and Main."

"10-4," he says, standing and turning for the door. "I need to run."

"What's a 10-66?" Rozanne asks.

"Suspicious person." The deputy nods at Rozanne's wide left eye. "Get well soon." He races out her bedroom door and down the hall.

"Now wait a minute," Mary yells as the deputy jogs out the front door and off the porch.

"Raincheck," Deputy Morris says before opening the car door. Mary frowns and shakes her head as he starts the car and backs out.

Gage walks down the hall to Rozanne's room. "Do you know why he bailed out of here so fast?"

"There was a radio call about a suspicious person at Bluff and Main." Rozanne drops the ice pack from her face and leans forward. "I think I need a half a pain pill."

"Sure thing," Gage says. He turns and sidesteps Mary.

"Men!" Mary says, coming into the room.

"I heard that!" Gage hollers from the kitchen.

"How are you doing?" Mary asks, tidying the blankets around the bed and picking up the smoothie glass and coffee mug from the side table.

"Minor pain, but okay," Rozanne says. "How are you?"

"Just fine," Mary says, smiling. "I've enjoyed being back in the pharmacy with Monroe." She winks before walking for the door. "He might not say the same, though."

Rozanne laughs.

Gage rattles the bottle as he walks in, and he plops down on the bed facing Rozanne. He holds up a whole pill. "You sure you don't want the whole thing?"

"Half is plenty," Rozanne says. "Do you know when I can have real food?"

Gage stands to fetch her discharge papers and the pill cutter from the dresser. He cuts the pill in half. He hands her the pill and the paper with the meal restrictions.

Rozanne frowns. "One-week liquids," she groans. "Two weeks soft foods or until a follow-up appointment."

Gage chuckles. "More burnt ends for me."

Rozanne tosses the wrapped bag of peas towards his face.

"Dude!" he says, catching the bag. "I was going to ask if you wanted ice cream but…"

"Gage," Rozanne says, "I apologize for throwing the peas at your face."

"Wow," Gage says. "Ice cream melts the ice queen's heart."

Rozanne smirks. "Mint chocolate chip with caramel."

"Yea, yea, the usual." Gage picks up the newspapers and places them back on the dresser. "Do you need anything else?"

"Ice cream only… please."

Gage salutes Rozanne and turns to Mary, walking in the room with a deck of cards in her hand. "Thanks for sitting with her," he says. "Do you need anything while I am out?"

"Chocolate shake," Mary says.

"You got it," Gage says. "Later Roz!"

21

Deputy Morris kills his siren as he nears Bluff and Main. He glances at the description: Caucasian male with light brown hair, approximately six-foot, mid-twenties wearing a blue polo shirt and tan pants. Last seen on foot heading south on Main. He scans the foot traffic on either side of the street. He sees two women leaving the church thrift shop near the corner, but otherwise there are no pedestrians. He turns right on Broadway and rolls to a stop behind a large red truck. He impatiently waits his turn at the four-way stop of Main and Broadway.

The truck rolls forward, and the deputy sees a young woman pushing a stroller, waiting to cross the street. When he rolls forward, he stops and motions for her to cross. He catches sight of a man watching her from a shop window. *If he is watching her, he may have seen Penny and whoever was with her.*

He turns north on Main and slowly takes a right on Bluff.

A girl darts out in front of his car. He slams on the brakes. She whirls, her face visible for only a second before she stumbles back and falls below the front of the car.

Deputy Morris shoves the gear into park and scrambles out, rushing to the front of the car but finds only pavement. He looks around, but the sidewalks are empty.

He shakes his head and walks back to the car. He slides in and taps the dash cam footage to replay. A girl appears, her face clearly in focus.

"No, that can't be," the deputy mumbles. He rolls back the footage and replays it again. A petite girl, maybe a pre-teen or teen with short hair, runs into the road. She twirls and falls back. "She was right there!"

Deputy Morris shakes his head. He looks to the left and scans Spa View Manor. He pulls his car into the empty parking lot. He starts for the front door but remembers the guy who was watching from the window at the intersection. He turns and walks towards the corner.

He pulls out his phone and pulls up the image of Penny and opens a second window with Maggie's image. He studies her face and all the hair on his arms stand at once. *The dashcam footage and this girl are the same.* He slowly turns, scanning the street, and his gaze rests again on the old manor. He feels someone watching him but can't find the source.

He shakes off the unease and continues down the street. He stops at the corner. A few parked cars dot the street, but there is no foot traffic either way. He makes a mental note to check with the salon across the street, but it looks closed at the moment.

He steps into the small artisan shop. He removes his hat and attempts to fan away the aroma of leather and juniper oil flooding his nose. He scans the display cases and racks of purses, wallets, and belts.

The man behind the counter straightens and places an open novel face down on the counter.

"Welcome, how can I help you today?" the man says, tapping a tablet on the counter. "We have a two for one sale on belts today."

"I just have a few questions." The deputy sidles up to the counter and looks out the window. There's no obstruction to the intersection from this angle. "I noticed on your sign out front, the shop is open Monday through Saturday from nine to six."

"That's correct," the man says, assessing the deputy.

The deputy faces the man. "And were you working this past Monday?"

The man looks down at the tablet and taps the calendar. "Yes, I worked from two to six so the owner could send out online orders from the weekend."

"Do you recall a lot of foot traffic on Monday?" the deputy says, scanning the shop.

"It's always kind of dead on Mondays." He picks up the novel from the counter. "I think I read an entire book during that shift."

"But you do watch the intersection?" the deputy says, meeting the man's eyes for the first time.

"I really only look outside when there is a loud vehicle or when the bus stops by in the afternoons. The kids are usually pretty loud."

"Earlier, when you watched that lady cross the street with the stroller," the deputy says. "Was that an exception?"

"A red truck was rumbling at the intersection for several minutes. I'm ninety percent sure he was on his phone." He lifts his chin towards the window. "I'm pretty sure he would still be there if a car didn't pull up behind him."

"Good to know," the deputy says, tapping his phone. "On Monday, did you notice or spot this young lady?" The deputy holds up the image of Penny.

The man studies the image and shakes his head. "She's a little older than the kids I see getting off the bus, but she looks familiar." He steps back. "Is that the missing girl?"

The deputy nods and swipes the screen. "And this girl?"

The man nods. "Yes!" He looks at his calendar again. "On Wednesday," he points to the large window near the counter, "she walked by several times but always stopped and stared down the street."

Deputy Morris stares out the window, and his scalp tingles. He pats the top of his head. "And did you ask her what she was staring at?"

"She's never come into the shop, just walks by now and again. But by close on Wednesday, I was curious enough to look where she was staring." He walks to the window and points up the street. "I think she was looking at the old homes that were flooded earlier this spring."

"How many times have you seen this girl?" the deputy asks, holding up the image of Maggie again.

"About once a month," the man says, pointing his thumb towards the rear of the shop. "I think she comes to visit someone at the old manor."

"Why do you think that?" the deputy asks, leaning forward.

"Once," the man says, and then smiles, "no twice. I saw her walking down the steps of the old manor when I took the trash out." He shrugs. "She's the only person I've actually seen come in or out of that creepy building."

"And is she… alone?" the deputy asks.

"Yes," the man says, nodding. "Which I always found a little odd with her age and condition."

"Condition?"

"She has down syndrome," the man says with confidence.

"But you told me you've never spoken with her," the deputy says, narrowing his eyes.

"My cousin's daughter also has down syndrome and she's nearly the same age as the wandering girl." He nods to the window. "And she paused long enough this week that I actually saw her eyes and round face close up. And real pretty hair. It was light, but a reddish color."

The deputy takes out his notebook and flips through a few pages until he finds Rozanne's description of Maggie. "Do you recall what she was wearing?"

"A dress and white knee socks with black shoes." The man holds up a hand up just below his chest. "I'd say she's fairly short, maybe just over five feet."

The deputy nods and jots down a line. "Great, thanks for your time."

"Is she missing too?" the man asks, gesturing to the deputy's phone.

The deputy looks up from his notebook. "I don't know who she is just yet. Let's hope she's just fine." He slides out a card and places it on the counter. "If you see her wandering around again, please call this number."

The man nods. "Will do!"

Deputy Morris nods, walks out of the shop, checks for traffic, and crosses the street. The salon is still dark. He checks the door for the hours and finds a sign, 'Closed for Remodel'. He makes a note to check back tomorrow for any signs of a crew. He looks across the intersection and can just see the porch of the first of the three flood-damaged homes.

He walks back across the street and up the block. The sensation of being watched stops him in his tracks. He looks up at the manor and his eyes land on a window near the top. *Was that a person or a shadow?* He looks up. The sky is clear, not a single cloud. He looks back at the manor and a face is staring back out at him from the same window.

The deputy bolts up the uneven steps to the front door of Spa View Manor, pausing at the gritty interior. He spots the stairs and sprints up the first flight. He pauses again at the open door on the second floor. He strains to see in the dim, narrow hallway. Closed doors line the hall and there is a flicker of light near the opposite end.

He listens, but only hears the faint hum of an air conditioner. He cautiously continues up and pauses on the third-floor landing.

The interior walls are toppled in piles of broken stones. Only a few supporting pillars remain. Graffiti tags are visible under the layers of dust.

He moves up the next flight of stairs with more haste. He looks down at a crack along one of the marble steps near the top. Then he looks up.

The wood paneling lining the staircase shines as if freshly polished. His eyes follow the paneling to a large, ornate wooden door. It's slightly ajar with a warm glow emanating from inside.

"What in the devil is this?" He unsnaps the holster on his belt and steps up onto the landing.

After five long seconds of listening to the silence, he pushes against the door, and it swings open with ease. He scans the well-lit hallway. His eyes fall on the gold and glass light fixtures evenly spaced down the hall. He blinks and takes a step in and stops at the first dark wood door. The number 401 is engraved on a brass plate centered on the door.

He reaches for the brass handle of the door, but feels the air shift behind him. He spins around. The hallway is vacant. He shakes off the feeling and opens the door. He steps across the threshold and gasps.

The suite is fully furnished with a brown upholstered sofa and four-post bed. Ruby-colored linens cover the mattress and match the long floor-to-ceiling curtains framing the large windows overlooking the businesses on Broadway. A large armoire sits in the corner near another open door.

Deputy Morris crosses the room to the open door and draws his weapon. The muzzle of his gun points at his own reflection in an antique mirror. He holsters his gun and takes in the small sink, round soaking tub, and a toilet under another window.

He looks out the window to the parking lot, assessing which window he saw the shadow pass by. A scuffle of footsteps passes the open door to the hallway, drawing his attention away. He cautiously walks out of the suite.

The four remaining doors on the left side of the hallway are closed, but there is a door ajar on the right. He swiftly moves down the hall, but it's not a door at all.

He inspects the piece of paneling on the wall that has been pried open. He clicks on his small flashlight and shines his light down the dark, narrow passage. A small click echoes back to him. He scrambles in and ducks his head to fit his height into the passageway. The passage comes to an abrupt end. He pats down the wall. *It's solid.* He steps back and shines his light along the edges, looking for any sign of a hinge. He pushes against the wall, but it doesn't budge. He checks and knocks on the walls on his right and then again on his left for any sign of an exit. He sighs and turns back to return to the hall as a shadow falls over the opening. His flashlight suddenly dims before falling dark. The hallway lights flicker and go dark a second later.

The deputy bolts forward and bursts out into the hallway. The hallway and fancy interior are gone. *What in the hell!* He barely balances his weight at the edge of a large hole. The third floor is visible from this vantage point. He can see the vague ruins of the space, like the lobby and the dilapidated third floor. There are piles of broken stone, dust and cobwebs clinging to every surface, and several pieces are missing from the floor.

He takes a gentle step along the giant hole and tests his weight. The floor crumbles and falls below. He scans the remaining bits of floor and finds a path still intact, leading back to a small doorway opposite the stairs he entered. He gingerly steps his way to the door. He twists the knob, and it falls loose in his hand.

"Hell." He looks down at the knob and sighs. He steps back and gives the door a solid kick, and it flies open to a rickety fire escape. He taps his foot against the metal grate. The ladder teeters and crashes down to the ground.

Tires screech to a halt in the street, and a man jumps out of a truck. He scrambles up the rise towards the building.

"I've called for help," the man shouts up, holding his phone. "Please don't jump."

"Sir, I'm Deputy—"

"All call 10-56A to Spa View Manor," the dispatcher calls from the radio.

"8413 to Dispatch," Deputy Morris says, tapping his radio.

"Copy," the dispatcher responds.

"Cancel the all call," Deputy Morris says.

"Sir?" the dispatcher responds.

"Send a fire truck with a ladder," the deputy says.

The man shades his eyes. "Deputy Morris?" he shouts.

"Yes," the deputy shouts. "Gage?"

"Yep," Gage says.

"Why are you here?" the deputy shouts.

"I had to get some clean clothes from the house before heading to my shop." Gage points to the east. "How did you get stuck up there?"

The whoop of sirens drowns out the deputy's response. A fire truck rolls to a stop near Gage. He directs the firefighters to the deputy standing at the open door on the fourth floor. They release the ladder.

A second squad car pulls up next to the deputy's car and Deputy Clawson steps out. He jogs over to Gage. "What's going on here?"

⚠

Gage points up to the firefighter climbing towards Deputy Morris with a harness. "Your friend appears to be stuck inside the building and his only exit crashed down as I was driving by."

Deputy Clawson squints up. "Is that Morris?"

"Yep," Gage says. "I thought he was a jumper. I called it in before I knew it was Deputy Morris."

A lady steps out of the front door of the old manor and waves to the deputy. Deputy Clawson nods. He pats Gage on the shoulder. "Please wait here for a moment."

"Sure," Gage says, watching Deputy Clawson jog over to a lady dressed in scrubs. Gage turns his attention back up to Deputy Morris and watches as he climbs down the ladder.

A radio call squawks out of the cab of the firetruck. Gage steps towards it to listen.

"Officer en route, suspect spotted near Bluff and Main."

Gage steps away from the truck. *This is Bluff and Main.*

Gage walks towards the corner. A firefighter rounds the back end of the truck, blocking Gage's view of the intersection. The man removes his jacket and turns his attention to the ladder.

Gage looks him over, but his eyes stay on the blue star with a white serpent symbol on the man's sleeve.

"Can I help you?" the man asks, glaring at Gage.

"What's the symbol on your shirt stand for?" Gage asks, ripping his eyes away from the man's shirt to read his face.

"I'm a medic and a firefighter," the man says. He straightens his slouched posture. "What are you doing here?"

"I was driving by and thought he was a jumper," Gage says, nodding towards the ladder. "Are there a lot of medics who are also firefighters?"

"Only four at Station 3, but most are trained first responders," the man says.

Two squad cars squeal to a stop, blocking the intersection at Bluff and Main directly behind the firetruck. A third squad car arrives, blocking the opposite end of Bluff.

Deputy Morris slips on one rung and clings to the ladder.

"What the hell?" Gage can hear Deputy Morris mutter as he assesses the commotion below.

Four uniformed officers step out of the squad cars. Gage notices their intense stare in his direction, and he backs away from the man wearing the medic shirt.

Deputy Clawson jogs back over towards Gage.

Gage leans close to Deputy Clawson and whispers, "I think they came for… him." He points a thumb towards the medic.

The medic is solely focused on the ladder above.

Deputy Clawson slowly nods and approaches the man, gently motioning for Gage to step further away.

"Hi, I'm Deputy Clawson," he says, sticking his hand out to the medic. "Have we met?"

"Um." The medic glances at the deputy and nods. "Possibly. I'm fairly new to the area." He peels back his lips into a smile. "I'm Logan Garnett, a new medic with Station 3."

Deputy Morris makes it down the last bit of the ladder.

Logan bends and picks up the medic bag and steps forward, but Deputy Clawson tugs on his arm. Logan glares at him.

"Let him catch his breath a moment," Deputy Clawson explains, nodding at Morris and the approaching officers. "You know, in front of his men and all."

Logan nods. Then he eyes the tactical formation of the approaching officers. He slowly turns to see more approaching from the far side of the truck. He wobbles from foot to foot as all color drains from his face.

Suddenly, he drops the bag and launches himself towards the firetruck's open driver's door.

Gage pushes the driver's door closed in a maneuver to get out of the way as Deputy Clawson and the other officers surround Logan.

Logan glares at Gage and scornfully eyes the other officers, two of whom have drawn their weapon, and a third who has cuffs out and ready.

One officer points at Logan. "On your knees, hands behind your head."

Logan complies and kneels. He slowly raises each hand behind his head, keeping his eyes glued on Deputy Clawson.

"Logan Garnett, you're under arrest for the kidnapping and assault of a minor," an officer says. "You have the right to remain silent. Anything you say can and will be used against you in a court of law. You have the right to an attorney. If you cannot afford an attorney, one will be provided for you."

A firefighter climbs down from the rig. "What's going on here?"

"We've just arrested your medic," the officer says, cuffing Logan's wrists. "Stand up," she says to Logan.

Logan complies and a second officer pats him down, removing the contents of his pockets and placing them in an open evidence bag.

"On what charges?" the firefighter asks.

"Kidnapping and assault of a minor," the officer says.

Logan shakes his head, but doesn't say a word.

The firefighter holds up a hand. "Are you sure you have the right guy? He's one of us." He points to the badge on his chest.

The officer nods. "Afraid so. Your captain is aware of the warrant for arrest and of said charges. He'll speak with you and the crew back at the station."

Deputy Morris jumps down from the truck and straightens his belt. "Clawson, a word."

Deputy Clawson nods, following Deputy Morris away from Gage and towards the front of the truck.

Gage watches the officers lead Logan to one of the squad cars and place him in the back. Two of the uniformed men get in front and back out onto Main, driving south towards Broadway.

Gage steps away from the firetruck and frowns at the confused faces and whispers of the firefighters. They are glaring at the backs of the police officers returning to their cars. The ladder is lowered and secured before the crew returns to the cab of the truck.

The deputies move away from the truck and wave Gage over to them. Gage walks with heavy steps to their sides.

"Was that the guy who took Penny?" Gage asks.

"To be determined," Deputy Morris says. "I need you to explain your whereabouts this morning."

Gage takes a step back. "What?"

"Were you following me and fucking with me up there?" Deputy Morris says, pointing up to the manor.

Gage laughs. "Up there?" He points to the manor.

Deputy Morris steps closer and glares down at Gage. "You think this is all a joke?"

"Dude, I've never stepped foot in that place, and I told you I had to run to my shop. I live about four blocks that way." Gage points over his shoulder to the west. "My shop is over there." He points in the other direction. Then he shakes his head. "And you saw me this morning at Rozanne's house."

"And you knew where I was heading when I left the house."

"Rozanne mentioned something about the call that made you leave without breakfast, but I didn't follow you here." He nods to his truck. "Check the passenger seat of my truck for the clean clothes I picked up from my house. And I have an appointment with an Officer Raleigh at ten to file a report regarding a break in and arson attempt at the shop."

Deputy Clawson steps between the two men and taps his radio. "8615 to dispatch."

A chirp squawks out before a woman says, "Go ahead, 8615."

"Is there an Officer Raleigh on duty this morning?"

"Yes, sir. Would you like me to patch you through to her?"

"Yes, please."

Deputy Morris glares at Gage over Clawson's shoulder, and Gage smirks.

Deputy Clawson's radio beeps.

"Officer Raleigh, over."

"What is your 10-20?" Deputy Clawson says.

"I'm on old 10 Highway," Officer Raleigh says. "About two miles south of Auburn Automotive."

Gage grins.

"10-4," Deputy Clawson responds. He looks at Gage, then at Deputy Morris. "I think we can take a step back and assess what just went down."

Gage taps his wrist. "If you want me included in that conversation, follow me over to the shop. I really need to get this report done and get back to Rozanne to relieve Mary."

"I think you have done enough," Deputy Clawson says before Deputy Morris can speak. "Thank you for your help today."

"On that note, gentlemen. Have a wonderful and protective day." Gage gives a mocking bow before jogging over to his truck.

22

Mary tucks the blanket around Rozanne. She collects the glasses from the side table and quietly walks back to the kitchen. She sets the dirty glasses in the sink, opens the freezer and takes out a new bag of frozen peas. She walks back to Rozanne's room and gently replaces the bag over Rozanne's bandages.

Rozanne mumbles, "Maggie, wait, come back."

Mary backs away from the bed.

"Mary, I'm back," Gage says, closing the front door.

Rozanne stirs.

Mary rushes out of the room and down the hall. "She just fell asleep. Keep your voice down."

Gage hands Mary a white cup with a straw. "Yes, ma'am."

Mary takes a sip and sighs. "Their chocolate shakes are so good."

"I agree, but I'm more of a root beer float kind of guy."

Mary smiles and pats his cheek. "You'd better put Rozanne's in the freezer." She follows Gage to the kitchen and starts washing the glasses. "How did the meeting go at the shop?"

Gage grabs a dish towel and steps beside Mary. "Good. They took an official report and dusted for fingerprints." He dries the last glass, rests his hip against the kitchen counter, and faces Mary. "But the best part of the morning was watching the local cops arrest a man they think took Penny."

"Really?" Mary says, drying her hands. "Who?"

"A medic named Logan."

Mary furrows her brow. "Logan Garnett?"

"You know him?" Gage asks.

"Monroe bowls with Steve, the captain at Station 3," Mary says, shaking her head. "He mentioned to Monroe that Logan was a little odd. And Logan came by the pharmacy on Tuesday asking about Rozanne." Gage stiffens. Mary continues. "Many people stopped by, so I thought nothing of it, but do they know each other?"

"I don't know all of Rozanne's friends, so it's possible. She hangs out with Darcy, who works in the dispatch office at the station."

Mary nods. "I have to run lunch to Monroe. Are you good here?"

"Yep," Gage says, patting his stomach. "Between breakfast and ice cream, I'll be good here for a while."

Gage follows Mary outside. He watches her back out and drive away before he grabs the clean clothes from the truck and walks back inside. He walks down the hall and stops at the open door to Rozanne's room. She has a hand up. He steps in and the floor squeaks under his weight. She stirs and drops her hand. He backs out and into the room across the hall. He sets the clothes down on the bed.

Gage pulls out his phone and does a quick search on Logan Garnett. A social media profile with a picture matching the man he met earlier appears in the search results. He clicks and swipes up. Most of the information and posts are blocked from public view, but Darcy is listed as a friend.

Gage's phone beeps with a low battery warning. He plugs his phone in, but the phone beeps again. A text message notification appears. He opens the text and an image of him with Deputy

Clawson outside of the old manor appears. The angle of the photo had to be from up high. He backs out of the image to look at the phone number, but it is unknown. "Shit!"

He forwards the text to the deputies before dialing Deputy Morris.

The line rings twice before the call connects.

"This better be important!" Deputy Morris shouts.

Gage moves the phone away from his ear. "Hello to you, too. Check your text messages." He pauses and hears the deputy grunt and fumble the phone on the other end.

"What the hell is this?" Deputy Morris says.

"I just received that text with the image about two minutes ago from an unknown number. From that angle, it has to be from either the ladder or inside the old manor."

"And you are where?" Deputy Morris asks.

"Back at Rozanne's house."

"Stay put!" Deputy Morris says.

Gage salutes the phone and chuckles. "Yes, sir." He ends the call and sets his phone down. *If I got a message, I wonder if Roz did, too?* He tiptoes into her room and taps her phone. Two text notifications fill the screen.

"Um," Gage mutters, trying to recall the swipe sequence to open her phone.

Rozanne sighs. "I can hear you breathing."

Gage covers his mouth. "Really?"

"Really." She opens her left eye and grins. "Why are you lurking over my phone?"

"I just received a photo message from an unknown number." He holds up her phone. "I wanted to check if you had any mysterious messages." She holds out her hand and Gage hands her phone over.

Rozanne unlocks it and taps the text notifications. "One from Darcy and one—crap, crap, crap." She turns her phone to show Gage.

Gage blinks several times before leaning closer.

An image of Deputy Morris standing in an open-door and there's a girl, covering her mouth with her hands, standing behind him just over his left shoulder.

"Is that Maggie?" Gage whispers.

Rozanne nods.

"I need to forward this to the deputies," Gage says, taking the phone from Rozanne. "Oh, and do you know Logan?"

"I know a Logan," Rozanne says. "He's a medic that works with Darcy at the station. Why?"

Gage looks up from the phone with a frown.

Rozanne sits up with effort. "What's happened?"

"He was arrested today for kidnapping Penny." Gage hands her back the phone.

"It can't be that, Logan, right?" Rozanne asks, looking at her unread message from Darcy. She swipes to the message and gasps. "Shit!"

"What?" Gage asks, leaning back over to see her screen.

"It is that, Logan." Rozanne frowns and sighs. "He finally had the nerve to ask for my number last weekend."

"Roz," Gage says, attempting to keep a straight face.

"Why are you laughing at me?" Rozanne asks, pointing at his face. "Is this because of Anthony?"

Anthony was the last guy she dated. Him and his dad were arrested for fraud. Apparently, they rolled back the miles on every used car they sold.

"Ah yea, Fony Tony." Gage throws up his hands and shrugs. "You really know how to pick them, Roz."

"Stop laughing."

"I'm not," Gage snickers, retreating towards the hall.

"Liar," Rozanne says, tossing a pillow at his back. It misses and hits the wall next to the door.

"You missed!" Gage laughs.

"Ugh! Did you at least bring back ice cream?"

"Yep, give me one second." Gage chuckles all the way down the hall. He checks the driveway and hears the rumble of the afternoon train. He ducks into the kitchen and grabs a spoon from the drawer before opening the freezer and taking out a white cup.

"Hey Roz, do you need anything else?" Gage calls down the hall.

"You've got to be kidding me!" Rozanne shouts.

"Okay, just the ice cream." Gage casually walks down the hall. He enters with a wide smile. She isn't there. "Roz?"

"Bathroom," Rozanne says. "Can you check the hall closet for, um… tampons?"

"Uh, sure." He sets the ice cream on the side table and returns to the hall. He scans the shelves and spots a blue box. He inspects the packaging and returns to the bathroom door. He knocks once.

"Thanks," Rozanne says, cracking the door. She takes the box.

"No problem," Gage says, backing out of the room and walking out onto the porch. He walks the length of the wraparound porch and jumps when he hears the snap of the screen door. "Roz?"

"I need some air," Rozanne says. "Don't tell Mary or Monroe I left the house." She points a spoon at him as he turns the corner. He smiles and nods. She carefully sits on the long bench that rests against the house.

"Do you know what I can't shake?" Gage says, leaning on the porch rail in front of her.

Rozanne looks up from her ice cream. "That you didn't buy enough ice cream?"

"There is another gallon in the freezer," Gage says, shaking his head. Rozanne wiggles her hips from side to side. "But seriously, Roz. Why are we getting messages?"

"Maybe they can fill us in." She points behind him as two cars pull up the drive.

"Is your phone with you or in the room?" Gage asks.

"Room," she says, handing him the empty cup.

He takes it and runs back inside. He returns with their phones as Deputy Morris and Deputy Clawson exit a car and a familiar woman hops out of a white van.

The woman waves to Gage. It's the same tech who assisted last night. He smiles and hands their phones to her.

"Thanks," she says, taking the phones. "Be right back with these." She nods to the deputies and opens the side door to the van.

"Welcome back, deputies," Rozanne says, adjusting her position to face them.

"Glad to see you outside for once," Deputy Clawson says with a smile.

"Beyond the photos you both received, we have some other concerns that we need to address with Rozanne." Deputy Morris turns to Gage. "Can you give us a moment?"

Gage looks at Rozanne. She nods. "Sure, I'll get started on her lunch."

Rozanne watches Deputy Morris take an awkward stance across from her. "What is your relationship with Logan Garnett?"

"Um, I would say acquaintance," Rozanne says. "I've hung out with the crew from the station socially, and he's attended a few of the gatherings."

"Have you ever been to his place?" Deputy Morris asks.

"No, I don't even know where he lives. I don't think Darcy, my friend at the station, ever mentioned his place."

"Did Gage tell you he's been arrested?" Deputy Clawson asks, sitting on the bench beside her.

"He did," Rozanne says. "But I also got a text from Darcy letting me know."

"If you are not in a relationship with Logan," Deputy Morris says, leaning forward, "why do you think Darcy felt the need to share that information?"

"Logan and I exchanged phone numbers last weekend," Rozanne says, feeling the flush of embarrassment rise to her cheeks. "She was just letting me know I shouldn't wait around for a phone call."

Deputy Clawson clears his throat. "And did Gage know about Logan?"

Rozanne chuckles. "There is nothing to know. Two adults exchanged numbers. Gage and I are nothing but friends."

"Okay," Deputy Clawson says, looking at Deputy Morris.

Deputy Morris nods. "We found fingerprints matching Logan's at Gage's shop and are under the assumption that he's responsible for the sabotage that nearly caught Gage's shop on fire."

"But… why?" Rozanne whispers.

"One possible motive would be the rumors of Gage hurting you," Deputy Clawson says.

"Ugh, fucking Viola!" Rozanne says under her breath. "Sorry, I didn't mean to curse. It's just that her gossip infects the community."

"We're aware of her role in this and are speaking with our superiors about slander charges," Deputy Morris says. "It will probably be a civil matter."

"Oh," Rozanne says, nodding. "It's good to know there can be some consequences for her actions."

"And the drifter on your land could not make bail and is awaiting his hearing in county jail," Deputy Morris says. "He was assigned a public defender, and they entered a request for one of the harassment charges to be dropped based on new information." He pauses and kneels level with Rozanne. "The drifter claims a man gave him one hundred dollars to activate two different phones." Rozanne frowns. The deputy continues. "His description matched Logan. We gave him fifty mug shots to look through, and he positively identified Logan."

"Wait, I'm not following…" Rozanne says, shifting on the bench.

"I received a text," explains Deputy Clawson, "from one phone the drifter activated during the search. The number matched the first message you received."

Rozanne dips her chin before looking up. "And Penny? Was it really Logan?"

"All evidence points to Logan so far," Deputy Clawson says, nodding. "And the case looks pretty solid."

"How's Penny?" Rozanne asks.

"She's been moved from critical to stable," Deputy Clawson says. "But she is still unconscious."

Rozanne's face pales.

"Rozanne?" Deputy Clawson says, placing a hand on her shoulder.

"Her poor parents," Rozanne whispers.

Deputy Morris nods. "It will be best if we can focus on putting this guy behind bars for a very long time."

The tech emerges from the white van. "Deputies. A moment of your time." She nods to Rozanne. "Two minutes."

"No problem," Rozanne says.

The deputies walk off the porch as Gage opens the front door with a bowl of soup.

Deputy Clawson turns and nods to him. "We're nearly done. Join Rozanne."

Gage nods and walks over to Rozanne. "How's the fresh air?" He assesses her pale face.

"Heavy," Rozanne says, taking the bowl from Gage. "They think Logan… torched your shop."

Gage sits down hard. "What? Why? I only met the guy today."

Rozanne shakes her head. "Vi," she says quietly, blowing the soup on her spoon.

"Son of a bitch," Gage mumbles, slamming his balled fist into the bench. Rozanne chokes a little before swallowing. "Sorry."

"Don't be," Rozanne says, wiping her lip. "It's not your fault."

"I should call and apologize to Dusty," Gage says, standing. Then he pauses. "They still have our phones, don't they?"

"Yea," Rozanne says. "And there is more news."

"Bad?" Gage asks, lowering back down to the bench. "Logan paid the drifter to activate two phones."

Gage's jaw flops open.

"What if the drifter and Logan were somehow connected…" She pauses and looks at the hanging chair. "It makes me very uneasy."

Gage stands and kicks the chair. "They were in on it!"

"Who were?" Deputy Clawson says, stepping back up on the porch.

"The drifter hurt Roz so she would call for help," Gage says, looking at the drawn face of Rozanne. He shakes his head. "Station 3 would be the first to respond. It's the closest station, and Logan would've been the knight that saves the day."

"Are you suggesting they planned the assault?" Deputy Clawson asks.

Deputy Morris holds up a hand. "According to the notes I have from the captain at Station 3, Logan was working a split shift on Monday." He flips the page. "He worked from seven to eleven in the morning and seven to eleven that evening. And his name was on the sign-up sheet for volunteers during the search party here on Wednesday morning."

Rozanne's hands tremble. She carefully sets the smoothie down and stands. "He's always been kind and pleasant the few times we've spoken. The suggestion that he would intentionally harm me, or Penny, just don't add up."

"Some of the guys I've put away have been squeaky clean on the outside," Deputy Morris says, frowning. "And terrible monsters on the inside." He hands Gage back the phones. "We're done with those for now, and the same number is attached to the images from last night and today."

Gage's eyes bulge. "Is there a third person involved?"

142

"We can't rule it out," Deputy Clawson says, shaking his head. "Both of the accused men were being interviewed at the time the messages were sent."

"The time stamp on the texts suggests they were sent at the same time," the tech says, sliding the van door closed. "It could be the phone was in airplane mode or roaming when the texts were sent. If the phone connected to the network, it would have sent all pending outgoing messages at the same time."

"The signal near the old manor is a little spotty," Deputy Clawson says.

Gage points to the deputy. "Logan took off his jacket before he was arrested. If the phone was in a pocket, it could've connected to the network or Wi-Fi when the truck returned to the station."

"We'll inquire about the jacket and a phone at Station 3." Deputy Morris closes his notebook. "The last thing we need to discuss is the appearance of Maggie."

23

Gage wraps a supportive arm around Rozanne as they watch the deputies drive away. "You look rough."

"My face pain is at an eight, plus my cramps are kicking in," Rozanne says, sipping the last of the soup. "I want to take another long hot bath and soak all of this madness away."

Gage nods and holds the front door open. "I know the feeling."

Rozanne stops and stares at her half-bandaged face in the foyer mirror. "How did they keep eye contact with me? I look ridiculous."

Gage pats her on the shoulder. "I'm pretty sure you're much prettier, half mummified, than the pricks they have locked up right now."

"Not by much," Rozanne groans, pressing on her hip.

"Do you believe Deputy Morris's description of the fourth floor?" Gage asks, shaking his head.

"It's nice to think I'm not alone in my bizarre hallucinations of a grand hotel."

"Or in being a little coo coo machoo," Gage says, following Rozanne down the hall.

"Funny." Rozanne rolls her eyes and opens a dresser drawer. "But the shopkeeper's theory that she is a visitor to the manor may turn up something."

Gage taps on the old journal sitting on the dresser. "Do you want to read some more of this?"

"By the time you call and apologize to Dusty," Rozanne says, grabbing a top and shorts, "the tub should be full. I'll leave the door cracked and pull the curtain. Grab a beer and pull the chair up near the bathroom door."

"Cozy entertainment." Gage takes a step out and then pauses. "I guess I can't bring you a beer?"

"Not funny Gage," Rozanne says.

"Pain pill?" Gage says.

"Half," Rozanne says.

"Got it." Gage checks the battery on his phone before walking out onto the front porch. He takes in a deep breath. He scans the woods as he dials Dusty's number from memory.

"Hey Gage," Dusty answers after the second ring.

"Good news," Gage says. "I owe you an apology."

"I'm sorry, this must be a bad connection," Dusty says. "Did you say apology?"

"I did, and here it is. I am sorry." Gage leans against the house.

"I might need a little more context," Dusty says.

"The deputies arrested a man today who's fingerprints match the ones they took from the shop door." Gage pauses for a response but is met with silence. He checks his phone to make sure the call didn't drop. "Dusty? You there?"

"Sorry, dude, just a little speechless," Dusty says. "Who was it?"

"Logan Garnett, a medic with Station 3. Do you know him?"

"I've seen him with some of the crew at the tavern, but I've never spoken to the guy. He was always tucked far back in the corner watching the room." Dusty pauses. "But why would he target you?"

"Apparently he had a thing for Roz," Gage says.

Gage hears Dusty slam a car door before answering. "Oh, and the gossip… shit Gage, that's messed up."

"It's a mess for sure. We also found out that the drifter squatting on Roz's land had a connection to Logan."

"Whoa," Dusty says. "I have a customer pulling in. Catch ya later?"

"Sure thing, thanks for taking care of the shop, and again, my apologies for blaming you for the bike."

"You got it."

Gage looks down at his phone. The battery is down to 2%. He walks into the house and takes two steps towards the kitchen, but turns back to the door. He engages the dead bolt.

"Stepping into the tub," Rozanne calls from the bathroom. "I'm going to need a whole pill. Oh, and an ice pack. My face is throbbing."

"And a cherry on top?" Gage doesn't hear a response. He grabs her medication, an ice pack, and a beer. He juggles his full hands and connects the phone to the charger in his room. He rattles the pill bottle as a warning that he's about to enter the bathroom. "Do you want it now or after the bath?"

"Mmm," Rozanne moans. "Ice pack for now, please." She sticks her hand out of the curtain and wiggles her fingers.

Gage shades his eyes and hesitantly extends the ice pack in the tub's direction.

"Thanks." Rozanne sighs, taking the ice pack. "I'm thinking we need to call in one of those paranormal investigation teams."

Gage chuckles. "Or a priest to do an exorcism for you and Deputy Morris?" He settles in the chair and opens the journal to the second passage.

"Not a bad idea," Rozanne groans. "I could use some divine intervention at the moment, but I'm listening. Read away."

Gage takes a long swig of his beer and swallows. He reads to her.

December 31, 1917

Two more days until I can sleep in and rest. The CR was booked solid for the last week, and I met the mayor of KC. It was surreal. He has bushy eyebrows and is bald on top; Thomas, the bellman, nicknamed him caterpillar. He's kind of cute...

146

Gage takes another long swig of his beer. "War in France, that would have been the first world war."

"Somebody paid attention in history class," Rozanne says.

"It was my second-best class," Gage says, smiling.

"Ah, that's right, home economics was first."

"Now who thinks they're funny?"

Rozanne laughs. "Who was the mayor back then?"

Gage pats his pocket. "One second, my phone is on the charger." He fetches his phone and returns, typing in a few keywords. "The author's description is pretty accurate." He clicks on the picture. "Look." He holds his phone facing the crack of the door.

Rozanne leans her head over the tub and draws the curtain open. She squints at the screen with her left eye. "His eyebrows are pretty epic. What's his name?"

Gage turns the phone back towards him and clicks back on the search results. "George Edwards, secretary of Edwards and Sloane Jewelry Company."

"Well, that explains the wife's jewelry. Are you good to keep reading?"

"Sure, the next one is just a few days later." Gage continues.

"Oh," Gage whispers.

"What is it?"

Gage clears his throat.

"Oh!" Rozanne says. Gage hears some sloshing and then
the tub starts to drain. "Getting out. Do not read a second more
until I am dressed."

Gage laughs. "I'm going to warm up some food. Do you
want more soup or a smoothie?"

Rozanne reaches blindly for the towel. "Chocolate or
pizza."

"I'll see what I can whip up."

Rozanne dries off and carefully steps out of the tub. Her
mind replays the conversation with Deputy Morris about the
hotel suite, which mirrored her experience at the old manor.
I'm not alone. We aren't crazy, right? She slathers on some
lotion, applies deodorant, and dresses in her top and shorts.
She glances in the mirror and curses. Her top is nearly sheer.
She steps out and grabs a cardigan from her closet and wraps
it tightly around her.

The throbbing of her face overwhelms her cramps for the
time being. She spots the orange bottle with her pain
medication on the bed. She opens it and slides one pill out but
lets it fall back into the bottle.

"Ibuprofen should be enough," Rozanne says, walking back
into the bathroom. She rummages around in a drawer until she
finds a white bottle with a blue label and shoves the orange
bottle in its place. She slams the drawer closed on her thumb.
"Crap!"

148

Gage comes into view, shading his eyes. "Did you fall out of the tub?"

"No," Rozanne says, firmly holding her left thumb. "Just smashed my thumb in a drawer."

"Ah," Gage says, peeking through his fingers. Seeing her clothed, he relaxes. "Do you need ice?" He gestures towards her hand. She shakes her head. He nods towards the bedroom door. "There was something left on the front porch."

"I haven't ordered anything," Rozanne says, starting for the door. "Did you bring it in?"

Gage follows her down the hall. "It's a little too large to bring inside."

Rozanne looks back at Gage.

He shrugs.

"What is it?"

"Take a look," Gage says, motioning towards the front door.

Rozanne huffs. She hurries to the front door and swings it open. She looks down at a wooden glider painted off white, matching the other pieces on the porch. She turns back to Gage.

He holds up his hands. "I don't know, honest. I saw the dust trail of a truck when I came into the kitchen." He nods to the setting sun. "I came out to get a better look and nearly toppled over this." He points to the glider.

Rozanne runs a hand over the wood. "Why didn't they knock or leave a note?"

"I suspect whoever commissioned this piece would know of your injury and the front room was dark," Gage says.

"You think this is a custom piece?" Rozanne asks.

"It matches the others too perfectly," Gage says, walking to the hanging porch swing and pointing at the bench. "It has the same paint and finish, plus the small willow tree carved in the center of each piece is identical."

Rozanne steps back, inspecting the similarities but gasps. "My wicker hanging chair is gone!"

Gage's eyes bulge. "You're right. I was too distracted by the new piece to notice." He chuckles. "My first guess is Monroe or Mary."

"No, this is not their style," Rozanne whispers. "They wouldn't just drop off something like this without notice and runaway with my chair."

"Well, have you checked your phone lately?" Gage asks.

"No," Rozanne says. She bends at the waist a bit and winces. "I'll check it and then lay down for a bit." She turns for the door but pauses. "Can you run down to the mailbox? Maybe there is a note there."

"Sure thing," Gage says.

Rozanne wearily walks back into the house as Gage steps off the front porch. She heads down the hall and pauses at the open door to Gage's temporary room. It's tidy, minus the pile of old newspapers on the side table. She hears her phone buzzing as she turns for her room. She catches her phone as it falls from the dresser. She swipes the screen to answer without acknowledging the caller's number.

"Hello," Rozanne says.

"Do you like it?" a warm, familiar male voice says.

"Pardon, but who is this?" Rozanne asks, looking at the screen. The number is not saved as a contact.

"Rozanne," he purrs in a whisper.

Rozanne's hair lifts from her arms and her scalp tingles. She shivers and tightens her grip on the phone. "Logan?"

"Of course," Logan says. "I see your porch has a lovely new addition. Replacing your old rickety chair."

"But you've never been here," Rozanne says, leaning on the bed.

Logan chuckles. "I was part of the search for the young lady at your home on Wednesday."

"The one you kidnapped," Rozanne whispers, fighting the urge to scream.

"Oh, Rozanne," Logan whispers.

The front door opens, and heavy steps come down the hall.

"No!" Rozanne throws her phone at the shadow filling her bedroom doorway.

Gage catches her phone. "No, what?" He looks down at the phone. A call end notification flashes on the screen. "What the hell, Roz? You look like you've seen a ghost."

She points a shaky finger at him. "It was Logan."

24

Gage ends the call with Deputy Morris and steps back inside the house. "It's just me."

"Me who?" Rozanne asks. Her tone suggests she's teasing, but Gage shakes his head, lengthening his stride down the hall.

"Gage, the mighty!" he says, casually leaning against the doorframe to her room. Rozanne's left eye is still red and slightly swollen from crying. "Deputy Morris is making calls to all the local wood craftsmen and will have a patrol car in the area until they locate the caller."

"He doesn't believe it was Logan?" Rozanne asks, sitting up a little higher. "I would swear on my Grandma Anne's grave that was his voice."

"They claim Logan was under video surveillance during the time of the call," Gage says, sitting on the side of the bed. "And they swept his cell after patting him down, but they didn't find a phone."

"I know what I heard," Rozanne says, looking out the window.

The evening dusk is painted with streaks of vibrant pink reflecting in the pond.

She sighs. "Do you think I'm crazy?"

Gage pats her leg. "Roz, based on the reaction I saw on your face, I know you heard someone that sounds like him, but what do you really know about Logan?"

Rozanne doesn't look at Gage, but lowers her eyes to the phone on the side table. "Well, he recently moved here from the Cleveland area."

"Ohio?" Gage asks.

"Tennessee," Rozanne says, looking up to meet his eyes. "He became a medic after a bad tornado ripped up a nearby town. It had a massive number of fatalities because of the lack of first responders with medic training."

Gage frowns. "That doesn't sound like a creepy kidnapper arsonist."

"I know, right?" Rozanne says, nodding. "But that's all I really know. We've only had one uninterrupted conversation. Otherwise, there was always one of the crew around."

"Dusty mentioned he's seen him with the other guys from the station at the tavern, but that he's always tucked back in the corner watching the room."

Rozanne shrugs. "Darcy mentioned he didn't joke around much with the others. She always called him the closet nerd of the crew."

"Speaking of Darcy, why didn't you call her the night you fell?" Gage points to her bandages.

"You were the last contact pulled up on my phone and it was dark." Gage frowns. "Plus, Darcy works evenings, so she can't always answer her phone."

"Hmm," Gage says, leaning back on the footrest. "How many kids does she have?"

"Two," Rozanne says, narrowing her eye at him.

"How does it feel getting dumped in the friend department for work and kids?"

"Darcy didn't dump me," Rozanne scoffs, "and we still hang out. It's called being adults; something you avoid at all cost."

"Hey now, I adult like the best of them," Gage says. Rozanne raises an eyebrow. "I own my shop, my house and four vehicles, including insurance."

Rozanne smiles. "You inherited the shop and house from your uncle and the cars are hobbies, not purchases."

"And this?" Gage says, waving his hand around. "Inherited, including your car. So, who is adulting now?"

"Point taken," Rozanne says, nodding. "Now before the regularly scheduled programming got all coo coo machoo, you were reading. Do you want to continue?"

"As you wish," Gage says, rolling off the bed. He grabs the journal from the chair and returns to the bed, fluffing the pillows against the footboard, before sitting to face her. "Where were we?"

"The entry about the cook's comment regarding Maggie," Rozanne says, adjusting an ice pack over the bandages and a hot water bottle across her hips.

Gage drags a finger down the page and pauses. He clears his throat and reads.

> *He said Miss Maggie is of the special kind and is always hidden away when her parents visit. I kin she is a mystery for another day, and they have a few days left during the visit. Maybe I will meet her tomorrow.*

Gage turns the page and mocks in a Scottish brogue, "I kin she is."

Rozanne chuckles. "Is that your impression of Ewan McGregor?"

"Aye," Gage says, winking at Rozanne.

"Oh dear, my sanity is truly waning," she says, touching the back of her hand to her forehead. "Is it fever dreams or true madness?"

Gage laughs hard enough to shake the entire bed.

"Easy, chuckles," she says, lifting the ice pack away from her face.

"Sorry," Gage gasps. "I think…" He wheezes out a final laugh. "I think I needed a good laugh with all the drama."

"I'm here all night," Rozanne says and gives a slight bow at the waist with a dramatic wave of her arm.

"Alright, joker," Gage says, lifting the journal to hide his smile. "The next entry is a few days later."

January 11, 1918
Mama received a letter from pa today. She let me read it. He is boarding a ship again. He saw a few whales on his last voyage and will try to describe them to me in another letter. He also mentioned another soldier receiving orders to return home. I pray he gets those orders soon. Mama misses him so much.
And today the family with the special girl checked out, and I finally saw her. Miss Maggie is beautiful. She appears to be a small teenage girl with the prettiest reddish blonde hair and the straightest posture.

Gage peers over the top of the journal. "Another confirmation?"

"Holy smokes," Rozanne whispers, nodding. "She's real, or was real?" She raises an eyebrow. "Do I see dead people?"

Gage shrugs. "Monroe said she was never declared dead."

"Ha, seriously," Rozanne whispers.

Gage turns the open journal towards her. "There's more. Should I continue?"

"Why not," Rozanne says with a shrug.

Gage nods and reads.

Why would they lock her away?
Thomas walked me home today and he thinks Miss Maggie is slow in her mind. He called her a slur I refuse to write. But why would they lock her up?

"She's not wrong," Rozanne says.

Headlights pan across the yard shimmering on the still water of the pond.

Gage closes the journal. "Are you expecting anyone?"

"No," Rozanne says, "but it sounds like Monroe's truck."

Gage nods. "Stay put." He moves off the bed and closes her bedroom door on his way out. He hears heavy footfalls on the front porch. He finds Monroe inspecting the glider when he swings open the door.

"Hey, Monroe," Gage says.

"It's odd," Monroe says without turning. "Bonnie had the porch swing and bench made for Anne's seventy-fifth birthday. And this piece… it matches."

"We noticed the similarities," Gage says.

Monroe points to the carving on the glider. "How would they get the tree design like this to match?"

"We were just as confused," Gage says, nodding to the front door. "Roz said the wood from Anne's set was from an old walnut tree that fell after a major ice storm."

Monroe nods. "This is super creepy."

"Do you recall who made the other two pieces?" Gage asks.

"Clyde Miller," Monroe says. Gage pulls out his phone to search for a number. "He passed away several years ago."

Gage frowns. He pushes open the front door while pocketing his phone.

Monroe pats him on the shoulder, stepping inside. "How's she doing?"

"The pain meds have been replaced," Gage says.

Monroe raises a single white eyebrow. "By what?"

"Ice, a hot water bottle and ibuprofen," Rozanne says, flipping on the hall light. She leans a metal baseball bat against the wall and opens the closet door. She places the bat back inside.

Gage chuckles. "And your weapon of choice is a bat?"

Rozanne shrugs. "Too lazy to open the safe."

Monroe side hugs Rozanne, and they walk to the kitchen.

Gage is standing at the open fridge. "What can I get ya, Monroe?"

Monroe pats his stomach. "Mary gave me orders to come here. She should be here any minute with a surprise for dinner."

Rozanne's stomach loudly rumbles. "I hope she figured out pizza in a blender."

Monroe and Gage laugh.

"How was the pharmacy today?" Rozanne asks after their laughter dies down.

"Nothing new to report," Monroe says. He holds up one finger. "Not true. The color of the diaper packaging is now pastel."

Rozanne rolls her eyes and smiles. "Hilarious."

A horn honks twice from the front drive.

"That's my Mary," Monroe says, dancing out of the kitchen to the front door.

Gage chokes on his beer. "Did he just do an old two step scoot out of the kitchen?"

Rozanne stares at the front door. "Aye." She smiles. "Their love is part of the reason I've never left the pharmacy for other opportunities. It's his joy and their love all day, every day." She sighs. "Truly admirable after that many years together."

"And the rumor is that you are cold and heartless," Gage says, twirling in a circle. "The ice queen has a heart."

Rozanne swings a backhand at Gage's shoulder. "That's twice today—you've called me an ice queen."

"Ice pack queen?" He laughs and steps out of her reach.

She glares at him as the front door opens.

"Dinner smells amazing," Gage says, jogging to the front door. He takes a brown paper bag from Mary. She pats his cheek. Monroe follows her inside with a casserole dish.

Mary hugs Rozanne. "How are you holding up?"

"I've had better days," Rozanne says.

Mary whispers, "Logan?" Rozanne nods. "You just never know with some people." Rozanne pulls away and shrugs. She gently pats Rozanne's left cheek. "Did you notice old Clyde's signature on the glider?"

Rozanne frowns. "What do you mean by signature?"

"Clyde's pieces always included his initials in the designs." Mary walks out onto the front porch.

Rozanne and Gage follow Mary.

She leans over and points to the inner side of the leg on the left. "He was a lefty and always carved his initials on the left side of every piece."

Gage takes out his phone and switches on the flashlight. He kneels and inspects the area she is pointing. "C.M. is carved in right here." He switches to the camera app and takes a closeup of the initials. He inspects the image before showing Rozanne.

"Wow," Rozanne whispers.

Gage stands and walks over to the porch swing. He lifts the left side and takes another photo. "Mary's right. It's the same signature." He lifts the left side of the bench and takes a third photo. "I'm going to send these over to the deputies. Monroe mentioned that Clyde passed away several years ago."

"He did," Mary says, shooing them back inside. "But his nephew took it over."

"Is he a C.M. as well?" Rozanne asks, walking in behind Gage.

Monroe is setting the table when they return to the kitchen.

Mary pats Monroe's hip. "Clyde's nephew is Chris or Curtis?"

"Hmm," Monroe says, wrapping an arm around her. "Curtis sounds right, but I guess we could as…"

Gage holds up his phone. "Or we could just look up, Curtis?" He frowns immediately. A picture of the glider is posted on a business page for C.M. Wood and Cabinets. "Just dropped off this beauty." Gage points to the caption as he turns the phone to Rozanne. "Mystery solved on who delivered, but who ordered and paid for it?"

25

Rozanne watches Gage pace the living room.

"Deputy Morris hasn't been able to locate Curtis," Gage says, pocketing his phone and sliding into the chair at the table next to Rozanne. "His truck was back at the shop, and it fits the description of the one I saw leaving the house." He shakes out his napkin and continues. "But his girlfriend said he hasn't returned home since leaving for work this morning."

"It's still early," Mary says, glancing at the clock hanging over the table. She scoops another serving of the seven-layer dip onto Gage's plate. "Was Curtis in your class at school?"

Rozanne shakes her head. "We did have a Miller in our class, but not a guy."

Gage nods. "Lindy was in our class. I have no idea if she had siblings. She always hung out with the band crowd."

Monroe taps his fork against the plate. "Clyde's brother Owen lived in Lawson. Curtis could be from Lawson originally."

"Regardless of who he is or where he is from," Mary says, scooting back from the table. "I hope he is not involved with this Logan fellow or Penny."

"Amen," Monroe says with a full mouth.

Mary swats her napkin at him. "Monroe, mind your manners."

He chokes a bit on his last bite and then winks at Mary. Her frown raises just a smidge.

Gage laughs.

Rozanne scoots back. "Mary, this was amazing. Real food for the first time in days, plus blending the chicken tortilla soup was so thoughtful."

"I aim to please, my dear." Mary picks up her plate and holds her hand out for Monroe's. He is eyeing Gage and the last bit of dip. "Mister, if you have another bite, you'll be sleeping outside."

Monroe pouts and scrunches his nose and eyebrows. He hands over his plate.

"I have dessert, you old sourpuss." Mary nods to the fridge.

Monroe bats his eyelashes. "Oh my goodness, what is on the menu?"

"Apple tart with vanilla bean ice cream." Mary winks at Rozanne. "I'll blend yours up with caramel sauce."

"Yep, this is Heaven," Gage says, whirling his napkin above his head.

Mary winks. "I'm glad you think so, because you and Monroe are on dish duty while I prep the dessert."

"Yes, ma'am," Gage says, standing and taking Rozanne's bowl and the casserole dish.

Monroe kisses Mary on the cheek on his way to the sink. "I'll dry."

Rozanne watches the three of them in her kitchen and sighs. "This is nice."

"What did you say?" Mary shouts over the sound of the blender.

Rozanne smiles. "I said thank you!"

Mary winks and pours the blended tart and ice cream into a large glass. "You can thank Mrs. Arber."

"What?" Rozanne and Gage ask in unison.

Mary sets the glass down in front of Rozanne. "The rotary club had a bake sale this afternoon. And the baker was none other than Mrs. Arber."

"Hmm," Gage says, shutting off the faucet.

"Did you two ever make heads or tails of that journal?" Monroe asks, drying the last plate.

"We've made it through a couple passages, and from what we can make of it, the author was a maid at the Castle Rock Hotel. Her father and uncle were overseas fighting in World War I." Gage pauses, taking a bowl with the tart and a heaping portion of ice cream from Mary. "And she mentions Roz's Maggie."

"Wow," Monroe mutters, admiring the dessert.

"Wow, to the journal entries or the tart?" Rozanne asks.

Monroe takes a seat back at the table next to Mary. "Wow to both."

"How do you know it was the Maggie you've seen?" Mary asks before taking a bite.

"The maid describes her how I've seen her," Rozanne says, "and she mentions her condition and that the parents locked her away while out." She frowns. "The parents from the article and this girl's description are nearly identical. Simply awful."

Gage turns to Monroe and Mary. "Did you hear Deputy Morris had a similar experience at the old manor?"

"Really?" Mary asks.

"He claims the fourth-floor transformed into a hotel with a fully furnished suite," Gage explains.

"Wow," Monroe says, shaking his head.

"But his grand hallucination dissolved after he got stuck in a tight spot," Rozanne adds.

"He was really rattled," Gage says, setting his bowl down with a sigh. "That was amazing, but I am beyond stuffed." He winks at Rozanne. "Between the beans from the dip and the dairy, if you hear thunder, it's not a storm."

"You're disgusting!" Rozanne groans.

Monroe snickers. "I know what you mean."

"Enough, you two." Mary stands, snatching the bowls from Monroe and Gage. "Did you check your manners at the door, Monroe Clarence?"

Gage's jaw falls open.

"Clarence?" Rozanne tilts her head. "I always wondered what the C stood for."

Monroe shrugs. "No big secret. I was named after my Grandma Clara."

Gage swallows. "Well, at least they gave you Clarence instead. Monroe Clara would be rather… actually, it's kind of elegant."

Mary laughs. "Elegant, Gage, really?"

Gage smirks. "What? You think this greasy mechanic can't come up with whimsical terms?"

Rozanne snorts into her glass.

Gage bumps Rozanne's shoulder. "See who is reading to whom later."

Rozanne chuckles and walks her glass over to the sink. She starts to wash it, but Mary shoos her away.

"Are you going to keep the glider?" Monroe asks, standing and stretching.

Rozanne swallows hard. "I haven't even thought about keeping it." She rubs the standing hairs on her arms. "The idea that somebody was this close to the house to get the design and paint colors for something like this is unnerving."

"Is there any chance that the piece was ordered by Anne and Clyde wasn't able to complete it?" Mary asks.

"Maybe, but the timing of Logan's call right after," Rozanne says. "It's just too… odd."

"What call?" Monroe and Mary ask in unison.

"Be right back," Gage excuses himself from the kitchen.

Rozanne sits back down and gives Monroe and Mary the play-by-play of the conversation with Logan right after she received the glider.

"And you know for sure it was Logan?" Monroe asks.

"I would swear on it."

"Does Logan have family here?" Mary asks.

"Here in town?" Rozanne asks, shaking her head. "I don't think he has any family here. Darcy may know." She pats her pocket. It's empty. She hears the familiar steps of Gage in the hall. "Gage, can you fetch my phone?"

"Aye, my lady," Gage says with the fake accent that raises Mary's eyebrows into her hairline.

"Gage thinks the journal's author may have had some Scottish roots, indicated by a few key phrases," Rozanne says.

Gage returns with the journal and her phone. He hands off her phone. He opens the first few pages and shows Monroe and Mary the author's description of Maggie.

Rozanne swipes open her phone and taps to open three new messages. She deletes the first, a reminder about her electrical bill, and opens two unread messages from Darcy.

Hi! How's it going?

Do you think you're up for a visit tomorrow afternoon with the kids?

Rozanne types back a response. *It's been an odd day. Tomorrow should be fine but fair warning. I look like a mummy and bruised. Not sure if your littles will be alarmed or not?*

Rozanne watches the three dots blink, and her phone buzzes again.

We might hold off on the kids. My eldest has had a series of night terrors since that girl was kidnapped. No need to rattle her. I'll swing by around five.

Rozanne responds. *Sounds good. An odd question, but does Logan have any family here?* Darcy's response comes almost immediately.

A cousin, I think. I'll ask Bryan when he comes back with more coffee.

"An accomplice," Rozanne mutters under her breath. Her ears go red, and her heart jumps out of her chest. She places a hand below her collarbone. She takes a deep breath in and slowly exhales. The heat in her ears subsides.

Only then does she respond to Darcy. *Thanks. See you tomorrow.* She sets the phone back on the table and looks up at Monroe, Mary and Gage huddled around the journal.

Their faces are pale.

"What is it?" Rozanne asks.

"Edith," Mary whispers.

"Your Great Grandma Edith is mentioned in the next entry," Gage says, sitting down next to Rozanne with the journal open.

Rozanne silently reads.

> *January 30, 1918*
>
> *A woman named Edith came by the CR today and spoke to the staff about an upcoming event to honor the Red Cross volunteers who helped give the pox vaccines to the school kids in KC. She wore a black hat lined with red silk. But her hair! She had two very long, dark brown braids. I've never seen hair so long. I hope she returns for the actual event.*
>
> *Thomas walked me home today. He asked if he could take me to the diner after our next shift. I asked mama, her exact response: Take your cousin Lucille, I will not have you unchaperoned in public. But Lucille is still up north visiting our grandmother. Someday soon, I hope we can go on a proper date.*

"But Edith was a fairly common name during this time," Rozanne says, looking up from the page. "Why do you think it is my Edith?"

"Maybe because of the painting hanging in the living room?" Monroe says and winks.

Rozanne stands but leans on the table for support. The throbbing pulses against her right eye down to her jawline. "I may need some ice."

Mary walks to the freezer and readies her pack. Gage helps support Rozanne as she and Monroe leave the kitchen.

Mary follows and flips on the track lighting over the wall with the small painting. She hands Rozanne the ice pack.

Rozanne stares at the old oil painting in its antique frame. Her great grandmother is painted wearing a black hat tilted back, allowing the artist to capture her full face. The tilt of the hat also exposes the red lining.

Edith has dark, full eyebrows, green eyes, high cheekbones, full lips, and an expression of confidence that reminds Rozanne of her own mother. Edith's two long braids fall over a grey smock with a small red cross painted on a white circular patch on the sleeve. She stands next to her grandfather in his formal Army uniform.

Rozanne's knees soften, and she sits abruptly on the couch behind her.

Mary smiles. "They were a beautiful couple."

"Wow," Rozanne whispers. "To be honest, I've always just admired him in his uniform and never even noticed Edith's attire."

Gage steps closer to the painting. "There's a date in the corner with the artist's initials." He points. "P.C. 1918."

Monroe steps back to the couch and sits next to Rozanne. "Do you know if Edith kept a journal or any letters during her husband's time in service?"

"There is a box of the letters sent back and forth between them when he was over in France," Rozanne says. "They're inside the old cedar hope chest in the attic, along with his uniform and medals."

Buzz, buzz

"I left my phone on the kitchen table." Rozanne attempts to stand, but Gage waves.

"I got it." Gage darts out and returns with her phone.

"Thanks," Rozanne says, fumbling the ice pack to swipe open her phone with one hand. She opens the response from Darcy.

According to Bry, Logan has an uncle and cousin that live out in Vibbard.

"A cousin?" Rozanne mutters. She quickly types back. *Thanks Darcy. See you tomorrow.*

"Darcy is coming by tomorrow evening," Rozanne says. "And Mary, you were right. Logan has an uncle and cousin in Vibbard."

Gage shakes his head and holds up his phone. "I'm calling Deputy Morris." He steps out onto the front porch.

"Surely the deputies know that already," Mary says.

Monroe nods. "I would hope so, but who knows? There are a lot of moving pieces with this investigation."

"My face and head hurt," Rozanne mumbles.

"You've had a long day," Mary says. "And it's getting late. We'll take our leave. Get some rest, love."

Monroe stands and offers his hand to Rozanne. She takes it and manages to stand without wobbling.

"Thanks again for the amazing dinner and the apple tart smoothie." Rozanne hugs Mary and then hugs Monroe.

Gage cracks open the front door. "Monroe. A word."

Rozanne drops her arms and narrows her left eye on Gage's grim face. "What's wrong?"

Gage swallows hard. "They found Curtis Miller."

"And?" Mary says, wrapping an arm around Rozanne.

"He's in the hospital and unconscious," Gage says as Monroe steps out onto the front porch. He closes the door.

Rozanne faces Mary. "Not a bad dream? I'm awake?"

Mary gently pinches Rozanne's left cheek. "Sorry, this is reality."

Gage and Monroe step back in. Monroe nods to Gage.

Gage clears his throat. "The deputies are assigning an officer to the house until they can make heads or tails of this situation."

Rozanne sits back down on the couch.

"The officer will screen any visitors," Gage says. "I've let them know you are expecting Darcy tomorrow. And, of course, the three of us." Gage points to Monroe, Mary, and himself. "But if there are additional people you want on the list, we can add them as needed."

166

"Do they know what happened to Curtis?" Rozanne's voice is cracking on the verge of tears.

"They aren't sure yet," Gage says, sitting next to her. "He was found in a ditch off Salem Road."

Rozanne sniffles and blinks away a tear. "And they think I am next?"

"They are just being cautious," Monroe says, patting her shoulder. "There hasn't been anything reported to make them think you are in danger."

"A tech with the department will place a tracer on your phone," Gage says. "If that creep calls again, they'll be able to trace the location and hopefully connect some of the dots."

"Did they know about Logan's family here?" Mary asks, watching Rozanne carefully.

"They did," Gage says. "His uncle works for the railroad. He has been on duty during the days in question and was cleared of any suspicion. However, Logan's cousin has a history of minor misdemeanors for petty theft and shoplifting."

"Who is he?" Rozanne asks.

"She," Gage says. "Her name is Francesca Garnett. Do you know her?"

"There was a girl that went by Fran at the last cookout with Darcy and the crew." Rozanne shrugs. "I'll ask Darcy tomorrow."

"One last note," Gage says, letting out a whistle. "Do you recall when I stepped out to take a call from the deputy right before you went into surgery?"

"Barely," Rozanne says.

"There was a girl trying to gain access to the house saying she lived here," Gage says. Rozanne nods. "The officer who encountered her said she gave the name Fran."

Mary gasps. "So, this is a family affair of crime?"

"But why the house or me?" Rozanne says, shaking her head. "What do they want?"

"No idea," Gage says, nodding to the front door. "But there will be an officer assigned here until that gets figured out."

Rozanne sighs.

"Do they know where this girl, Francesca, is at the moment?" Mary asks.

"No," Monroe says, taking Mary's hand.

Rozanne feels a slithering tingle glide down her back. She shifts and stiffens her spine. "Well, I'm not going to sit here and be terrified." She pushes off the couch. "What did you have to tell Monroe that you didn't want me to hear?"

"The young girl, Penny," Gage says, pushing down a lump in his throat. "She didn't make it."

Mary lets out a sob and clamps a hand over her mouth. Monroe places an arm around her.

"But," Rozanne says in disbelief, "they said she was stable!"

Monroe nods. "Gage was confirming the scientific terminology the deputy gave for her passing. They believe it was a pulmonary embolism."

Rozanne opens her mouth but can't find the words.

Mary hugs Rozanne and Gage. She pats Monroe on the cheek and sniffles. "I'll meet you at home."

Monroe nods. "See you soon."

Gage helps Mary out to the car with the casserole dish from dinner.

Monroe folds Rozanne into a gentle hug. "We'll keep you safe. I promised Anne."

"I know," Rozanne says, her voice muffled by his chest.

Monroe steps back and looks her over. "Ice and bed rest." He taps the drainage tube. "I don't think you are supposed to be this vertical for this long."

"Yes, sir." Rozanne salutes.

Gage comes back up to the porch and holds the door open for Monroe. "We've got this."

Monroe smirks and pats Gage on the shoulder and leans in. "Let's hope so, otherwise I'm sending Anne's ghost to your house."

"Ha, ha," Gage says. Monroe waves and steps out. Gage locks the door behind him and walks past Rozanne to the back door. Then he locks the back door. "You heard Monroe. Bed rest." He points down the hall with the journal in hand. "And I'll read until you fall asleep."

"Gage," Rozanne says. "What else are you not telling me?"

Gage shrugs. "Am I that obvious?"

Rozanne nods. "You've always had a tell." Gage opens his mouth. "And no, I won't tell you what it is. I enjoy winning at poker."

Gage scowls at her.

"Spill it."

He sighs. "They found Penny's DNA on the white socks found with the shoes by the creek."

"Seriously?"

Gage nods. "I'm afraid so."

Rozanne bends at the waist. "I think I might be sick." She cups her mouth and hustles down the hall to her room and collapses in front of her toilet just in time.

26

Rozanne rinses out her mouth and pats her left cheek dry. She hears the front door close and cracks open the bathroom door. "Gage?"

"Are you ok?" Gage asks, walking into the room.

Rozanne nods and walks to the bed.

"An officer arrived about five minutes ago." Gage sets her phone and a glass of ginger ale on the side table after Rozanne sits down on the bed. "Take small sips."

Rozanne sighs and takes the glass. She slowly swallows and squashes a belch. "Did they bug my phone?"

"Not a bug, but a tracing app," Gage says. "Are you still up for some reading?"

"One or two entries," Rozanne says, leaning back on the pillow. She adjusts a new ice pack over her face.

Gage nods and circles the bed, returning to his spot at the end, facing her. He opens the journal.

"Gage," Rozanne whispers. He looks over the journal. "Could we have saved her?"

Gage sets the journal down. "We did what we could. You did more than me." He pats her leg.

She shakes her head once and her lip quivers.

"Remember, you made me go out and look for her."

"But we were too late!"

"Roz," Gage says, leaning forward. "She was gone by the time I made it down to the creek and we called for help immediately. What more could we have done?"

Rozanne chews on the corner of her lip. "She was just so close… and now she's gone. Her parents…" She dips her chin to her chest.

Gage scoots up and wraps his arms around her. "We can't take the blame for the cruelty that took her."

Rozanne feels a drip on her forehead. She tilts her head back and looks up. *Is Gage crying?*

Gage is focusing on the ceiling.

Rozanne reaches up and softly smooths the drops on each cheek with her thumbs.

His watery hazel eyes look down at hers.

He leans down, kissing her exposed left temple.

Rozanne's cheeks ignite. She stops breathing.

Gage kisses her ruby red cheek.

Rozanne exhales and turns her lips to his. Their lips meet with a gentle kiss. Gage withdraws with a smirk. She focuses on his eyes, which are still watering. He strokes the line of her neck with his thumb.

Rozanne gives him a slight nod.

Gage doesn't hesitate and kisses her until her ice pack falls on his exposed knee. He hisses and sits back.

Rozanne touches her lips. "Who taught you to kiss like that?"

Gage levels his gaze to hers. "Who says I'm not self-taught?"

Rozanne smiles and laughs. "Spin the bottle, ninth grade."

"We were forced to kiss," Gage says. "And it was my first kiss. Yours too, right?"

"Nah, Luke, seventh grade on the bus ride home from a track meet."

"You kissed Luke Dudley?" Gage asks, scrunching his nose.

"No, he kissed me," Rozanne says, bouncing her exposed eyebrow.

"Well, la dee dah," Gage sings. "I had a room full of horny teenagers watching me kiss the one girl who would be my end."

Rozanne's jaw falls open. He leans forward and kisses the tip of her nose. Then he places a finger under her chin and gently pushes her mouth closed.

"Now, where were we?" Gage says, sitting back with the journal.

Rozanne, still reeling from his confession, swallows. "Your end?" she whispers.

"Oh, that's right," Gage says, ignoring her question. "She fancies Thomas."

Rozanne debates placing the ice pack somewhere south as he opens the journal and begins reading.

February 3, 1918

Mama received another letter from pa today. His company is afloat, pending further orders. He saw two whales and seven sharks. The largest shark attacked a school of fish near the ship. He described the fleeing fish as organized chaos. I've tried to picture this like a swarm of bees in a thick forest, dodging limbs and leaves to stay clustered together and protect the queen.

Gage pauses and looks over the journal. "That's not a bad analogy of the bees versus the fish."

"She's clever and descriptive," Rozanne says.

Gage nods. "She may be the glue that can hold the chaos of our current situation together."

"True." Rozanne shifts another pillow under her head.

Gage continues reading.

I had to assist the ballroom staff with a large luncheon this afternoon and received a compliment from that woman I admire, Edith. She said I had the prettiest red curls she had ever seen. I found my words after a moment and I told her I admired her long braids. She leaned close and said it's because she has curly hair

Gage lowers the journal. "What are vamp lace boots?"

"I think they have pointed toes with a small heel and laces that go up the boot."

Gage is typing on his phone. "Ding, ding." He turns the screen towards Rozanne. "You're correct."

Rozanne takes his phone and zooms in on the advert. "It's from a 1918 Sears catalog." She hands back his phone and when their fingers touch, she freezes. She fights the tingling sensation and risks a look up.

Gage winks.

"Ugh, what in the hell, dude?" Rozanne groans.

"Speaking of dead giveaways," Gage teases. "Your 'tell' is just as obvious to me."

"Just read," Rozanne says, hiding her burning face with the ice pack.

Gage turns the page and laughs. Rozanne lifts the ice pack. He holds up a finger and reads.

February 6, 1918

He kissed me!

Gage smiles.

"That's it?" Rozanne asks.

"Yep," Gage says, turning the journal to face Rozanne.

The author took the whole page to write the three words in big, bold letters.

"Well, I guess the mystery author and I have something in common," Rozanne says.

Gage lifts an eyebrow.

"He kissed me… too."

Gage leans forward and hovers his face over hers. "So, when does she… kiss him?"

"Wouldn't you like to know?" Rozanne says and winks.

Gage sighs and shifts to lay next to her. "It's after ten. Do you want to call it a night?"

"One more," Rozanne says, poking him in the ribs.

Gage squirms. "Not cool, dude."

Rozanne laughs.

Gage leans forward and stacks the pillows behind his head so he can remain lying next to her. He shares the journal so she can see the page.

She reads to him.

Gage chuckles. "She has a point."

"I think obesity was a sign of wealth back then," Rozanne says. "If you had enough to eat to become obese, you were considered well off."

"Oh, the plague of societal acceptance," Gage mocks.

"Not so far off from today's judgement-at-first-glance and make a meme culture."

"Miss Rayvern," Gage says, lowering his tone. "Are you saying we need to address the plague of social media?"

"Why, Mr. Auburn, do you have a cure?" Rozanne says.

"Destroy all smart devices," Gage says in a monotone, robotic voice. "This will shift our minds into learning first before accepting face value."

"My word, ladies and gentlemen," Rozanne says, holding her hands in the shape of a crown and placing it on top of Gage's head. "Miss America 2018 goes to Mr. Gage Auburn." She claps her hands. "Bravo, bravo."

"Miss America," Gage muses. "Try Mr. Universe."

"You wish," Rozanne says. "Your turn to read."

He sighs and picks up the journal.

Lucille has agreed to chaperone another date this Saturday. She flirted with a tall waiter during our last date. I hope he is there again to distract her. Thomas left me a note in my apron pocket last night since he was off today. He said my lips taste like honey and sweet blueberries. He signed with a heart. The other maid overheard him telling the cook that he has something special planned for our next date. I've been racking my mind with possibilities. Top three guesses, toffee from the candy store, a flower, or another kiss… oh hurry up Saturday!

"Young puppy love," Rozanne says, turning the page.

"We still have no idea how old she is," Gage says, "or even who she is."

"But we have some clues," Rozanne says. "Her cousin's name is Lucille. Lucille's parents are Martin and Gerty, and the author's father served during the first world war with his brother or brother-in-law."

"And we know her place of employment," Gage says. "Well, we can navigate that rabbit hole tomorrow. And I'll get the letters from the attic if you think they can be helpful."

"It's worth a shot," Rozanne says. "Maybe check the papers from February 1918. There may be an article about the luncheon."

Gage closes the journal and rolls over her without physically touching her. He just hovers and stares at her for a few seconds before pouncing off the bed.

Rozanne stares at him as he casually walks towards the door like nothing happened.

"Good night," Gage says, pausing at the door. "I'll be over here." He winks and nods to the room across the hall. "If you should need anything, ring or shout!" He turns off her light and closes her door.

"What the actual hell?" Rozanne mutters into the knuckle she was biting. She shakes out her hand. *Did he really just casually kiss the hell out of me and then pretend for the next half hour like it was no big deal?*

Rozanne flips on her lamp and opens the drawer to her nightstand. She fumbles her hand through the contents until her fingers find the soft binding of her journal she kept in high school. She pulls it out and thumbs through the pages, pausing when a post-it slips out. She flips it over and gasps.

Gage's scratchy handwriting spells out two words. *My end.*

"Son of a..." Rozanne whispers, recalling the day Gage stuck this to her jacket.

It was junior year. Rozanne was in her fifth-period class when Darcy noticed the post-it.

"Who did this?" Darcy had asked, holding up the note.

"Damn him, that's Gage's handwriting and he sits behind me during science. I've been wearing that note since second-period."

"Your hair was down until now," Darcy had said. "It was probably hidden behind all those curls. 'My end' is kind of dramatic. Are you two in some kind of neighbor feud?"

"I beat his highest score on the old Donkey Kong game in their basement. He was pretty pissed."

Darcy had rolled her eyes.

176

Rozanne stuffs the post-it back in the journal and flips towards the front. She scans the pages of her favorite lyrics and lines from comedy sketches. She pauses at one entry.

I fell off the skateboard for, according to Gage, the hundredth time today. He leaned over me and just stared directly into my eyes for like five seconds. It was super weird and made my stomach queasy. Why are boys so awkward?

Rozanne laughs. "Why indeed? The skateboarding phase… I would have been… twelve." She stuffs the journal back in the drawer and flips off her lamp. She rests back on the pillow.

Her mind spins, and she feels the pull of a knot unraveling deep in her chest. "We can't—we know way too much about each other."

She recalls her Grandma Anne's voice. *"It's a wonder you two don't sleep in the same bed."*

And her mom scolding grandma's attempt at humor. *"Don't you dare encourage teenagers to sleep in the same bed!"*

"Ah geez," Rozanne says, pressing her hand over her chest.

<h1 style="text-align:center">27</h1>

Gage's phone buzzes so hard it falls off the nightstand and thumps onto the floor.

He reaches down and grabs it. When he taps the screen, he sees two missed calls from Deputy Morris and one missed call from Deputy Clawson.

He sits up and calls Deputy Morris.

"Gage!" the deputy immediately answers.

"Hey, sorry I was…" Gage says, but Deputy Morris cuts in.

"Is Rozanne there with you?" Deputy Morris says with a tone that has Gage up and out of bed.

He runs across the hall and swings open her bedroom door. The bed linens are slept in, but empty. "Roz!" He checks her bathroom. *It's steamy.*

"Gage," Deputy Morris says, "is she with you?"

Gage ignores his question. "Roz, where the hell are you?"

"Gage!" Deputy Morris shouts.

Gage checks the other bedroom, bathroom, and kitchen. He opens the front door and scans the front yard to the woods. He jogs the wrap-around porch, eyes scanning the surrounding area.

"She's not here," Gage says breathlessly. "I don't understand."

"We received a muffled call to dispatch. The caller was whispering, but the dispatcher made out a few words. Based on what she said, we're assuming Rozanne is in the trunk of a white sedan, and that she was taken by a tall man with a hood and a girl dressed as a cop."

"What!" Gage shouts. "How? You had an officer here, right?" He jumps off the porch and circles the house. "Where is the officer's car?"

"Dispatch got a call about a half hour ago regarding suspicious activity at the old Clevenger property near Rozanne's house. The shift replacement was en route to Rozanne's house, and he was the closest officer. He accepted the call to investigate, but never responded with an update."

"Useless," Gage mutters, running back inside. "He left us exposed with no warning."

Deputy Morris ignores his comment. "Since the other officer didn't respond after several calls from dispatch, the officer en route to Rozanne's bypassed her house to check on the unresponsive officer. He found him knocked unconscious by a hard blow to the head."

Gage falls against a dresser as he tries to hold the phone and put on his jeans. He curses, putting the phone on speaker. "When did the call come in from Roz?"

"Four minutes after the second officer arrived on scene at the Clevenger's place."

"Morris!" Gage ties his boots and stands. He uses every ounce of self-control not to kick the wall.

"I know," Deputy Morris says, his tone level. "We think the girl posed as the officer on duty and the tall man surprised Rozanne." He clears his throat. "Did you hear anything at all?"

"No, damn it! I was still dreaming when you called." Gage jogs back down the hall and checks the kitchen. "She was up at least long enough to shower and to put on a pot of coffee. It's full and still hot."

"Gage, we have every available officer on duty looking for a white sedan, and Deputy Clawson should be pulling in now to dust for fingerprints and check tire tracks. We will find her!"

"Shit!" Gage yells at the phone as the call ends. "This can't be happening!"

The siren of Deputy Clawson's cruiser disrupts Gage's shock. He opens the front door and stares at the deputy jumping out of the car. "This is your fault!" he says, pointing at the deputy. "Well, your department's fault!"

Deputy Clawson nods and raises his hands. "I don't disagree."

A white van pulls up next to the cruiser. A man in a plain blue polo hops out.

"Dust the front and back doors first," Deputy Clawson says to the man. "Gage, walk with me."

Gage moves off the front porch with lead legs. "If they hurt her, I swear to God…"

"You do love her, don't you?" Deputy Clawson asks, assessing Gage's face.

Gage scowls. "What?"

"Morris called it the first night he met you two."

"What the hell are you talking about?" Gage spits.

"Lifelong friends, sure." Deputy Clawson smiles. "But you're mad in love with that girl, and everyone can see it but you two."

Gage deflates. "You don't know anything about us or her."

Deputy Clawson holds up a hand. "Of course."

"Why is this happening?" Gage asks. "Why her?"

"We found a connection between the Garnett family and Rozanne's family late last night."

Gage stops walking.

"Explain," Gage says, between clenched teeth.

"Rozanne's parents," the deputy says. Gage frowns. "The drunk driver who killed them was Francesca Garnett's mother and Logan's aunt."

"No," Gage says, shaking his head. "The woman's name was Lisa Terrence."

"Correct," Deputy Clawson says, "she never married Francesca's father."

Gage balls up his fists. "Do you think it was her? Francesca? Did she take Roz?"

"She is a person of interest." Deputy Clawson frowns. "We had an officer waiting at Ray's diner to pick her up this morning with regards to questions about her connections with Logan and Penny. But she didn't show up for her shift."

"Penny," Gage whispers. "Oh God, she's dead. What if they…"

"We'll find Rozanne," Deputy Clawson says. "We put the tracer on her phone last night, remember? We've been tracking her signal since she placed the call."

Gage runs a hand through his hair. "Then why are we just standing here?"

"We need evidence to put these people away for good."

Gage glares at him. "No, we need Roz safe and away from these psychos."

"Sir," the man calls from the front porch. He's holding up a red cloth. "Is this hers?"

Gage and the deputy jog back to the porch.

Gage nods. "It's the cloth we've used around her frozen bags of peas or corn. Where was this?"

"Bottom step of the back porch."

Gage and the deputy jog around to the back of the house. Deputy Clawson points out a few yellow kernels of corn leading to tracks visible on the dusty gravel drive.

"I need these tire impressions sent to the station immediately," Deputy Clawson says, kneeling to get a closer look. There is something shiny in the dirt near one of the pieces of corn. He takes out a glove from his pocket and puts it on. Then he picks up the object—an hourglass shaped piece of smooth metal with two prongs at either end.

"Did Rozanne have these securing her bandages?" Deputy Clawson asks, showing Gage.

"Yes," Gage says. "Ugh! We were going to change her bandages this morning." He staggers back to the steps and sits down hard. *Who is screaming?* Gage can't hear the deputy over the noise, but he can see his lips moving.

"Gage, I need you to just breathe and remain calm," Deputy Clawson says.

The deputy places a hand on Gage's shoulder and the screaming stops.

Gage inhales a big gulp of air. His throat aches. "Who was screaming?" He reaches up to massage his throat and looks past the deputy.

"You were," the deputy says, kneeling to be eye level with Gage. "You're in shock. It's normal under severe stress or trauma."

Gage blinks and looks at the deputy. "Roz—she's gone."

"Do you want me to call a family member or a friend to come here and be with you?" the deputy asks.

"Darcy," Gage says, attempting to stand. His knees buckle and he falls back on the step. "She knew Logan and is friends with Rozanne. Call Darcy."

"Is she the dispatcher at the fire station?" the deputy asks, flipping through his notes.

"Yes," Gage says.

The deputy nods and stands. He uses his radio to call dispatch, and his phone pings a few seconds later. He dials the number, puts the phone on speaker, and waits.

"Hello," Darcy answers.

"Darcy, my name is Deputy Clawson."

"One second." Darcy mutes a cartoon blaring in the background. "Sorry, my kids only know one volume… loud."

"We have a request for your assistance at Rozanne Rayvern's home."

"Is Rozanne okay?" Darcy asks.

"Ma'am, can you come to her home immediately?" the deputy asks.

"Is she okay?" Darcy asks again.

Gage stands and takes the phone from the deputy. "The bastards took Rozanne this morning. Get your ass over here."

"What? When? How?" Darcy stammers.

The deputy yanks the phone back from Gage and glares at him. "We have a situation, and we need your assistance."

"I'll be right there," Darcy says, ending the call.

"Never touch my phone again," the deputy scolds Gage.

"This isn't the time for delicate answers," Gage says, straightening his spine to match the deputy's height. "She asked you a question, and Roz is not okay. We can't afford to pussyfoot around with her lost out there."

"I'm going to chalk your insults up to shock and get back to work," the deputy says, pointing to the house. "Stay here and answer your damn phone when we call!"

"Just find Roz," Gage says, walking back up on the porch and around to the front door. His phone pings with a text from Darcy.

On my way. Had to drop kids off at my sister's.

Seriously, what the hell is happening?

Gage types back. *A fucking mess.*

28

Gage hears the deputy's radio explode with a series of calls. Gage runs after Deputy Clawson as he sprints for his cruiser.

"Gage, if you follow me, I'll arrest you. Stay put and wait for Darcy."

"Did they find the car?" Gage asks, catching up with the deputy.

"Yes," Deputy Clawson says. "Stay here! That's an order."

The deputy starts the engine and peels out of the driveway, barely missing Darcy's car on the way out.

Darcy screeches to a stop and hops out of the car. "Gage!"

"Do you have your radio?" Gage asks, looking in her car.

"Yes," Darcy says. "Explain what the hell is happening!"

"Rozanne has been kidnapped. She called for help from the trunk of a car."

"Why?" Darcy says, shaking her head. "Why would anyone abduct Rozanne?"

"They fucking took her and stuffed her in a trunk," Gage says, waving a hand at her car.

"Okay, calm down," Darcy says, pacing back and forth. "I'm assuming the deputy received the call of shots fired."

"They're shooting at the cops?" Gage says, stepping in front of Darcy. She nods. "And did they find Roz?"

"I don't know," Darcy says, returning to the car and pulling out her radio. "I didn't flip it on until after I dropped the kids off." She adjusts a knob, and a call streams out.

10-52 times three. 10-99 Bluff and Main.

"What does that even mean?" Gage says.

"Three ambulances and a suspect, armed and dangerous, last seen near Bluff and Main."

"Darcy," Gage says. "That's Spa View, the old manor."

"It's an intersection, Gage," Darcy says. "It's also close to the condemned houses where they found Penny."

"Fine," Gage says, throwing his hands in the air. "What do you know about Logan's cousin, Francesca?"

"That's his cousin's name?" Darcy says, scrunching her nose.

Gage nods.

"Hmm," Darcy says, "there was a girl named Fran at the last cookout, about a month ago. But I thought she was the fling of the week for one of our rookies."

"Her mother, Logan's aunt, killed Roz's parents," Gage says. Darcy takes a step back.

"Shit," she whispers. "But it's been years."

"Six years," Gage says.

"This weekend," they say in unison.

"Do you recall how many years the woman was sentenced?" Gage asks.

"Twenty years or so," Darcy says and shrugs. "But what does that have to do with Rozanne and the abduction?"

"Francesca is a person of interest," Gage says. "And I bet she conspired with Logan's planned assault that caused Roz's injuries."

"Whoa," Darcy says, holding up a hand. "I was on duty with Logan the night that Rozanne fell."

"Turns out the drifter was paid by Logan to activate two phones," Gage says. "And one theory is that Logan also hired the drifter to harm Rozanne. If she had called for emergency services instead of calling me for help that night, it would've been your station to respond to this location. And he would be the medic on duty to assist her."

"That's insane," Darcy says.

"And disgusting," Gage says. "And then he took his vengeance out on me via the shop for stealing his role."

"I heard about that," Darcy says. "But I thought it was because of the lies Viola spread about you harming Rozanne."

"I don't really care at this point," Gage says. "I just want her back."

Darcy smiles. "Gage Auburn, are you in love with our best friend?"

"Why do people keep saying that?" Gage says, shaking his head. "For fifteen years, Rozanne has been a pain in my ass, but she doesn't deserve to be taken or stuffed in someone's trunk."

A radio transmission bleeps. It crackles again and Gage leans closer to the radio.

Shots fired. Officer down, I repeat, officer down.

The man in the blue polo jogs around the side of the house.

"Ah!" Darcy screams.

The man stops mid stride.

"Darcy," Gage says, turning her towards the white van. "He's a tech from the station. He's collecting fingerprints and tire impressions."

"Sorry," Darcy apologizes as the man climbs into the van. He nods without a word and backs the van away from the house.

They watch the dust rise from the van's departure. The radio beeps and they jump a little startled.

Fire!

The distant sirens and honks of a fire engine start within seconds of the call. Darcy takes a step for her car, but Gage grabs the antenna of her radio and pulls it out of her grasp. He holds it over his head.

"The deputy gave me orders that I couldn't leave the property," Gage says. "But he said I could listen with you."

Darcy tilts her chin up and places her fists on her hips. "One, two, thr—" She kicks him hard between the legs.

He folds and collapses.

"You think you can bully a short girl? You've got another think coming!" She picks up the radio and nods towards the car. "Are you getting in? Or are you going to lie there and cry all day?"

"Darcy," Gage wheezes, crawling towards her car. "You could have just asked for it back."

"I started counting with my mom voice," Darcy says and opens her car door. "It's the same thing."

"I'm not four years old," Gage groans, sliding into the passenger seat.

All call. We have four officers cornered and under fire.

SWAT two minutes out, fall back.

Darcy drives at full speed down the driveway.

Gage braces against the dash as she jerks the car out onto the main road.

Gage fumbles with the seat belt and clicks it into place. "Where did you learn to drive?" he asks, bracing around the next corner.

"Mind your manners," Darcy says, cutting him a look. "We'll be there in sixty seconds."

Darcy is right. They slide into a spot outside the station in a minute flat. She hops out and impatiently taps her foot. Gage moves slowly, attempting to stand tall, but ending up hunched over. They walk into the station. She waves her hand. "Go to the second door on the right. I'll bring you a bag of ice."

Gage follows her instructions into a conference room.

Darcy returns with a bag and gently tosses it in his direction.

Gage catches it and pulls back one chair from the table. He carefully sits and positions the bag.

Darcy turns on a large screen and logs in. She pulls up the live feeds from the firetruck's cameras and positions the three views on the screen.

"The three abandoned homes are on fire," Darcy says, pointing to a middle structure. "It looks like the blaze started here and spread to the other homes on either side."

Gage squints at the screen. "What's that on the right?" He points to an object hovering in the sky in the far-right-hand corner of the screen.

Darcy taps on the live feed from that camera and zooms in. "That's a hobby drone." She zooms back out and the drone flies out of view. She pulls the multi-camera view back up.

"When I talked to the deputy last night, the techs have a theory that a drone captured the pictures Roz and I have received based on the angle it was taken."

"What photos?" Darcy glances over at him.

"The first was a girl in a window. The reflection from the window showed Penny walking with a tall figure with a medic's star on their sleeve. I'm assuming that was Logan with Penny."

"You've seen the photo of the two of them?"

"Yea, it was sent to Rozanne's phone," Gage says.

"What?" Darcy turns her back to the screen and faces Gage. She narrows her eyes to small slits.

"I thought you knew," Gage says, holding up a hand.

"We haven't had a chance to properly chat since her fall. I mean, assault."

The radio squawks. *SWAT in position.*

Darcy turns her focus back to the screen. A swarm of black uniforms comes from every direction. "Where are they heading?" She taps the keyboard. All the cameras go wide. "There!" She points to the far-left-hand corner where a white car is parked in a church parking lot.

Gage holds his breath as they bypass the car and surround the church. "Why aren't they checking the car?"

"The trunk is popped open," Darcy says, squinting at the screen. "Sorry Gage. I've got to turn the cameras back to the fire. The captain will have my hide already for messing with the footage."

Gage pounds a fist against the table.

Darcy jumps.

188

"Sorry," Gage says.

"I get it," Darcy says, focusing the final camera on the fire.

"So now what?" Gage says, watching the streams of water hitting the middle house.

"We wait," Darcy says. "How's your um…"

Gage lifts the bag before she can finish. "Numb."

"Sorry," Darcy apologizes with her hands folded. "Forgive me?"

"On one condition," Gage says, narrowing his eyes at her.

"Name it," Darcy says.

"Never even think about doing that again," Gage says.

"To you or to anyone?" Darcy asks.

"To me!" Gage says, shaking his head.

"Deal." Darcy extends her hand. Gage takes it with a firm grip. "I wish we could hear the SWAT teams radio coms."

"Dude we can!" Darcy stands. "We can't stand in the dispatch office, but we can hear from the room next door. They have the live channel for the SWAT communications, and it's only audible in there."

Gage pushes back from the table. "Then why are we still in here? Let's go!"

Darcy leads Gage to another room. She heads to a closet with extra gear and points up to a vent. She places one finger over her mouth. Gage nods.

Balcony clear. First floor is clear. Lead two to basement. Copy lead two.

Gage stiffens and braces against the wall.

"Just breathe," Darcy whispers.

Basement clear of people, but there is a second passage with a ladder leading down. Copy lead two, hold position.

Darcy turns to Gage, eyes wide. "The bootleg tunnels," she whispers.

"Those are real?" Gage asks.

Darcy nods. She pushes him out the door. "That is one of the oldest churches in the historic district. All the old structures have access to the catacombs, it was mainly for water line and utilities before prohibition. They run all the way from Spa View to the Elms Resort."

"I thought those were just urban legends," Gage says, shaking his head.

"Nope, I think some parts were caved in after the last major flood, but most are still intact."

"Francesca works at the old diner on Broadway. Is there an access point there?"

"Most likely," Darcy says, fumbling for her phone. She taps her screen. "The new salon on the corner just pulled the original floor plans of the buildings on the south side of Broadway to keep the esthetic the same while refurbishing the place."

"How do you know that?" Gage asks, looking over her shoulder.

"My brother-in-law is the contractor on the project," Darcy says. She pauses at one image and then takes off running towards the conference room. Gage follows her in.

She links her phone to the big screen and a black-and-white image of a floor plan appears. Gage leans closer to read the text in the corner.

"Ray's Diner?" Gage asks.

Darcy nods. "Here," she says, pointing to the cellar and access ladder. "If it is Francesca, and she knows about the tunnels, this could be an exit. Plus, there are a few parking spots at this end of the alley."

"And if they have a car waiting…" Gage says.

"Let's go!" Darcy grabs her car keys and sprints out of the room.

Gage is in the car with the seatbelt on before she has the car started. He pounds the dash. "Go!"

190

Darcy throws the car in gear and peels out of the station lot. She barely brake checks three intersections and hurdles down the back streets away from the action. She pauses at a dead end, a baseball field parking lot. She turns the car to face the steep, grassy hill up to the diner. "Hold on!" She drops her car into the lowest gear and charges up the hill.

"Darcy!" Gage mutters, grabbing the handle above the passenger window.

The car rocks side to side as the engine revs to crest the hill. She pops over onto the pavement next to a giant dumpster.

"You good?" Darcy asks Gage.

"Wicked high on adrenaline at the moment," Gage says a little breathless.

"That's the owner's van," Darcy says, pointing to a white transit van. "I've seen him in it enough times, but that red truck could be hers."

"Keep the car running," Gage says, jumping out. "I'll check the cellar door."

"I'll call in the plates," Darcy says, patting her pocket. "Crap, I left my phone and radio at the station."

Gage tosses his phone at her and runs for the back of the diner. He slides to a stop at a wooden door set at an angle next to the back door. He yanks it open and squats down, inspecting the narrow stone steps.

"To hell with it." He quickly but carefully steps down into the darkness and feels around for a switch. He whacks his head on an object that swings away. He reaches up, and his hand lands on something. *A light bulb.* He pats it until he finds a string. He pulls it and blinks away the brightness. He spins around. *Just crates of vegetables, no door.*

He stomps in frustration, and something rattles. He searches the floor and finds a chain attached to a metal loop. He pulls up, and a hatch door budges but won't open. He bends and finds an eye hook. He releases the hook and stands. He pulls it open with ease. He finds another hook anchored halfway up the wall. He hooks a few links of the chain and tests the weight of the door. *It should stay open.*

Darcy scrambles down the cellar steps. "That truck is registered to a Rector Higgins, and according to Francesca's social media pages, that's her boyfriend."

"Does he work in the diner?" Gage asks, pointing up.

"Maybe, but we may not have time to ask," Darcy says, looking over her shoulder towards the door. "I spotted officers heading down the alley. We need to hightail it out of here."

"But Roz…" Gage argues.

"Won't be happy if we get shot," Darcy says, tugging on his arm. "Come on!"

Gage shouts down the open shaft. "Roz!"

"Gage!" Darcy shouts. "We've got to go now!" She pushes him towards the exit.

Gage stumbles and climbs up the steps. Darcy steps out on his heels and looks down the alley. "Go to the car. I've blocked the truck in."

"Where are you going?" Gage asks.

"To check if Rector is inside the diner."

Gage slides into the driver's seat and starts the car.

Darcy goes in the back door of the diner. She pops back out a second later and jogs to the car.

"He does work here, but he was a no show this morning," Darcy says. "Let's get back to the station before the entire SWAT team comes this direction."

"But the truck…" Gage says, waving a hand at the large red truck.

"… has two flat tires," Darcy says with a wink.

Gage whips his head around and inspects the truck. It's leaning to one side, and he can see the rear tire is completely flat.

Darcy taps the dash. "Drive or get out and let me."

"Alright." Gage puts the car in gear. He turns to drive the long way back to the station, opposite of the shortcut up the hill. "Did you warn the owner about the cellar and tunnel?"

"I suggested he lock up both doors with a possible shooter on the loose and heading in his direction." Darcy taps her knee. "I didn't want him down there in case they popped up, locked and loaded."

"Good thinking," Gage says, pulling back into the station. He opens the door and gets out. He tosses her the keys. "How did you flatten the tires, anyway?"

Darcy pockets the keys and pulls out a small pocketknife. "Thankfully, the tires were old and thin."

Gage grins. "Thankfully, you kicked me instead of using that."

Darcy holds the door to the station open for him. "You're lucky I had coffee this morning, otherwise that would have been an option in my sleep deprived state."

Gage laughs, but her face remains flat of expression. "Dude, really?"

"If you ever have kids who don't sleep for more than two hours at a time, you'll understand," Darcy says, walking to the conference room. She retrieves her phone. "Crap! My sister called nine times."

"Oh, not good," Gage whispers.

"Slow down!" Darcy says when her sister answers. "He what? When?" She listens and then grabs Gage's arm and squeezes. "I'll check, I promise." She listens again. "I'll call you right back." She stares at her phone.

"What's happened?" Gage asks.

"My brother-in-law was working on the salon remodel on Broadway this morning when the shooting started. Two bullets shattered the large front window while him and his crew were laying tile." Darcy sucks in a shaky breath. "My brother-in-law was struck in the thigh and another man…" She taps her right temple.

Gage lets out a long, low whistle. "Darcy," he says, following her out to the car. "I'm so sorry. I'll call Dusty for a ride."

"Yea, okay. Good idea. Call me when they find Rozanne." Darcy tosses the radio at him. "Keep it on channel three and don't go anywhere near Broadway."

Gage nods and adjusts the dial to three. He sits on the curb, watching Darcy back out as he dials Dusty. It rings once.

"Hey Gage," Dusty says.

"Hey, can you swing by Station 3 and pick me up?" Gage asks.

"Sure," Dusty says.

"Don't cut down Broadway. Come up the long way around."

"Okay, why?" Dusty asks.

"I'll explain it all when you get here."

29

"Why are you doing this?" Rozanne asks, her voice hoarse from screaming. "What do you want?" She wiggles her fingers, trying to get feeling back. She looks up at her wrists. They are tied over her head and anchored around a curved metal hook. *Is that a meat hook?*

The woman takes off the officer's cap and tosses it in the corner. "You have no clue who I am, do you?"

"You said your name was Officer Terrence," Rozanne says, searching her face and uniform.

"And Terrence doesn't ring any bells?" the woman says, stepping closer to the single light bulb hanging in the dark, damp space.

Rozanne squints. "Are you Logan's cousin, Fran?" She recalls her conversation with Gage. "You came to a cookout a few weeks ago."

Fran slowly claps. "You didn't answer my question." She pokes Rozanne hard in the chest. "Does the name Terrence ring any bells?"

Rozanne winces. "I don't know, maybe. I see a lot of names at the pharmacy."

"Lisa Terrence."

Rozanne's mouth falls open.

"So, it does ring a bell?" Fran says, circling Rozanne. "She's my mother."

"I was fifteen," Rozanne says, fighting back tears. "When my parents were…"

"And I was twelve," Fran says, squaring her shoulders in front of Rozanne, "when they locked my mother up."

"I don't understand," Rozanne says, blowing a piece of hair away from her face. "And this," she wheezes, shaking her wrists against the metal. "All of this is because your mother destroyed our childhood?"

"It wasn't her fault," Fran says. "Hell, she wasn't even driving that night."

"What are you saying?" Rozanne asks.

"She was at home with me that night," Fran says, gritting her teeth. "I had my first period at school that day, and she was showing me how to wash the stains out of my clothes."

"But they found her unconscious at the scene," Rozanne says.

"That was my father's doing. Did you know the accident was less than a hundred yards from our house?"

"No?" Rozanne says, trying to breathe through the stabs of pain emanating across her right cheek.

"He came home stumbling drunk and dragged my mother out of the laundry room shouting about the sacrifices he has made for her, and it was her turn to step up and shut up. She tried to defend herself, but he knocked her out on the second punch to the head. He didn't stop. He just kept punching her limp…"

"Stop!" Rozanne sobs. "Just… just let me go."

"But you want to know the why, right?" Fran says, leaning closer to Rozanne's face. "Why you, why them, why now?"

Rozanne glares at her. "Them?"

Fran circles Rozanne and ignores her question. "The bastard even went as far as shattering a mirror and cutting her in a few places." She shakes her head. "At this point, I charged him—all one hundred pounds of me—but he hit me hard enough that I flew across the room and into a cabinet." Fran stops in front of Rozanne. She lifts her hair and points to a faint white scar over her left eye. "Almost as bad as your face." She smirks. "He dumped my mother's beaten body next to the car and returned about twenty minutes later. He complained about pouring out perfectly good whiskey while attempting to clean and dress my cut."

"That's sick!" Rozanne says. Her knees soften and her wrists ache from extra weight pulling on them.

"Did you know the police never did a blood alcohol test on my mother?"

Rozanne scrambles to get her feet back under her. "Why?"

She clicks her tongue three times. "Just because she reeked of whiskey and the empty bottle was found at the scene."

"Why didn't you tell the police?"

"I tried, over and over again!" Fran says, pacing back and forth in front of Rozanne. "They wouldn't listen. They said I made it all up because of my concussion, which my father said was from a fucking bike accident." She points at the scar again. "I didn't even own a bike, but they believed him. He claimed my mother was a closet drinker and said he was going to leave her for my sake the night of the accident." She spits on the floor. "And they ate it up."

"Why would he make her take the fall?" Rozanne asks.

"One alcohol violation involving a death is immediate termination at the railroad."

"That's… I don't know what to say!" Rozanne shakes her head and sways, trying to focus on Fran. "If he's the bad guy here, why am I tied up?"

"It was your statement read at the trial during closing arguments that sealed her fate." Fran stops pacing. "She tried to plea out, but the prosecuting attorney wanted to make it a spectacle. And your words about mommy and daddy broke the jury and my mother."

"I was fifteen and grieving," Rozanne says. "I had no idea she was innocent. Why didn't she share that with the jury?"

"My father beat her frontal lobe so hard that night that she barely remembers her name let alone mine!"

"But why do this?" Rozanne asks, shaking her wrists again against the metal.

"Logan," Fran whispers. "It's his fault, really. I was sent to live with Logan's family after the trial." She holds up air quotes with her fingers. "I was a 'liability' to my father's guilty conscience." She kicks the wall. "It was mostly fine until Logan's parents were killed in a tornado. I was a minor at the time, and my only legal guardian… my joke of a father." She faces Rozanne again. "I had almost forgotten your name by the time I moved back, but then Logan kept going on and on about this pretty girl from the pharmacy."

"And his interest in me triggered this nightmare?" Rozanne asks.

"Did you even like Logan?" Fran asks.

"I barely knew him," Rozanne says.

Fran laughs a little manically. "Well, it's too late for that love to blossom. He wanted your eyes only on him," she says, smiling. "He's an intense stalker, by all counts of creepiness. I even found pictures of you, your house, the mechanic guy, and that old dude you work with on his phone. I would not be surprised if your house, car, and work are all bugged. He had recording software on his phone and laptop with loads of files."

Rozanne bites her bottom lip and flares her nostrils.

"I even caught him bribing an old homeless dude to spy on you." She faces Rozanne. "Did the cops tell you about him?"

Rozanne nods.

"He was going to be the white knight to swoop in and pick up the pieces after you had a little accident." Fran chuckles. "I suppose he failed to recognize the other man. Gage, is it?"

Rozanne sighs. "We've been friends for fifteen years."

"Must be nice," Fran says, cracking her neck. "Friends were a luxury I never really understood, especially after being labeled the daughter of a murderer."

"Look, for what it's worth, I'm really sorry about your mom and about what your dad did," Rozanne says, trying to keep her left eye open. The pain throbbing in her right cheek was getting harder to ignore.

"Not worth a penny." Fran circles behind Rozanne. "And that girl, Penny," she says, shaking her head. "Wrong place, wrong time."

"Why her?" Rozanne says through gritted teeth.

"The Monday Penny went missing," Fran says, ignoring Rozanne. "Logan came by the diner to tell me how you two finally exchanged numbers. He kept checking his phone." She frowns. "But you had not sent him a single message all day and his anxiety was out of control."

"I was waiting on him," Rozanne says.

"Ha, too late!" Fran takes a few steps closer to Rozanne. "Penny walked into the diner with a stack of papers. She hung up a flyer for babysitting services on the bulletin board with her name and number cut on the bottom. Logan followed her out of the diner."

"He was listening…" Rozanne whispers. Her mind was reeling, thinking back to the conversations with Monroe and Gage about Maggie. *Did I ever say Penelope or just Margaret?*

Fran circles Rozanne. "I could see he was chatting with her by the time they got to the corner, but I had tables and didn't see which direction they went to." She laughs. "The police are so useless. That flyer is still hanging on the bulletin board, right next to the missing flyer with her face on it."

"Why didn't you help Penny?" Rozanne asks.

"Why would the cops listen to me now?" Fran asks, facing her again. "It's not like I stood by and did nothing. I tried to volunteer for the search."

"More like trying to gain access to my house," Rozanne says. "They told me you claimed to be a roommate or something like that."

Fran laughs. "I just wanted to see what all the fuss was about." She waves her hand around the space. "Is it as cool as my dungeon?"

Rozanne sighs. "Is that what you call this place?" She looks around at the shallow puddles dotting the floor and grey cement walls. "What are we under? The diner?"

"You think I'm foolish enough to bring you closer to my work, where they would likely look first?" Fran laughs again. "How much prohibition history do you know about this town?"

Rozanne reels back with the whiplash of another subject change. "You honestly want to discuss history… now?"

"Fine." Fran huffs. "I'll give you the short version. The catacombs were built for utilities and sewage from one large hotel to another, but parallel shafts were dug out during the prohibition to transfer moonshine from one place to another unseen. Some speak easy establishments, like this one, were created as well." She waves a hand around the room. "Oh! And years later, the great mafia boss, Al Capone, had a secret stairway built into the Elms Resort to access the catacombs in case of a raid."

"Fascinating," Rozanne says with as much sarcasm as she can manage. "What does this have to do with me here and now?"

"Many secrets are buried in the catacombs," Fran says, leaning her ear against the only door. "I've heard that if you listen long enough, you can hear the old hum of conversations."

"You're stalling," Rozanne says, fighting the pain radiating from her fingers to her face.

Fran laughs. "Did you really see Penny on your property?"

"I saw a girl by my pond and evidence would suggest it was Penny," Rozanne says, trying to adjust her wrists.

"Logan loved to play hide and seek in the woods," Fran says, stepping away from the door. "He would send me out at dusk and tell me to hide. If he found me before full dark, I had to do his chores for a week. But if I could stay hidden until after dark, I won."

"Send you out?" Rozanne asks, shaking her head. "Like you were forced to run and hide?"

Fran shrugs. "It's complicated."

"Would you be stuck out there all night?" Rozanne asks, biting down a ripple of fear. *Trauma manifests in many ways.*

"That only happened once," Fran says. "I fell asleep behind a large bush and didn't wake until the sun hit my face."

"Sun would be nice right about now," Rozanne says, nodding for the door.

Fran frowns. "You think reverse psychology will work on me?"

Rozanne rolls her eyes. "I still have no idea what you want with me. And you're an adult. Just turned eighteen, right?"

"Yea, what of it?" Fran says.

"So, whatever you do to me today will have adult consequences," Rozanne says. "Is getting back at Logan or your father really worth ruining your life?"

"You think this is about revenge?" Fran laughs.

"How the hell would I know?" Rozanne asks. "You've not given me a why, just some stories about my statement in court!"

Fran holds her hand up and steps back, opening the only door.

A tall guy in a hoodie ducks his head to enter. He sets down a semi-automatic rifle and empties his pockets.

"Were you followed?" Fran asks, assessing the man and the remaining ammo.

"No," he says.

"Who are you?" Rozanne asks as he pulls back his hood.

Fran pauses from counting the ammo and glares up at Rozanne. "He's mine."

The man stares down at Fran and crooks up a small smile.

"I wasn't calling dibs," Rozanne mutters.

Fran ignores her and loads the gun with practiced ease. "Are you ready?" She shoulders the gun. He nods. "Gag her and smash the bulb."

"Wait!" Rozanne bucks her head back. "Why are you doing this? Just tell me."

"Logan will explain everything," Fran says, picking up the gun. "If he wins."

"What…" Rozanne is cut off when a cloth is shoved into her mouth. The man ties another around her face, surprisingly careful around her bandages. "Please." She mumbles over her gag.

He just shakes his head and unscrews the light bulb.

Rozanne searches the darkness as she hears the bulb shatter. Shoes crunch over the shards, and the air shifts around her as the door snaps shut.

Just breathe, don't panic.

30

Dusty pulls into the station's lot.

Gage jogs over and hops in. "Thanks," he says, closing the door.

"I can hear the sirens from here," Dusty says, nodding toward Broadway.

"All hell broke loose this morning," Gage says. "Let's head to Rozanne's house."

Dusty nods and pulls out, heading south, away from the action.

"Roz was stuffed in a trunk this morning," Gage says.

Dusty immediately taps his brakes.

Gage braces a hand against the dashboard.

"Sorry, man, but seriously?" Dusty asks, facing Gage.

Gage nods. "We aren't positive, but we think the people who took her are Francesca Garnett and her boyfriend Rector."

Dusty returns to his previous speed. "Who are they?"

"Francesca is Logan's cousin," Gage says.

Dusty mumbles, "Arson twat!"

"And her mother was the drunk driver who killed Roz's parents."

"What?" Dusty says, turning down the county road that leads to Rozanne's house.

"It's so messed up," Gage says. "They died six years ago this weekend."

"What do they want with Rozanne?" Dusty asks.

"That's a million-dollar question," Gage says. "All the action down off Broadway and Main is related. Roz made a call for help after she was taken." He shakes his head. "Dude, it's bad! There were officers down on the scene, the three old homes were burning, and a few stray bullets caught a crew working on a remodel off Broadway."

Dusty slows and turns on his blinker to turn down Rozanne's driveway. He almost makes the turn but pumps the brakes as a cruiser with its lights blinking and siren blaring speeds past.

"That guy is flying!" Dusty waits a few seconds and then hastily turns down the drive.

Gage leans forward and squints past the blinding sun.

"Whoa, who's that?" Dusty says, pointing at the front porch as he slows to a stop.

"That's Logan," Gage says, digging out his phone. "Stay in the truck, keep the doors locked." He dials Deputy Morris and places the phone on speaker.

Deputy Morris answers in a clipped tone, "Morris."

"Why is Logan Garnett sitting on Rozanne's front porch?" Gage asks, gripping the handle of the truck's door.

"His bail hearing was this morning," the deputy says. "He had no priors and probably made bail. I'll send an officer immediately. Do not approach him. Stay inside, out of sight."

"I'm not in the house," Gage says.

"Deputy Clawson gave you an order to stay put."

"I'm not under anyone's command, deputy." Gage ends the call.

Darcy's radio blares with a long emergency beep. Gage covers the radio and turns the volume knob to silence the incoming transmission.

"They just let a murderer walk the streets?" Dusty asks, his eyes still focused on Logan, who is casually sitting on the glider. "Is he armed?"

Gage sits up a little taller. "I can't tell from here, but with everything that has happened this morning, I'm not sure we should find out."

"There was a tall, suspicious-looking guy who came by the shop yesterday," Dusty says. "He was asking questions about when you would return to work."

"What did you tell him?" Gage asks.

"I asked him what repairs or body work he needed done. He got all weird and jumpy." Dusty glances over at Gage's white knuckles gripping the door handle. "He left without answering my questions."

"What did he leave in?" Gage asks.

Dusty taps on the steering wheel. "A red Dodge truck."

"It was Rector, Francesca's boyfriend." Gage shakes his head. "What is this all about? Why are they after Roz, and why are they digging around in my business?"

"Dude, we've got movement coming out of the woods at nine o'clock." Dusty reaches under the seat for what Gage can only assume is his pistol. Gage places a hand on his arm to still his movement.

"It's an officer," Gage says. "Or shit, is that a girl? That could be Francesca."

"She's not alone." Dusty says. "There is a dude standing in the shadows with a rifle."

Logan stands and looks towards the woods. Then he nods toward Dusty's truck.

"Back up," Gage says. "Now!"

Dusty punches the gas. The truck lurches backwards.

Pop

The wing mirror on the driver's side shatters.

"They're shooting at us!" Dusty gasps, dropping the truck in drive and flooring it down the driveway.

Gage is fumbling for his phone. He hits call.

"What now!" Deputy Morris answers.

"They're here and shooting at us!" Gage screams as another shot hits the side of the truck.

"Who's they!" Deputy Morris shouts.

"Francesca and Rector just showed up." Gage looks back down the driveway as Dusty turns onto the county road.

"All units, be advised. Suspects are at 1219 County Road 812. They are actively shooting. I need eyes in the sky immediately." Deputy Morris ends the transmission. "Gage, where are you now?"

"Heading north in Dusty's grey truck," Gage says, checking the mirror.

"Did you see Rozanne?" Deputy Morris asks.

"No!" Gage says, pounding his fist on the dash.

"We have a search team in the tunnels," Deputy Morris says. "Was there a vehicle on site?"

"No, just Roz's car and my truck," Gage says.

"Head to the police station off, Thompson," the deputy says. "They'll process Dusty's truck and file a report." The deputy sighs. "Gage, I need you to stay put at the station."

"I can help with the search," Gage argues.

"Not when you could be next," the deputy says. "Just stay put and out of sight."

The deputy ends the call. Gage stares at his phone. "Dusty."

"Yea, dude," Dusty says, not letting his foot off the accelerator. "I heard the cop. I'll head to the station."

"They know," Gage says, rubbing the hair standing up on his arms. "They know why all of this is happening."

Dusty turns again in the station's direction and slows down. "What's 'next' mean… death, kidnapping, or what?"

"If Roz is hurt again…" Gage mumbles.

"Dude, your phone is ringing!" Dusty says, turning into the packed police lot.

"Hello," Gage says

"Gage!" Mary yells.

206

"Yes, ma'am." Gage responds, watching an officer jog towards them.

Dusty rolls down his window and points to the shattered mirror. The officer waves them through and directs them into a spot.

"Where are you?" Mary asks. "Why are there dozens of police cars blocking the road and driveway?"

"Mary, can you please come down to the police station off Thompson?" Gage asks, exiting the truck. The adrenaline is gone, and the weight of his legs makes him stumble. "It's been a terrible morning. I'm sorry I haven't had a chance to call you or Monroe."

"On my way." Mary ends the call.

Dusty shows the officer and a tech the damage from the bullets.

Gage slumps to the curb and puts his head between his knees.

"Are you hurt?" a woman asks, sitting next to Gage.

"Define hurt." Gage lifts his head to look at the woman. She smiles and Gage sits up straight. "Are you um, Mrs. Arber?"

"Call me Peggy." She points to her hair. "It's my hair, isn't it?" Peggy laughs. Gage nods. "It's been my identity for the last forty years, but if I dyed my hair, I think I could walk around like a total stranger."

Gage smiles. "For Rozanne, that would be a guarantee."

"You know Rozanne from the pharmacy?" Peggy asks.

"I do," Gage says. "Did you leave the journal?"

Peggy frowns. "What journal?"

Gage runs a hand through his hair. "It's not important at the moment."

"They need your statement," Dusty says, waving Gage over.

"Thanks for checking on me," Gage says, standing up from the curb. He offers a hand to Peggy. She takes his hand and stands.

"No problem," Peggy says, brushing off her slacks. "Tell Rozanne hello."

Gage nods and whispers, "I hope I can," under his breath as she walks away.

Dusty pats Gage on the shoulder. "Do you know her?"

"Not really," Gage says, walking with Dusty to the side door of the station.

"She doesn't look like the other officers," Dusty says, glancing back at Peggy.

Peggy remains standing at the curb watching the tech remove a bullet shell embedded in the side bed of the truck.

"She is our victim liaison," the officer says, following Gage inside and directing them into a conference room. "A volunteer." The officer points to a couple of chairs. "She'll be into address any aftercare or needs you may require after your traumatic event."

Gage and Dusty glance at each other and nod before taking a seat at the table.

"I'll need your names, current addresses, and phone numbers on these forms." The officer hands them each a pen and a form. "And then we can start with the events leading up to bullets in your truck."

Gage clicks the pen. "Is there any update on Rozanne Rayvern?"

"No, sir," the officer says. "Still searching."

They finish filling out their forms just as Mary barges into the conference room.

The officer whirls and steps forward to head off her entry. "Ma'am."

"Don't you dare ma'am me," Mary says, pointing her finger at the officer. "I need to talk to that young man, and I will lay you flat if you stand in my way."

Gage stands up quickly and walks to the officer's side. "Start with Dusty. I'll be just outside with Mary."

The officer nods and waits for them to exit before turning his back on the door.

"Where is Rozanne?" Mary asks, the second the door clicks shut.

"She's missing," Gage says, "or I should say, she was taken."

"Explain." Mary pokes him in the chest. "Gage Auburn, do not skip a single detail."

Gage walks her through the day's proceedings. Mary's face fades from beet red to white onion.

"Are you okay?" Gage says, steadying her wobbling frame. "Let's get you a chair and maybe some water before I continue."

Mary walks with Gage's help to a chair in the small lobby outside the conference room.

An officer walks in from the side door.

"Is there a way to get her a glass of water?" Gage asks the officer. The officer looks Mary over and nods. They return a minute later with a glass of water. "Thanks."

Mary takes a sip and sighs. Some color returns to her face.

"Maybe we should call Monroe and wait for him." Gage pulls out his phone.

"He's on his way," Mary says, nodding to the door. "He had a few customers to check out. He's going to put the 'Closed for an Emergency' sign on the door."

Gage pats her free hand. "That's good."

The officer in the conference room opens the door. "I'm ready for you."

"Give me ten minutes or so to help file the report." Gage stands. "And I'll be right back to fill you both in on everything, I promise."

Mary nods but cuts a narrow-eyed look in the officer's direction. "Ten minutes."

"Yes, ma'am." The officer salutes Mary as Gage walks back into the room. He closes the door behind them and faces Gage. "That woman may be barely five feet tall, but she is terrifying."

Gage laughs. "Oh, I know, but she's also harmless."

"If you say so," the officer says. He motions for Gage to sit down next Dusty at the table before looking over the report. "I only have a few additional questions." Gage nods. "Dusty covered the shots fired and the three individuals at the house. But the vehicles on the property belong to you and Ms. Rayvern?"

"Yes," Gage says.

"So, why did you get a ride to town and need a ride back?"

"Darcy, a dispatcher at Station 3, gave me a ride to town," Gage says. "She had to leave for a family emergency."

"Why didn't you just drive?"

"She had her dispatch radio and offered me a ride so we could listen for any sign of Rozanne."

"And what is your relationship with Ms. Rayvern?" the officer asks.

"Friends and temporary caretaker," Gage says.

"Caretaker?" The officer frowns. "What do you mean?"

"She's technically on bedrest."

The officer jots down a few words. "What time did you and…" he scans the paper, "Darcy, leave the house?"

Gage pulls out his phone. "She texted a few minutes before she arrived. And we left less than ten minutes later." He scans the timestamp on the last text from Darcy. "We left between nine and nine fifteen."

"And you remained at Station 3 until Dusty picked you up just before eleven?"

Gage chews on the inside of his cheek. "No, sir."

"Where else did you go?" the officer asks.

"To check on the diner," Gage says.

The officer leans forward. "Gage, we don't have time for vague answers."

Gage sighs. "We overheard the radio transmission from the church about the entrance to the tunnels. And Darcy was familiar with the tunnel routes in that area." He takes a breath. "We didn't want them to pop out and drive away with Roz."

"Why the diner?" the officer asks.

"That's where the deputy said Francesca worked."

The officer shakes his head. "Bold but stupid, considering the active shooter in the area."

"Can we maybe not mention that to Morris or Clawson?" Gage asks with a pleading smile. "They asked me to stay at the house, but I could not just sit and wait."

The officer smiles and nods. "If you can make sure we get out of here before that little lady comes back in, then it's a deal."

Gage checks the clock hanging on the wall. "I think we should probably wrap it up. Did you have any more questions?"

"What is Logan Garnett's relationship with Ms. Rayvern?" the officer asks.

"They recently exchanged numbers," Gage says. "But beyond a few crew cookouts with her friend Darcy, she hasn't had much interaction with him."

The officer nods and stands. "I'll send Mrs. Arber in to address your needs."

"Thanks, but we don't need any trauma care," Dusty says, standing and pushing in the chair. "Right, Gage?"

"All good," Gage says, standing.

"Alright, well, you can pick up a copy of the police report for your insurance claim later today."

"Thanks," Dusty says. He follows Gage to the door. "But I don't really need that either. I work for him, a.k.a. Auburn Automotive. We can manage the repairs."

The officer points at Gage. "Auburn, right. I knew your name sounded familiar."

Gage shrugs and holds up his hand. "Guilty." He opens the door.

"Guilty of what, Gage?" Monroe asks with his hand raised to knock.

"Hey, Monroe," Gage says, shaking his head. "Of being the Auburn of Auburn Automotive."

"Oh," Monroe says. "Are you ready to share what the hell has this town turned upside down?"

The officer leaves the door to the conference room open. "You can use the room."

"Thank you," Gage says, waving Mary over. He stands back, giving Dusty room to exit, and Monroe and Mary room to enter.

"I'll catch up with you later," Dusty says. "Do you want Darcy's radio?"

"Can you run it by Station 3?" Gage asks. "I don't think she is home."

"Sure, dude," Dusty says. "Let me know when they find Rozanne." Gage sucks in a breath. "And good luck in there."

"Thanks," Gage says, exhaling slowly. "I'm going to need it."

31

It's just dark, not small.

Rozanne pushes her tongue against the gag and wiggles her fingers. The rope loosens. She twists her wrist and feels some slack give. She pauses as a wave of throbbing pain slithers down the right side of her face.

Just breathe, Rozanne!

She starts a deep inhale through her nose but coughs. She stomps her foot.

Somebody will find me soon. Right?

She closes her uncovered eye and feels a sense of falling. Her bound wrists drop from the hook. The sensation of blood returning to her hands makes her writhe and her knees buckle. She yanks the gag out.

"Agh," she cries out, crumpling to the floor. She pulls on the rope around her wrists. She finally shakes them off and rubs her wrists and hands against her sweats.

"All better?" a girl whispers.

Rozanne searches the darkness. "Who's there?" She pats the bandages covering her stitches and tucks back in a loose piece. "Are you hurt too?"

"Not hurt," the girl answers. "But lost."

"Lost?" Rozanne gets to her feet. "I can't see a thing. Can you come closer?" She takes a step and feels the crunch of the glass from the lightbulb under her. "Be careful of the glass."

Rozanne takes another step with her arms stretched out. "Are you still there?" She walks forward until her hands touch the wall.

Rozanne searches the darkness, and says with a little more force, "Hello?"

A cool breeze drifts over the base of her neck. She rubs her prickled skin under her sleeves, holds her breath, and listens.

Silence. I'm alone.

Her pulse quickens and she moves forward, patting the wall for any change. She traces her finger up and down a long straight crack.

"It has to be the door." She finds a handle and fumbles with a latch. The door hisses open when she pushes against it. "It's freaking heavy." She takes a hesitant step forward, patting the ground with the toe of her sandal. She finds a solid surface and steps out of the room and into a narrow corridor.

If I call for help, who will come? She sighs. *Just keep moving.* She keeps her hands on the walls for balance and some sensation of reality. Her eyes adjust to the levels of darkness, and she hastens forward with a little more ease.

Her hand makes contact with a piece of metal. She pauses and pats it down for further inspection. "A ladder?" She tests her weight against one rung. "Up versus wandering around in the darkness… Up it is."

She makes it up ten rungs and hits her forehead on the lip of a hole over her head. "Damn it!" She leans closer to the ladder to hold her weight. She gently presses her stitches over her right eyebrow.

Rozanne sighs and adjusts her grip. She pats the smooth surface over her head. *Maybe a utility shaft? But it's really tiny.*

"Get a grip, Rozanne," she mutters to herself. She hugs the ladder as she ascends into the small space. Sweat immediately starts dripping off her. She pauses a third time to dry her hands on her cardigan and finally looks up. A small pinhole of light wavers.

Vroom

Rozanne lets go of the ladder with one hand to cover her ears over the echo of sound. Her balance shifts, and she slips down a rung. She clings to the ladder and gasps for a breath.

"A car! That means a street!" She climbs up faster and finds fresh air seeping in from the two tiny holes in the metal cover.

"Help!" Rozanne shouts, attempting to balance and push the metal cover up. "Can anyone hear me?"

Vroom

"Hello!" Rozanne shouts, rolling up on her tiptoes. Her sandal comes loose, pinging off the sides of the shaft as it falls. She screams, "Damn it!"

"Is somebody down there?" a voice whispers over her head.

"Yes, please help!" Rozanne shouts. "I need help!" She climbs up and bangs on the cover. "I can't get it open!"

"Hold on, I'll get help!" a girl shouts. "Dad! Dad! Come quick."

"No, means no," the man says. "I said no sweets today."

"Dad! There is someone stuck down here!" The girl stomps on the cover.

Rozanne grimaces as her ear drums vibrate.

The man comes to stand at his daughter's side. "She's down here!" She points down and steps off the cover.

"Sir! Can you hear me? My name is Rozanne Rayvern. Please, sir, I can't lift it on my own."

32

Gage reaches across the table and takes Mary's hand. "They'll find Rozanne."

Monroe frowns. "We know she's tough, but this…"

Deputy Clawson knocks once and then peeks his head in the door. "Ah, good. Mrs. Arber said you were in here." He looks over his shoulder. "Morris, they're in here."

Deputy Morris and Deputy Clawson walk in and closed the door behind them.

Gage, Mary, and Monroe stand immediately.

"What is it?" Mary asks, taking Monroe's hand.

"We've located Ms. Rayvern," Deputy Morris says, holding up a hand as each of them tries to ask a question. "And she is on her way to the hospital," he says, speaking over them. They quiet immediately. "For assessment only. She has no major injuries."

Gage starts for the door. "What hospital?"

"Hold up," Deputy Clawson says. "We're not done."

Gage shakes his head. "Yes, we are. Rozanne's safe, that's all that matters. The rest can wait."

"When we arrived at Ms. Rayvern's home, it was vacant," Deputy Morris says, blocking Gage's path. "They are on the run and until we know their whereabouts, you and Ms. Rayvern will be under our protection."

"Why am I a target?" Gage asks, folding his arms across his chest.

Deputy Clawson sighs. "The surveillance footage we pulled from Logan Garnett's devices would indicate that your interest in Ms. Rayvern would impede his goal."

"His goal?" Gage asks, lifting his chin.

"Ms. Rayvern's full, undivided attention and affection," Deputy Morris says.

Gage takes a step back.

"We swept Ms. Rayvern's home and car, including your truck for listening devices, cameras, and such, after we found files on Logan's computer," Deputy Clawson says. "We found twelve devices and are sending another team out to look for more around the property to ensure they are all located and destroyed."

Gage grasps the back of the chair. "He's been spying on her… us. How long has he been doing this?"

"The first file was dated the second of June," Deputy Morris says.

"Almost an entire month?" Gage mutters.

"And if you had this much evidence," Monroe says. "Why in the hell was he released to await a trial?"

"Up until now, Mr. Garnett had no record, not even a speeding ticket." Deputy Morris removes his hat. "And none of this evidence was related to Penny. We searched Logan's apartment again after the phone call Rozanne claimed was from Logan, and we found Mr. Miller unconscious. We found a hidden pantry full of surveillance gear and his laptop. His files were encrypted and the tech's worked all night, but they only retrieved files after the bail hearing. They are still sifting through each for evidence. And we let the prosecutor and judge know immediately, but they had already released him."

Gage raises a hand. "If you only found out about the files this morning, why did you post an officer at her house last night?"

Deputy Clawson nods. "Well, to be honest, between Curtis Miller and the sound files on Logan's phone we discovered last night…"

"Wait, what?" Gage says, leaning forward. "Neither of you mentioned anything about sound files last night."

"We think the voices are Ms. Rayvern and you, Gage," Deputy Clawson says. "But we couldn't connect the dots or confirm that until we found the other files this morning."

"We are now building a second case against Logan with regards to stalking and abducting Ms. Rayvern," Deputy Morris says. "Monroe, we would like a tech to sweep the pharmacy, and Gage, the same with your shop."

Monroe and Gage nod.

"Well, we will not sit around and wait for you two to drop the ball again," Mary says, shouldering her purse.

"Ma'am…" Deputy Morris says, raising his hand.

"Don't you dare interrupt me," Mary says, tugging on Monroe's arm and marching for the door. "You tell us where they took Rozanne right this minute."

Mrs. Arber knocks once and steps inside the conference room. "Ms. Rayvern was taken to North Kansas City Hospital. I have an officer waiting just outside to escort the family over to her, if you'd like… or you can take your own vehicle."

Monroe smiles. "Thanks Peggy. Gage, go with the officer. I'll drive Mary and myself down in my truck."

"Happy to help," Peggy says, moving to allow Mary and Monroe room to exit. "Deputy Morris, the captain is waiting for you and Deputy Clawson."

Gage smirks. "Looks like you're done with me." He pushes past the deputies and follows Mary and Monroe outside. He gives Mary a quick hug. "See you there. Drive safe."

"Right behind ya," Monroe says, walking Mary towards his truck.

Gage assesses the officer loitering by a dark unmarked sedan. "Are you my ride to the hospital?"

"Are you Mr. Auburn?" the officer asks with a smile, opening the door.

"Yes," Gage says. "And you are?"

"Patrol Officer Thorne," he says, offering a hand. Gage shakes his hand. "Is it just you?"

"Yes, they are going to follow us to the hospital," Gage says, sliding into the passenger seat. He buckles in and closes the door as the officer rounds the car.

The officer nods to Mrs. Arber as she steps out of the station. She nods in return and the officer slides into the car.

Gage watches Mrs. Arber as the officer puts the car in drive. "Do you know where they found her?"

"Who? Mrs. Arber?" the officer says, turning out of the lot.

"No, Rozanne," Gage says, checking the mirror for Monroe's truck.

"In a utility manhole near the Mill Inn," the officer says, merging onto the main road.

"Seriously?" Gage asks, glancing at the mirror again for Monroe.

The officer nods. "A little girl heard her call out and persuaded her dad to get help."

Gage shakes his head. "This is such a mess." He rubs his hands down his thighs. "All for what?" He balls his hands into fists.

"If you are thinking about punching something," the officer says, glancing over. "Please wait until we are out of the vehicle."

"Ugh." Gage claps his hands together. "Sorry, it's been a very long morning."

"I know what you mean," the officer says. "I am supposed to be knee deep in a river casting a line, but I was called in when the chaos started downtown."

"Well, let's hope the other officers can cast a line and catch these…" Gage's knee bounces. "What do you call sick fucks?"

The officer coughs and chuckles. "Pretty sure your explanation is enough."

"Sorry," Gage mutters.

"Nah, I get it," the officer says. "If my other half had been abducted, I would be just as angry."

"We're friends," Gage says, rolling his eyes. "Just friends."

33

"We lost them," Francesca says, breathlessly. She slows to a stop.

"Not if they bring the hounds back," Logan says, nudging her forward. "We need to get Rozanne and get back to my place."

"We can't go back there," Francesca says, turning to face him. "They found everything."

Logan shakes his head. "No, I would have never made bail if they had."

"Logan, listen," Francesca says, "I went in the back way through the tunnels like you showed me. The false wall was gone." Logan flinches. "Your laptop and photos… all gone."

Logan punches the wall and mumbles a curse. "You can't be serious."

"Sorry," Francesca says and shrugs. "But I don't think they found the room until after the girl died. So maybe the timing saved your ass. I'm sure they are sifting through every file now."

Logan punches the wall a second time and shakes out his hand.

"How did they find the girl?" Francesca asks.

"I called in an anonymous tip once I found her unconscious," Logan says.

"You said she was only a pawn and that you wouldn't hurt her."

Logan shakes his head. "I know. But she fell when we were climbing down the shaft at the old farm on Tuesday. She was pretty banged up and had a large bruise on her thigh. My lawyer showed me the autopsy report. She had some genetic condition that made her develop clots."

"So, technically, her death is not your fault, but an accident?" Francesca asks, patting Logan on the shoulder.

Logan shrugs off her hand.

"Well, on the upside, Rector set the fire at the old abandon houses at the time you requested," Francesca says. "Did you get what you needed from the station?"

Logan nods and pulls out a thumb drive. "The station was a ghost town, and they didn't find my stash." He pats his pocket. "We should have what we need for the next phase."

"Is it a right or left up here?" Rector calls from up ahead.

"Right." Francesca sighs and turns away from Logan.

"Why did you have to bring your seven-foot boyfriend?" Logan mumbles. "He's not exactly easy to hide."

"He was the muscle and gun power I needed to carry out your absurd plan," Francesca says, nearly catching up with Rector. "Plus, he's mine. And I keep what is mine close."

"Understatement," Logan says. "Do you know if he actually hurt anyone today?"

"He's not sure," Francesca says. "He mostly aimed over their heads."

"Guns were never part of the plan."

"Piss off," Francesca says. "This next phase of your plan, will it involve more accidental deaths?"

Logan pulls on Francesca's ponytail, yanking her head back.

"Let go!" Francesca says, whirling to face Logan. She lands a punch to his ribs. He releases his grip on her hair but doesn't blink.

"This plan is everything," Logan whispers. "And if you think for one moment about screwing me over, just remember I have enough evidence to link you and that lurch of a boyfriend to all of this." He grins. "It's tucked safely away for my lawyer to retrieve if I don't call him by this evening."

"All threats have consequences, Logan," Francesca says. "And Rozanne doesn't even like you."

"Careful, cousin," Logan whispers, leaning close to her ear. "You might want to play your hand after you've got the money."

Rector pauses when the tunnel opens to a large space and stretches to his full height. "What are you two whispering about? We are burning daylight."

"Go get Rozanne," Francesca says, pointing to a tunnel on the other side. "Rector and I will get the other car and bring it to the ball field below the diner. They should have already swept that route since we left his truck parked in the rear." She tosses Logan a phone. "The only number saved on that phone goes to this one." She holds up an identical phone. "We'll wait one hour, Logan. Not a minute longer."

Logan leans his forehead to Francesca's. "I promise, she's worth it." He opens his jacket and shows her a worn journal. "We have something she wants."

Francesca shakes her head. "We'll see if she comes along willingly… after you and Penny."

Logan frowns. "I'll make her understand."

"Good luck," Francesca says, taking the tunnel away from Logan. Rector follows her without a word or a look back.

Logan adjusts his head lamp and ducks into the tunnel. He rehearses his lines. "I'm here. Don't worry, you're safe. I've got you, just relax." He grins and picks up his pace. "Two lefts, straight past five turns, and then right to the love of my life."

34

Rozanne shifts on the cold, narrow table.

A tech draped in a lead apron adjusts the x-ray tube directly over her face. "Just relax. I'll be done in two quick shots. For the first one, inhale and hold your breath for five seconds when I say go. And for the second, you can just breathe normally."

"Okay," Rozanne says, staring up at the tube.

The tech walks back behind a wall and says, "Go."

Rozanne inhales and counts backwards. *5, 4, 3, 2, 1.* She releases her breath.

"Great," the tech says. "Last one."

Rozanne hears the machine click a few times and the tech returns. They move the apparatus away from the table and help her up to sit with her legs dangling off the side. The tech lowers the table with a foot pedal until Rozanne's feet find the floor.

"Alright, slowly stand up, and we'll get you back in the chair and up to your room." The tech holds one hand under her elbow, and she pivots towards the wheelchair.

"What do you mean, my room?" Rozanne says, lifting her feet up while the tech lowers the footrests. "I'm just going back to the emergency room, right?"

"You were given a room on the med surge floor," the tech says. "Likely just an observation order until you are cleared by the surgeon." The tech points to her face. "A precaution and because his reputation is on the line."

"Well, any damage from today wouldn't be his fault," Rozanne says as the tech pushes her into an elevator. She sucks in a breath as the door closes, but the panic never kicks in. She laughs. "Have you ever heard of anyone getting over a phobia after a traumatic event?"

"It's usually the other way around," the tech says as the elevator dings. They push her chair forward out of the elevator and down the hall.

"Roz!" Gage runs towards the tech as they turn a corner. The tech stops pushing and quickly stands in front of Rozanne.

"Gage!" Rozanne says, pushing the tech aside.

Gage nearly tackles the chair out from under her.

"Careful!" Rozanne says, laughing.

Gage loosens his bear hug and lowers her back to the chair. "Sorry. Did they hurt you?"

"No, I'm okay," Rozanne says, still holding on to him. "And I might be over my fear of small spaces."

Gage laughs and releases her with a grin. "Well, look at you, Ms. Rayvern."

"I know, right?" Rozanne says. "Is that officer with you?"

The officer nods.

"Just until they find them," Gage says.

The tech steps back behind the chair. "I take it he is a friend of yours."

"Yes, sorry," Gage says, waving his hands next to his face. "I didn't mean to look all crazy running towards her."

"Crazy is one way to put it," the tech mumbles, stopping outside of a room. "I'm going to get her in a bed. Can you wait down the hall in the waiting room for a few minutes?"

Gage nods. "Monroe and Mary are on their way up with some food."

Rozanne's stomach audibly growls. "Oh, thank goodness."

"I'll stay outside the door," the officer says. Gage nods.

Ten minutes later, the admitting nurse steps inside the waiting room. "Ms. Rayvern is ready for company." The nurse points to the food. "She is not cleared for regular food."

Mary nods and holds up a pudding cup and smoothie. "Got it." The nurse smiles as they file out.

Gage hangs back at the door and lets Monroe and Mary fuss over her. He smiles and wipes the tears falling down his cheek. He slowly walks to her side. "Did you tell them the good news?" He winks.

Rozanne smiles. "I may have conquered my claustrophobia."

"Isn't that something?" Mary says, opening the pudding cup and handing her a spoon. "The smoothie has a scoop of protein powder, so make sure you drink up."

"Thanks, Mary," Rozanne says. "Who's at the pharmacy if you're both here?"

"The 'Closed for Emergency' sign was dusted off and hung for the first time since I took over," Monroe says.

"I'm sorry, Monroe," Rozanne apologizes.

"Child, don't you dare think about being sorry for what you went through." Monroe's lip quivers. "I'm just happy you're safe and here with us."

Rozanne reaches over and squeezes his hand. "I'm not that easy to get rid of. You should know that by now."

Monroe nods and leans forward, kissing her temple. "I just hope this nightmare is over."

"Me too," Rozanne whispers.

"Well, eat up," Mary says, waving to Gage. "He can fill you in later on what happened while you were… missing."

Rozanne glances at Gage.

He nods. "Later, I promise."

Knock, knock

Gage opens the door and Darcy pushes past him.

"Rozanne Edith Rayvern," Darcy says, hugging Rozanne.

"Hello to you too, Darcy Megan," Rozanne says into Darcy's hair. "How did you get here so fast?"

Darcy releases her and leans back. "Gage didn't tell you?"

"I haven't had a chance." Gage holds up a hand when Darcy glares in his direction. "We just got here."

"My brother-in-law has a broken femur."

Mary whispers, "Is he okay?"

"He'll recover just fine," Darcy says.

"What happened?" Rozanne asks.

"He was shot by a stray bullet this morning during the chaos," Darcy says, shaking her head.

Rozanne drops her spoon recalling the ammo and gun Fran's boyfriend carried in. "What do you mean by chaos?"

Darcy looks at Gage. He nods. Darcy spends the next ten minutes going over their morning.

"And after you left Gage at the station," Rozanne says. "What happened?"

Gage sighs. "It's not good. Are you sure you don't want to eat and rest for a bit?"

"Rip the Band-Aid off and tell me," Rozanne says.

Mary scoots a chair up next to the bed and pats it. "Gage, sit and tell her everything. We'll give you the room."

Darcy watches Monroe and Mary leave the room. "I need to go help my sister with our kids." She leans over the bed and taps Rozanne's nose with her finger. "I'll be back later."

Rozanne's face pales. "Tell your sister I'm sorry."

Darcy frowns. "You didn't shoot him. Don't even think about taking that guilt on."

Rozanne forces a smile and nods again. The door closes with a loud click. She flinches.

Gage circles the bed to the chair but plops on the bed next to her.

She frowns. "How bad did it get?"

Gage leans forward and softly kisses her cheek.

"That bad," Rozanne says, turning her cheek and pushing her nose to his.

He sighs and softly kisses her.

Rozanne's cheek blushes a deep crimson.

Gage pecks her cheek.

Rozanne swallows. "I can handle it."

He strokes her cheek and nods. "I know."

Rozanne swipes two fingers over her closed lips and twists her hand.

Gage laughs.

He spends the next hour replaying his morning, starting with the phone call from the deputy to his ride to the hospital. When he finishes, he reaches up and makes the unzipping gesture across her lips.

Rozanne sighs. "Francesca told me about his stalking activities while I was down there."

"How did they take you?" Gage asks.

"Coffee," Rozanne says, shaking her head. "I stepped out on the porch to offer the officer on duty a cup of coffee, but was taken from behind. I saw their faces for just a moment as they closed the trunk. My hands were tied, but I was able to retrieve my phone and call for help before I dropped it. It's probably still somewhere in that trunk."

"Wow," Gage says.

"Here's the kicker," Rozanne says. "Fran claims that her mother is innocent."

Gage reels back. "What, how? They found her passed out at the scene."

Rozanne explains their conversation about Fran's dad framing her mother and her escape.

When she finishes, Gage slumps back. "Do you think taking you was, in some part, a distraction to make sure the deputies were tied up and guaranteed Logan a chance at bail?"

"Logan knew about their plan to take me," Rozanne says. "I would bet my life on that."

"Son of a…" Gage stands. "But why? What do they want?"

"I may have a theory, but it's muddy." Rozanne pulls on a strand of her hair and starts gently winding it around her finger. "Fran mentioned he had been super anxious the Monday when he took Penny, because I had not called or texted."

"Okay," Gage says.

"If he'd been listening," Rozanne says, "and has the pharmacy bugged as well, then he knew about my morning with Mrs. Arber and the confusion with Maggie. He would also learn about my encounter with Maggie at the manor."

"He played on your encounter to make sure you would react when you saw Penny by the pond." Rozanne nods. Gage claps. "Do you think he planted the pennies and old shoes at the creek?"

"I mean it's possible," Rozanne says. "But he would have had to have access to an old pair of shoes and two wheat pennies with less than a few hours' notice." She pauses. "And the blue rocks. We didn't even put the Vance connection together until after the incident."

"There are two antique shops across from Station 3," Gage says. "And Lorraine Michaels, who identified the rocks, owns the new mineral and rock shop off Broadway. She mentioned they sell those rocks there."

"And it was the headline of the newspaper Tuesday morning," Rozanne says. "But seriously, how could he have just by chance picked a girl with a similar name and age to Maggie?"

"Maybe it wasn't those factors but her uniform," Gage says. Rozanne frowns.

"Her school uniform was very similar to how you described Maggie's appearance during previous encounters in the pharmacy."

"It's my fault," Rozanne whispers and lays a hand on her chest. "If I would have just…"

Gage leans over her. "Roz, literally none of this is your fault. You are the first victim. He is the villain, not you."

Knock, knock

Gage backs away from the bed as the door swings open.

Monroe sticks his head in. "Mary and I are going to head back to town. I have had a few calls for some refills."

Rozanne nods. "Thanks for coming down to check on me."

Mary bustles past Monroe, leans over the bed, and hugs Rozanne. "Call us when you get released, and we'll come right back." She taps the smoothie. "Drink up."

"Thanks, Mary." Rozanne squeezes her hand. "I promise I'll finish this one and another soon."

"And you," Mary says, pointing at Gage. "Young man, do not let her out of your sight."

Gage salutes. "Ma'am, yes, ma'am."

"Mary," Monroe says low and slow. Mary rolls her eyes before turning to face Monroe.

"Monroe," Mary mocks in the same low and slow cadence.

Gage and Rozanne laugh.

Monroe cannot keep a stern face and smiles.

Mary turns back to Rozanne and winks.

Rozanne laughs harder.

"On that note," Monroe says, "see you soon."

"See you later," Gage says, shaking his head and biting his knuckle to suppress a second round of laughter.

Mary waves a hand over her head and closes the door behind them.

35

Logan trips as he makes the final right turn. He tilts his headlamp to scan the ground and hovers the beam over a shoe. *That's a sandal. Rozanne's sandal.* He runs down the corridor. *Why is the door open?*

"Rozanne?" Logan shouts.

"On your knees!" a woman shouts, stepping out from the room with a flashlight and weapon pointed at his chest. "Show me your hands!"

Logan whirls around, blinded by additional light. "No!"

"Logan Garnett," an officer says, "it's over. On your knees, hands above your head."

"No, no, no!" Logan stomps his feet. "You're ruining everything!" He reaches inside his jacket.

The woman behind him releases the safety and cocks her gun.

Logan freezes when he hears the sound and takes a knee, slowly raising his hands above his head. "I'm unarmed. Don't shoot."

Another officer cuffs him and pats him down. They remove the worn journal and a small paper bag with four vials of ketamine and three syringes from his jacket pockets. They pull a set of keys, a thumb drive, a phone and a wallet out of his pants pockets.

"You have to find Rozanne," Logan says, looking up at the officers. "They took her!" The officers shake their heads. "Officers, please, I'm not the bad guy. Rozanne needs my help." He takes a breath and stands at the urge of the officer holding his cuffs. "It wasn't me. I swear!"

"Save it for the judge," an officer says from behind him and nudges him forward.

"Honestly," Logan pleads. "She could be hurt."

The officers remain silent and lead him down a series of turns.

"Why aren't you listening?" Logan turns to the officer holding his phone. "Call the only number saved on that phone. That's who you should be after!"

They reach a small narrow staircase. The officer nudges Logan forward.

"I'm not going up there until Rozanne is safe," Logan says, locking his knees.

The officer unclips the snap around her gun. "You either walk up or go up in a body bag. Your choice."

"Why aren't you listening?" Logan pulls on the cuffs. "Rozanne Rayvern was taken and held down here. Her shoe was in that corridor."

"Yea, yea," the leading officer says, opening the shaft at the top of the steps. "We know. Up or bag."

"She's safe?" Logan asks, looking up at the officer.

The officer nods.

Logan climbs the steps without another word. They enter a small root cellar with canned goods and vegetables. He squints at the sunlight streaming from the top of a second staircase. The officer nudges him forward. He climbs the steps and looks around. They're in an alley behind his house.

"Don't even think about running," an officer says, assessing Logan. "You're done."

"He has two minutes," Francesca says, pulling the car around and pausing at the exit to the baseball field parking lot.

Rector rolls down his window. "I hear sirens over towards his place." He points north. "I don't think he's coming."

"One more minute," Francesca says, tapping on the steering wheel. "Come on, Logan."

A small white truck pulls into the lot. The driver glances over at Francesca and Rector and immediately stops. They throw the truck in reverse and peel out of the lot.

"Rector, they saw us," Francesca says, putting the car in drive. "We can't let them call it in!"

Rector nods and folds his large frame out the window with a revolver raised. He fires. The bullet strikes the bed of the truck.

"Go for the tires!" Francesca says, gaining on the truck. Rector fires again, hitting the rim of the tire.

The driver honks their horn repeatedly as Rector fires a third time, finally hitting the tire as they peel out on Thompson.

"Shit!" Francesca screams. "He's heading straight for the police station!" She makes a hard right down a narrow alley and slams on her brakes. "A freaking dead end!"

She shoulders the door open and looks around. "The car's burned. We need to get as far away from it as possible."

Rector squeezes out of the car and points up to the large, red brick building. "It's the old Royal Hotel. We could take the tunnel back to the farm and hide out there until the heat simmers down."

A squad car, lights swirling, blows by the alley.

"Okay, let's go! Grab the bag." Francesca picks the lock on the back door. "Leave the phone."

Rector smashes the phone with his heel and follows her inside a dark hallway.

Francesca coughs and covers her nose.

Rector sneezes. "Cats!" He snarls. "I'm not going to sleep tonight." He sneezes again. A few cats hiss in response.

"Keep it down," Francesca says, fumbling with the bag and removing two headlamps. She hands one to Rector. She clicks hers on and slides it onto her forehead. The light flickers. She taps it and the light vanishes. "Batteries are dead."

Rector clicks his on. The light shines over Francesca's frown. "It's fine, just stay close."

"How allergic to cats are you?" Francesca pokes his swollen face. "Can you see anything?"

"Kind of," Rector says, rubbing his eyes. "Here, take the light. I'll follow you." He sneezes five times in a row as they run down the hall to the abandoned, dust-covered lobby. She adjusts the lights angle and carefully navigates the steps down near the old front desk. "Watch your step. Some of these boards are weak or missing."

Rector pauses and sneezes again. "Feline hell!" Red and blue lights dance over his head. "We got company! Fran, run!"

Francesca picks up her pace and races down the final steps. She hears a board snap and Rector curses. She stops and looks back. "Rector!"

"Go! I'm coming!" Rector squirms his foot out of a jagged hole. He sneezes again and the sound echoes back.

"Did you hear that?" a man shouts.

Rector jumps down the steps two at a time, following Francesca's bouncing head lamp. He catches up with her just as she turns down the next hallway.

More shouts echo.

Francesca slows and holds a finger to her lips. Rector nods. She turns off her light. She carefully opens a door, it squeaks. She pauses and swings it open faster. She swats away cobwebs as she enters.

Rector follows, ducking his head. He shimmies sideways through the narrow passage. He holds a hand over his nose, fighting another sneeze.

Footsteps shuffle outside the door, and they freeze.

"Come out with your hands up!"

The door crashes open, hitting Rector in the shoulder.

Rector slams the door back in the officer's face. "Go," he whispers, holding the door closed. "I'll meet you there before sunrise. Don't wait a second longer."

Francesca nods and darts down the passage. She flicks on the light and navigates the steps down to a metal grate. She pulls on the grate. It won't budge. She panics as the noise escalates.

Pop, thump

"Roll him over and I'll cuff him," an officer says. "Which direction did the girl go?"

Francesca frantically looks around for anything to pry the grate open. She panics when a beam of light blinds her. She ducks to the corner, flipping off her light.

"You're cornered," the officer says. "Come on up and we'll take you in with dry pants, unlike your boyfriend."

Francesca pats her pants down. Her pockets are empty, no weapons. A second beam of light filters down the steps. *I can't take on two.* She sighs and steps out of the shadow. She holds both hands up and walks back up the steps.

"Face the wall," the officer says. "Do you have any weapons on you?"

"No," Francesca says, fighting back tears.

The second officer pats her down and cuffs her wrists behind her back.

"Call it in," the officer says, nudging Francesca forward.

36

"Knock, knock," a friendly male voice says from the door. Gage stands up.

A man dressed in a white coat walks over to Rozanne's bed side. He nods to Gage. "I'm Dr. Klostra, Ms. Rayvern's surgeon."

Gage nods. "I'll step out and grab a cup of coffee."

"I could use one too," Rozanne says, sitting up a little higher in the bed.

"Doc," Gage says, pausing at the door. "Coffee?"

"No thanks," Dr. Klostra says. "I hit my limit about an hour ago."

"Be back soon," Gage says, stepping out into the hall. He gently closes the door behind him. He turns to the officer standing by the door. "Where can I find good coffee around here?"

"Main lobby, if you like it fancy," the officer says. "Otherwise, you can try the kitchen near the waiting room." He points down the hall. "I think it's the last door on the right."

"Thanks," Gage says. "Do you want one?"

"No thanks," the officer says.

Gage walks past the elevators to the kitchen and finds a half a pot of coffee that's still warm. He finds a few creamers and one packet of sugar on the small table. He fills two cups, dumps the creamers in Rozanne's, and splits the sugar pack between the two. He carefully walks back down the hall and waits outside the door.

The officer answers a call and steps away.

Gage's phone pings twice. He contemplates setting a cup down to check his phone when the door to Rozanne's room opens.

Dr. Klostra holds the door open for Gage.

"Thanks. Is she free to go?" Gage asks, sidling past without spilling.

"Almost," Dr. Klostra says, "we're starting her discharge papers now." He closes the door behind Gage.

Gage sets down the two cups and smiles at Rozanne. "So, you're good?"

Rozanne nods. "Everything was fine, minus the swelling over my right eyebrow. He showed me the images to assure me there is no further damage. However, he did ask about the abduction and if I felt safe to return home."

Gage raises an eyebrow.

"I assured him I had the best caretakers looking after me."

"And he bought that line?" Gage's phone pings again. He takes out his phone and swipes open his messages. Three texts from Deputy Morris appear with the same two words: *Call me.* Gage frowns.

"What's wrong?" Rozanne asks, leaning forward to see his screen.

Gage dials Deputy Morris and places the call on speaker mode. He sets the phone down between them. It rings once.

"Morris," the deputy answers.

"It's Gage and Rozanne," Gage says.

"All three are in custody," Deputy Morris says.

Gage squeezes Rozanne's hand. She blows out a long breath.

"Bail is no longer an option for Logan Garnett. He is looking at aggravated stalking, invasion of privacy, arson, kidnapping of a minor, attempted murder, and second-degree murder." The deputy pauses for a breath. "He was found in the tunnels heading to the room you were held in with three syringes, a drug lethal enough to kill a person and a USB drive with a key to access his bitcoin account. There were enough funds in there to make him and a few others disappear."

"He was going to kill me?" Rozanne asks.

"We aren't sure of his intentions, but possession of the substance is enough grounds for the charge, considering his obsession with you," Deputy Morris says. He clears his throat. "The prosecutor has suggested a press gag order to ensure a fair trial without bias." He sighs. "We want a clean conviction and sentence without the media circus. Can I get you both to agree to no social media posts on the topic or interviews with any press until after the trial is over?"

"On one condition," Rozanne says, surprising Gage. He frowns at her. "I want Francesca's father to submit to a lie detector test regarding the night of the accident that killed my parents. If her mother is innocent, I want him behind bars. And her mother freed, with a full pardon."

They overhear the deputy talking to someone in the room.

"Deal."

"Then yes, we agree to the gag order," Rozanne says. "What charges are being brought against Francesca and Rector?"

"That list is growing by the minute," Deputy Morris says. "The property damage downtown, arson of the three homes, the officers and bystanders hurt and killed, plus the kidnapping and assault. And Mr. Miller's awake now and recalls a partial plate matching Rector's red truck. Rector ran him down, eventually hit him with his truck, and left him for dead. So that's another charge for attempted manslaughter, at the least. Plus a few stolen cars."

"Did Mr. Miller mention who ordered and paid for the glider?" Rozanne asks, chewing on the corner of her lip.

"It was a piece his uncle had started but never finished," the deputy says. "The invoice was signed by an Anne with instructions to remove the old wicker chair. It appears to be entirely a coincidental that the glider appeared when it did."

"So, it was my Grandma?" Rozanne whispers. "But why go after the delivery guy?"

"Mr. Miller spotted a man standing in the woods when he delivered it," the deputy says. "And then he was followed back to his shop."

"How did Logan know about the delivery?"

"The phone call you thought was from Logan was traced back to a phone found inside the holding cell next to where Logan was being held. We still don't know who or how it was smuggled in."

Rozanne lightly punches Gage's arm. "See, I'm not crazy."

"Thanks, deputies," Gage says, rubbing his arm with fake concern. "We are heading back to town. Did you find any additional devices on the property or elsewhere?"

"The last count was forty-six," Deputy Clawson says. "The pharmacy had nine, your shop had three, and there were eight trail cameras stuck up high in the trees around your property. We caught him with Penny on your property on his own camera. It's one of the clearest pieces of evidence we have."

"Wow," Rozanne says, rubbing her arms. "He knew my every move."

"And we have the original picture that was texted to you with the girl you call Maggie in the window on his hard drive," Deputy Clawson adds. "We can't explain the girl in the manor's window or your encounters with Maggie, but I hope you agree that is a low priority at the moment."

"Logan sent the photo of himself with Penny?" Rozanne asks, furrowing her brow. "That seems odd."

"We think Francesca may have sent the photos," Deputy Clawson says. "We'll see how much they spill during the interviews and what our techs can put together."

"Is it safe to return home?" Rozanne asks, fixing her eyes on Gage. He takes her hand.

"We believe everyone involved is tucked safely inside the jail," Deputy Clawson says.

"We also have an old journal," Deputy Morris adds, "recovered during the arrest of Logan. I believe you two might want that back."

"Yes!" Gage and Rozanne respond in unison.

37

"Are you two ready?" Mary asks, stepping inside the room.

Rozanne nods. Gage takes her hand as they leave the small office outside of the courtroom.

"We've waited a year and a half for this day," Rozanne whispers. "I want to be able to talk and post without having to censor anything." The gag order restricted everyone outside of Mary, Monroe, and Gage after a few 'friends' leaked information to the press.

"At least today is the last one," Gage says, holding the door open for Mary and Rozanne. Monroe stands from his bench and ushers them into his row.

Deputy Morris and Deputy Clawson nod to them as they take a seat across the aisle.

The jury enters from the other side of the courtroom and hands over a copy of their verdict.

The judge reviews the papers. "Mr. Garnett please rise."

The accused stands and straightens his tie.

"The jury finds Mr. Brand Garnett guilty of two counts of vehicular manslaughter," the judge says, flipping a paper over, "guilty of domestic assault, guilty of abusing a minor, and guilty of felony perjury."

Gage wraps his arm around Rozanne. She leans in with a sigh. "Something good in all the chaos," he whispers into her hair.

Rozanne looks up through watery eyes and gives a slight nod. Mary pats Rozanne's leg. "It's finally over."

Rozanne nods again and listens to the final proceedings of the court, unaware of the tears streaming down her cheeks.

The judge smacks the gavel, and Brand Garnett is led away. The judge rises to leave but pauses. "Ms. Rayvern, may I have a word with you in my chambers?"

Rozanne nods. Gage frowns. "It's fine," she says. "I'll be fine."

The court deputy escorts Rozanne out of the courtroom and into a secured hallway. They walk together to an open door.

The judge shows Rozanne a chair. "Thanks for your time. Have a seat." The judge moves to the chair beside her. "Today's conviction overturns the sentence and charges for Lisa Terrence." Rozanne nods. "Francesca's testimony to secure her father's conviction was done without any reward. She waived the offer of a lesser sentence to ensure her mother receives compensation for her time served and a medical facility for her mother's memory care."

Rozanne nods again. "I understand, and I hope her mother thrives outside of prison."

"Mrs. Arber stated you've declined the application for the Crime Victims Compensation program," the judge says.

"Yes, ma'am," Rozanne says. "Brand's conviction, although six years late, is all I need for my peace of mind. Especially with the others tucked safely behind bars."

The judge nods. "That's pretty remarkable, Ms. Rayvern."

"Thank you," Rozanne says, pressing down on her bouncing knee.

"The reason I asked you to come speak with me is that my chambers received a letter a week ago asking me to deliver a sealed letter to you regarding M.P. Vance. I didn't see the harm in passing the letter along. I hope you understand the delay, but I had to wait for the trial to conclude."

Rozanne whispers, "Vance?"

"Do you know anyone by that name?" the judge asks.

"I don't know anyone living by those initials or last name," Rozanne says and snorts to squash the rising laughter. "Do you believe in ghosts?"

"Ghosts?" The judge shakes their head. "Ms. Rayvern?"

"Never mind," Rozanne says, shaking out her sweaty hands.

"I'm still not sure how the sender knew you would be in my courtroom," the judge says, handing Rozanne the sealed envelope. "But I do see this as an opportunity to right a few wrongs today."

"May I?" Rozanne asks, tracing the seal.

"In your own time," the judge says. "I hope it brings you some comfort." The judge stands. "Merry Christmas, Ms. Rayvern."

Rozanne stands and smiles. "Merry Christmas to you." She steps towards the door and pauses. "You're not at all curious?"

The judge smirks. "Beyond curious! But it's your ghost, not mine."

Rozanne nods and holds up the letter. "Thank you." She rushes down the hall and through the door.

Mary and Monroe are speaking with the deputies, and Gage is sitting on a bench reviewing index cards next to her purse and coat.

Rozanne slides the letter into her purse. "Thanks for grabbing my stuff." She pecks Gage on the cheek and puts on her coat. "Are you ready to read your statement for the press?"

Gage is pale and sweating. "I hate public speaking." He shakes out his coat. "Is it hot in here?"

"You'll do great," Rozanne says, taking his arm as they walk to the front of the courthouse. She can see a few reporters standing near the bottom. "Let's just hope we don't become a meme."

"Ugh," Gage groans, watching the deputies answer a round of questions.

Mary and Monroe put a hand on Gage and Rozanne's shoulders. Mary squeezes once and leans close. "It's like riding a bike. You may fall, but you always get back up and try again."

Gage and Rozanne glance at each other and laugh. They bump elbows and walk to the reporters when the deputies wave them over.

"We've prepared a statement," Rozanne says.

Gage blows out a breath. "We would like to first thank Mary and Monroe for their hospitality, kindness, and company during the last eighteen months. It was their unwavering support that made our silence to you, the media, possible. And to the deputies and officers who worked hard to secure the justice served today. Thank you." Gage takes a breath and continues. "And last, Ms. Rayvern and I would like to thank the media for only slightly badgering us during this time. We will take a few questions."

"Ms. Rayvern, Brett Clark, *Channel Four News*," the first reporter says, waving a hand with a microphone. "Do you have a message for Lisa Terrence?"

Rozanne nods. "She has a very strong and stubborn daughter who fought like hell to give her justice. Despite her actions, I want her to know that her little girl never gave up on her."

"Ms. Rayvern, Nita Darren, *Lawson Review*," a second reporter says. "Do you think the proposed sentencing for Brand Garnett fits the crime?"

Rozanne nods. "My parents are dead. I was subsequently a target because of his lies and actions over six years later. Not to mention his actions against his own daughter and her mother. I think the verdict today speaks for itself." She feels Gage's hand on her back and takes in a deep breath. "I'll take two more questions."

"Moore with the *KC Star*. Do you feel that your home and town are a safe place to live?"

"We have a beautiful community who was willing to step up and look for a missing girl with no warning and who are present to lean on during crisis and grief." She nods. "Yes, it's a wonderful town I am happy to call home."

"Amy Luther, *Channel Five News*," a woman says, pushing her phone between two reporters. "Have you two set a date?"

Rozanne blushes and covers her left hand.

Gage grins. "If we do, the media will be the last to know." He winks. "Thanks for your time." He nudges Rozanne away from the crowd. The deputies step up for final questions, giving them space to exit.

Mary and Monroe are waiting by Rozanne's car.

"Great job!" Monroe says, hugging Rozanne. "Are you ready for some burnt ends?"

Rozanne steps back. "Am I that predictable?"

"Yes!" Mary and Gage say in unison.

Rozanne smiles and nods. "I'll own it. It may be my one vice."

Gage laughs.

Monroe opens her car door. "We'll meet you there. The reservation is under Auburn."

"Gage," Rozanne says, getting in the car.

"Roz," Gage says. He leans over the console and kisses her. "You were saying?" He grins and puts on his seat belt.

"Hmm…" Rozanne murmurs. She pats her purse. "The judge gave me a letter."

"Do you want to read it now?" Gage says, glancing at her purse.

She shakes her head and puts the car in drive. "Later."

He claps and rubs his hands together. "Great! I may have ordered a few pounds ahead of time to ensure we don't have to share."

"It appears your hand will survive a fork stabbing today." She winks.

Epilogue

Dear Ms. Rayvern,

I know this letter may come as a surprise, but I wanted to be sure it found you at the right time. I was the one who left the journal at the pharmacy to help you understand the time surrounding Maggie's disappearance. My Great-Grandmother, Mina Grady, was the author of that journal. The last passage of her journal was torn out, and we thought it had been lost. By chance, we recently found it in our family Bible. I've enclosed the final passage.

It could be nothing or everything.

~Minnie

July 1, 1928

I found her! I found Margaret Penelope Vance. She walked into the café with Edith. I would recognize Edith's braids anywhere. I watched from the corner booth as they ordered a slice of pie and sat down. It's been ten years. I saw nothing in the papers about them finding the missing girl and she's here. I stood up before I could talk myself out of it and walked to their table. The girl looked up from her pie and said, hello Mina. She remembered my name.

Edith asked me to join them after mentioning my lovely curls again. I sat down because I don't think I could have stood up for too much longer. We talked about the weather and the pie. But I finally asked are you the missing girl, from the Castle Rock Hotel. The girl frowned. Edith patted the girl's hand with the love of a mother before she turned to look at me. She said, Miss Maggie is not from anywhere but here and points to her chest. She winked at me.

They left the café with smiles and waves. I sat there staring at the door so long that the lady behind the counter came out to check on me. I asked her if she had seen Edith with Miss Maggie in here before. She nodded and said… every Sunday for the last ten years. I think she is her guardian.

I stood up so fast I nearly turned the table over. I had to apologize to the frightened lady several times before I stumbled out of the café. She must be the same girl. Her hair is exactly how I remember and her eyes, plus she knew my name!

I had to tell somebody, but the last time I went to the sheriff, they ignored me. But she's not missing. Maybe it's not my place to say. And what is there to tell if she is loved and cared for?

Author's Note

My author's journey started in the fantasy world, but there was a little small-town mystery brewing on the side. The location for this novel was inspired by the years I spent visiting my Great Grandma Twyla and my Great Aunt Myra Beth at the old Spa View Manor. It was demolished and no longer stands, but it still holds a piece of my childhood and some fond memories. Although this book is a work of fiction, it holds little gems and nods to a small Missouri town near where I spent the first eighteen years of my life.

And if you ever connect the dots, stop by Wabash for a plate of burnt ends, take a tour of the old Elms Resort, and finish with some delicious ice cream at Dari-B.

Acknowledgements

Who is Maggie is only possible because my dearest love and partner for life, Art, gave me the creative space and time to release the story whirling around in my head. His support means more than I can express. I hope that my readers have or had a partner in life that can hold or held the torch to light your path as you pursue or pursued your passion and cheer them on.

And to my faithful editor, Jenny Leonard, and my beta readers. Your feedback and time dedicated to this book have made it possible. Without you, it would still sit in a 'saved for later' draft pile. THANK YOU!

And to my readers, as I step outside of my fantasy genre and wet my feet on a mystery/thriller, let me know your thoughts in the reviews. Did I hit the mark and leave you wanting to turn the page?

About the Author

Kim Malaj lives on a vineyard and homestead in northern Albania with her husband, Arti, author of Northern Albanian Folk Tales, Myths and Legends. Although she is a Show Me State (Missouri) lady at heart, she loves her life at Homestead Albania.

When she's not writing, she tends to the garden, orchard, vineyard, and livestock. She also brews up batches of raki and wine, and other sweet and savory treats made from the fruits and veggies produced in the garden. She is an avid photographer, an active blogger about the homestead, and a hobbyist drone pilot, learning the art of aerial photography and filming.

Visit the blog: www.HomesteadAlbania.com
For publishing news:www.KimMalaj.com

www.ingramcontent.com/pod-product-compliance
Lightning Source LLC
Chambersburg PA
CBHW021128190726
48288CB00008B/2548